Dying to Live

Sam Carter

This is a work of fiction. Names, characters, places, and incidents either are the product of the author's imagination or are used fictitiously. Any resemblance to actual persons, living or dead, events, or locales is entirely coincidental.

First paperback edition February 2019

Book cover by Edward Bettison
Interior Design by Word-2-Kindle

To my best friend, favorite person and biggest fan, Amy.
Thank you for never giving up on this book and me.

Chapter 1

Four years ago, Stacy changed Dr. Harlan Allred's life forever. Today, as he prepared for a busy day with his pediatric patients, he had no idea she was about to do it again.

This morning, like almost every morning, Harlan went over his schedule name by name with his nurse, Clara. Seeing that Stacy Montgomery was his first appointment put a smile on his face. Throughout all the changes and stress in his life, Stacy always made him feel better. Every doctor is thankful for patients like her, patients that help them remember why they do what they do.

"You've got that look in your eye, Doctor. The same one you always do when you see Stacy on your schedule," Clara said with a smile on her face. She had been a pediatric nurse for over fifteen years and had spent the last seven with Harlan. She knew him, and she knew what she was doing. She wasn't afraid to remind him of this every chance she could.

"And what look might that be? It can't be any different than how I look every morning—exhausted and wishing it were 5:00!"

"Shut it. You know that's not true." Most people would be surprised to hear a nurse talk to a doctor that way, but Harlan loved it. Kept them on the same page. "It's a combination of happiness and sadness—like you are excited that she is here to see you, but wish she never had to come in."

How Clara could read Harlan like a book he would never know, but she hit it right on the head. Stacy shouldn't have to come in for visits with a surgeon. And it was his fault.

Stacy was only six when she was first rushed to the ER at Seattle Children's Hospital after a horrific car accident. Harlan was on call that night and performed the surgery that would ultimately save her life.

On that fall night four years ago, the weather was doing what it does best in Seattle—raining. Not raining hard, just spitting. But it had been spitting long enough that the roads were quite slick. As Stacy and her mother drove home from one of Stacy's dance classes, a car coming from the opposite side of the road headed right toward them in a busy intersection.

Stacy's mother tried to move out of the way but overcorrected and slid fast into the middle of the oncoming traffic in the crossing road. This movement, this quick and sudden movement, put them right in front of the glaring headlights of an SUV speeding directly toward them.

That was the last thing Stacy saw before opening her eyes to see Harlan staring at her as she was wheeled into the emergency department. No one knows what caused the other driver to be in their lane because, unfortunately, the driver of the car that caused the accident drove off like nothing happened and was never found. People have speculated it was either someone who had too much to drink, or an idiot sending a text instead of paying attention to the road. Either way, it remained a mystery. It didn't really matter. At least it shouldn't, but it always would to Harlan.

Harlan clearly remembered the looks of both horror and peace in this young girl's eye—she could only open one eye at the time—but that look of peace amazed him even then. How anyone could look anything but completely terrified during a time like that was beyond Harlan, but somehow Stacy looked calm. She looked like she knew she would be ok. She looked like she knew that Harlan would save her and help her come out of this even better than before. That very moment Harlan swore to himself that this little girl, this angel, would be ok. Better than ok. She would be 110 percent better and completely back to normal. He was going to do it.

Unfortunately, he could not completely reverse the damage caused to Stacy by this horrible accident. She would always walk with an awful limp, and the burns on her face would always be a part of her life. Stacy didn't care; she was always happy. She helped make Harlan's job worth it and was the reason why he chose such a challenging field.

At the same time, cases like Stacy's were partly why Harlan had let his life spin so far out of control—why his wife had left him and, until recently, why his son would hardly talk to him; why he spent so much time at Alcoholics Anonymous meetings; why he wasn't the person that he knew he should be.

The questions and second-guessing were sometimes more than he could bear. Why couldn't he have saved her legs? If he had just been quicker or maybe made better decisions in the ER that night, she would be out running around with friends like a normal ten-year-old.

Maybe if he had been by her side the second the ambulance rolled into the hospital, he could have lessened the damage to her face, and then in a few years she would be getting the attention from boys that an extraordinary girl like her deserved. Harlan had too many maybes in his life. Too many wrong decisions. Too many what ifs.

"Doctor? You still here? Get out of dreamland, it's time to get to work."

"I'm here. Just thinking about what it would be like to finally fire you," he said with a smile that caused Clara to let out a full belly laugh.

Before they got to the room where Stacy was waiting, Clara, true to form, started talking Harlan's ears off. If Clara wasn't talking about the patients, she was usually talking about one of two things: reality TV or whichever man she was seeing at the time. As much as Harlan despised shows like *The Bachelor* (none of those beautiful people could find a date on their own, really?) or *Survivor* (was he supposed to believe those contestants lived off the land without any help the whole time?), he would rather hear about who got a rose or who got voted off the island than get the latest news about Clara's love life.

He couldn't keep track of all the different men and stories, and he didn't want to either. As she started to talk, Harlan said a silent prayer that last night someone had lost a lot of weight on *The Biggest Loser* or that some team had cheated on *The Amazing Race*.

Unfortunately, Harlan's prayers were not answered. "Last night I had the time of my life with Dalton. You remember me telling you about Dalton? The big ol' sexy, delicious policeman?"

Harlan nodded because even though he had no clue what she was talking about, he didn't need to hear the details of how they met or specifics about what he looked like. He just wanted her to get on with her story.

"Good. Let me tell you, Harlan, this boy is yummy. With a capital Y-U-M. First, he took me out to a fancy dinner downtown where he fed me bacon-wrapped shrimp. It was divine, Harlan, divine." Harlan could tell she was just getting started, and he was afraid of what would come out of her mouth next.

"After that, he took me on a picnic and fed me some chocolate-covered strawberries, not outside because of that pesky rain we live with here. But it turned out much better that we were inside because the strawberries were not the dessert, my friend. Not at all," Clara said, emphasizing every word just in case Harlan couldn't picture the vivid painting she was creating with her words.

He thought he was going to be sick. Good thing they were near a hospital.

Just as Clara was about to give Harlan details that would make a porn star blush, they reached the door. Clara stopped talking, thank the Lord, and put on her figurative nurse hat. She was so amazing at being where she needed to be and putting everything else in the periphery. Harlan could not do that, which led to the need for weekly AA meetings. He wished he could.

Harlan opened the door to where Stacy was waiting, but the normal feelings of hope that filled the air whenever he met with her were noticeably absent. Stacy was still smiling, but it seemed more out of habit than because she actually meant it. Something was different. Something was wrong. The question wasn't just what was wrong, but what in the world Harlan was going to do to fix it. And if he even could.

Chapter 2

Stacy's father, Phil, was the first to talk. Harlan had been a physician for fourteen years and always felt it was important for the doctor to begin the conversation, but in this case he had no idea what to say.

"This morning Stacy woke up in tears. I know what you're thinking, and it wasn't a nightmare this time. She woke up crying in pain, drenched in sweat, and looked like she was lost. I have no idea what is going on. Please help, Dr. Allred. Please."

The hopelessness in Phil's voice was apparent and strong. Stacy was all he had now. On that horrible night, Stacy lost more than her ability to run and play. She had also lost her mother. Harlan could hear in Phil's voice that he could not handle even the thought of losing anyone else. Stacy was his world, and he just needed her to be ok.

Harlan took a deep breath and began to examine Stacy. Everything looked normal. Her breathing was fine, her temperature was normal, and her pulse was what it needed to be. There were no obvious symptoms that showed something had changed in her health, but something had changed.

Just as Harlan and Clara were about to end the visit so they could leave to discuss what they had seen, Stacy screamed out in pain and grabbed her legs as if they had caught on fire. Harlan rushed to her side while Clara calmly placed her arm around Phil to give him the comfort he so desperately needed.

Stacy grabbed her stomach as the pain appeared to move throughout her body. The look of worry on Stacy's face was something Harlan had never observed in any of their visits, and he knew he had to act fast. But before he could do anything, the pain was gone. Stacy stopped screaming and the tears dried up. It was almost as if nothing had happened at all.

Now it was Harlan's turn to be in shock. He stood there, almost frozen in time. Clara reached over and calmly took him by the arm, waking him up from his momentary absence. They looked at each other, and trying their very best to be the professionals that they were, began to decide what the next steps would be.

"Stacy, we are going to need to admit you for the night. The best thing for you—and for you, Phil—is for you stay at the hospital so we can have a better chance at discovering what is going on."

"What else will you do? How will you stop this? What is going on with my daughter?" Phil said through sobs. He was lost, and honestly, so was Harlan.

"The best thing is for her to be here where we can watch over her. We will also draw blood and run tests so we can see if she has some sort of infection. If we can figure that out now, we will be able to get Stacy out of here in no time. How do you feel about that, Stacy?"

Stacy smiled—thank goodness for that trademark smile. "Sounds great. You saved me once, Dr. Allred. I know you will save me again."

Harlan could hardly hold back the tears as he left the room for his next appointment.

Harlan and Carla walked through the halls in complete silence. Both were baffled by what they had just seen. Stacy was making so much progress. Today was supposed to be the day when they let her know they would not need her to come back for regular visits. What could have happened that would lead to such a reversal in her fortunes? Harlan wanted to be confident they would figure it out quickly. He wasn't sure he could stomach any more tragedy.

Chapter 3

The rest of the day grew more difficult for Harlan as his clinic filled with patients showing symptoms similar to Stacy's—one moment they were fine and happy, playing and interacting as kids do, and then, without any warning, everything would change. Their whole world would come crashing down, their faces reflecting complete pain and shock, while everyone else was at a loss for what to do.

As Harlan went to each patient, he could not understand what he was seeing and became more and more concerned. Each patient had recently shown signs of improvement and had appeared to have turned a corner, but now they seemed to be worse off than before.

But there was something else that made Harlan stop and think. As he checked their charts, he found that each of them had been scheduled for appointments with their doctors over the last few days, and each had some lab work done prior to coming in. He needed to figure out what the link was between these events. If there was one at all.

Harlan was researching each case more closely when his phone let out the annoying text message beep. No matter what, it startled him every single time. But this one was worth it because it was from his sixteen-year-old son, Jack.

"C U at the game. Gonna be amazing! Thx!"

No matter how hard Harlan tried, he would never understand why kids couldn't write out the entire word, but it didn't matter. Jack wanted to be with him that night, and that was all Harlan needed to hear.

Jack was Harlan's oldest child. He had a little girl named Leslie, too. While Leslie had stayed by her father's side during the divorce, Jack had wanted nothing to do with Harlan. Jack never returned a phone call or text message and wouldn't talk with Harlan during their visits. He had done everything that he could to cut his father out of his life. Until three months ago. Now they were as thick as thieves, and tonight would be another opportunity for that new bond to grow.

Tonight they would witness history together as father and son. They were going to go watch their beloved Seattle Mariners play the last game of the season as they prepared for what Harlan hoped would be a long postseason run, finally leading to a championship for Seattle. Plus, and this was probably the best part, they would get to watch their favorite player, Luke Masterson, become the first player in over seventy years to finish the season with a batting average over .400.

To the non-baseball fan, maybe this wasn't a big deal. But it was huge to those who followed and unhealthily obsessed over it. And that was Harlan and Jack. They had gotten that trait from Harlan's father, Dr. Alan Allred. That's right, Harlan had gone into the family business. He wasn't sure if he was grateful for that or not.

Harlan's life had been difficult for the past few years and he knew he had done it to himself. But this year was different. He was five months sober, his teenage son was finally talking to him on a regular basis, and the Mariners were going to the playoffs. And Harlan gave all the credit to one man and one man alone: Luke Masterson.

Chapter 4

Luke Masterson had accomplished the impossible, or at least he almost had. On the last day of a long 162-game Major League Baseball season, he was about to do something most people thought would never happen again. He only had to hold on for one more game. Luke needed to show up to the ballpark and do what he had been doing his whole life—hit. If he did that he would be the king of all sports, at least until the twenty-four-hour news cycle moved on to the next "great thing." But that's not what Luke was thinking about.

In fact, Luke was barely thinking about that at all. He was thinking about everything that would happen, everything people would learn, everything he alone had accomplished to ruin the lives of so many, and all those fools had no idea. He was thinking about the ridiculous looks on their faces as they realized their lives had changed forever, and they didn't even know how it happened or how to stop it.

Luke thought he had accomplished something impossible that would change humanity. Maybe he was being a little dramatic, but he felt he had earned it. After all he had been through just to get to this point, he had earned a moment of self-indulgence. So he took that moment to bask in the glory of being Luke Masterson and to revel in the fact that no one would ever be able to reach his heights or ability. Ever. And those thoughts, those all-consuming thoughts, were the reason he could not wipe the smile off his face; and no one knew it.

No, all the idiots surrounding him scribbling in their notepads and taking countless pictures thought Luke was smiling because he was about to make history. Reporters asked the questions they had been waiting their entire careers to ask an elite athlete. Talking heads on every radio and TV show filled the air with endless comparisons to the best players of all time and attempted to rank Luke's season among the all-time greats. Journalists began to write the books they had waited their whole careers to write about the greatest season they had ever witnessed.

Little did they know that in just a few days from now, the questions they would be asking and the stories they would be telling would transcend sports in ways they could not comprehend. And with that knowledge, Luke's smile grew to a point that would make even the Cheshire cat jealous. He was almost home and no one could stop him.

Chapter 5

Harlan wasn't able to enjoy the thought of going to the game for very long because Barry Michaels, the CEO of Seattle Children's Hospital, rounded the corner and called out to him. Harlan had been taught by his father to despise hospital administrators. His father told him that all they cared about was profit, contribution margin, and other pointless financial numbers that had nothing to do with the actual reason for hospitals—to care for patients.

Barry, however, was a sort of personal savior for Harlan. The year Barry was hired was the darkest and most difficult of Harlan's life. For the first time, his then-wife, Emily, was starting to question their relationship, and Harlan began drinking more heavily than ever. Until then he had mostly been a social drinker, and that was about it. But when Stacy was rushed through the emergency room doors and he couldn't make her whole again, Harlan sank to the lowest of lows.

He started working late and then going to the bar even later. He would stagger home about an hour before Emily was to get up with the kids and then roll out of bed in time to shower and go into the office. He missed recitals, sporting events for the kids, anniversaries—things that before, he would have never missed for the world. He was absent at home, and because he was getting little sleep and drinking enough for a small army, his worked suffered, too.

At least Harlan liked to tell himself that it only started just four years ago, but he knew better.

He had started being aloof with Emily and his kids years before. He had allowed work to take over his life and his focus too often switched to his next surgery or busy clinic day. Worse yet, when he finally left for the day, he often didn't find his way home, but to a bar where he drank his life away. Truly, he had already started to lose himself and, most importantly, his family years before Stacy's accident.

But he allowed what he considered a failure to make everything worse. And it had just kept getting worse every single day.

Barry saw the changes and felt it was important that they did not lose Harlan. He pulled Harlan aside on more than one occasion just to talk. To talk about the Mariners, the Seahawks, the University of Washington football team, politics, and anything else that would keep Harlan's mind off life. As soon as it was obvious Barry cared about Harlan as a person and not just as a physician employed at his hospital, Barry pulled him into his office and gave him an ultimatum.

"Harlan, you're one of the best doctors and, for that matter, people I've ever worked with, but you are killing yourself and your work. You're losing your family and your patients. It's time to get help, because if you don't, you will never be able to help the people you took an oath to serve."

Harlan knew he was right. He probably could have been fired and no one would have batted an eye. The next day Harlan made his way to his first AA meeting. This may not have saved his marriage, and it may not have meant he was sober for very long at a time, but he began to gain perspective on what mattered. He was still in the process, but he was finally in a better place. Barry was a good man who had saved Harlan's life. He was a good man who cared about the life of every patient in that hospital, too.

So it wasn't a shock that on that day Barry would be walking around and trying to find out what was going on. Harlan was more concerned this time around though; he didn't have clear answers for Barry. He had some leads and some ideas of what they could do, but he really had no idea why the hospital was filled with patients who were once doing well and were now sicker than they had been before. What were they going to do?

"Harlan, I think you already know this, but we need to talk," Barry said as he approached. "We should probably go upstairs."

Great. Upstairs. Upstairs meant that Harlan would need to accompany Barry to the C-Suite and spend some time in administration. But mostly it meant that it wouldn't just be Harlan and Barry talking about the events of the day and what they could do to make things better. No, they would be joined by the hospital's Chief Medical Officer, Josie Silver. Of all the people Harlan did not want to see today, or any day for that matter, Josie was the one.

Josie had become CMO at Seattle Children's about two years ago, and to say she was a disaster would be putting it lightly. She was pompous, ego-driven, over-bearing, and undeserving. And those were her best qualities. What Harlan would like to say about her he couldn't, because, well, there were children around.

She had gained a nickname during her years at the hospital: Hi-Ho Silver. Clever and extremely original, but it made sense when you broke it down. Hi because she was always on her high horse looking down on everyone and everything. Ho because she was, and this is the only way to put it, a ho. At least that was the word around the office, the city, and the entire medical community.

Harlan didn't call her this or get involved in any of the normal gossip that was the constant plague of any office setting. There was plenty to say about him, and all of it was most likely true. Who was he to judge? So, he stayed out of it, but he still laughed when he heard it. It was funny. And sometimes you've just got to laugh.

As they walked, they attempted some small talk to distract them from all that was going on in the hospital, but it wasn't long until they entered Josie's oversized office—the one she hardly ever left to see what was actually happening. Now it was time to get back to reality and Harlan was not looking forward to it.

Chapter 6

There was only one good thing that Luke could say about his scumbag of a father: he taught him how to play baseball. That was all he ever did for him. When Luke was old enough to walk, his father made sure that he carried a baseball around with him wherever he went. They would play catch, run the bases, and hit for hours.

Baseball had been his father's life growing up in Australia because he had been a budding star. At eighteen, William had signed with the Queensland Rams and helped bring them back to their glory years. Luke loved hearing stories about all that his dad accomplished: youngest MVP of the Claxton Shield, Australia's premier baseball competition, at age twenty; first player to ever hit over .400 during the International Baseball League of Australia season, and then first to accomplish the feat in back-to-back seasons. Luke could listen to his father talk for hours about baseball and his accomplishments, but the stories didn't last long because there weren't many to tell.

At twenty-one, Luke's father was coming off his second .400 season and finally about to win the Claxton Shield. He was the talk of all of Australia, which was basically impossible in a land that couldn't care less about baseball. He graced the cover of every newspaper and every magazine. He was their star, their future, and their hope of breaking into the American sports market.

"There I was, son, standing on second base. The winning run, in the deciding game, just 180 feet away from bringing the Shield home. The crowd was loving it, loving me after I ripped that two-out double. You should have been there to hear them chanting my name."

The first time Luke heard this story, he loved every second of it. At least at the beginning when his dad seemed so happy.

"First pitch, Tony Fields slams this line drive right up the middle. Perfect for a guy with my blazing speed to score easily. I rounded third base and the crowd—Luke, the crowd was screaming. They could taste it. Hell, I could taste it. The Shield was really going to come back to Queensland. The only place it should really be."

At this point, Luke's dad's face always started to become dark and his eyes would turn fire red with anger and a hint a sadness. The first time, Luke didn't know why. But he would soon learn that it was never a good sign for Luke or his mom.

"Baseball, more than any other sport, is a game of inches. A game of split-second decisions. You've got very little time to make that perfect decision. When I saw the throw was coming in, I thought the best thing to do was slide headfirst. It hadn't failed me before. Stupid catcher. Moved just a few inches right in front of me, and I didn't see it. I had no time to react."

This was always the point in the story that Luke hated the most, but not because it meant that his dad was out and the Victoria Aces would go on to score in the next inning and win the Claxton Shield once again.

No, it was because his dad would always pull out his constantly shaky and claw-like left hand for Luke to see. It was because his dad would explain in perfect detail how he felt his arm explode in pain as it slammed into the catcher, breaking in every place imaginable. He would put that hand right in Luke's face. Then, without any hesitation or any sign of remorse, he would beat him with it until Luke passed out in a puddle of his own tears.

Two things happened that day to Luke's father. First, he could no longer grip the bat with the same force. His ability to hit for power, or really at all, was gone. Long gone. He would never be the same player again.

Second, his confidence was shot. He would forever question his decision to slide headfirst when he may just have had a better chance to slide around the catcher feet-first. William would have been able to see him move those tiny inches and he would have scored. He wouldn't have gotten hurt, they would have won, and he would have been the talk of Australia. He would have signed to play the game he loved in America, at least that's what he told himself, and his life would have been better. Instead he was stuck with a dead-end job and a family he didn't want. A family he never wanted.

He pretended he did want the family life for a while, but it didn't last forever. As a kid, Luke loved his dad. But Luke was just a stupid child who didn't know better. It didn't take very long for Luke to realize that his dad didn't care about him or anyone else, especially his mother.

By the time Luke turned eleven, his father was rarely home. When he was home, he wasn't just drunk, he was a monster. Truthfully, calling him a monster was unfair to real monsters like Godzilla, Frankenstein, and Dracula. Luke was sure those guys at least had hearts, because he knew his dad had nothing of the sort. As soon as his dad stumbled through the door he would spend the first hour or so telling Luke's mother what a worthless sack of excrement she was, and then, as he sobered up, he would go outside and make her play catch with him for hours. Except she didn't get a glove. Or the use of her hands.

When Luke had too much time to think, these were the horrible things he dwelt on. And as he sat alone in his Seattle apartment, waiting for the two biggest moments of his life to come, it was all he thought about. About his father and his mother and his miserable life growing up in Australia. He thought about how much time he had to spend cleaning up his mother whenever his father "made time for them."

He thought about how his mother just sat there and cried like a helpless little baby. He thought about how he had no friends because he didn't care for their stupid games of rugby or cricket. He thought about how the kids at school would tease and pick on him because he carried a baseball glove everywhere. He thought about how much he wanted to get away from that home and be anywhere but there.

It was a miserable childhood, and he was sure people would use this as a way to explain why Luke was the way he was, and why he had committed so many heinous acts in his life. But they had no idea. Everyone who would ever try to psychoanalyze him would be wrong. And that thought made Luke do something he rarely did—laugh.

In truth, Luke was not Luke because of his father. Yes, he hated his father, but he was not angry with him for all that he had done. And, to be perfectly honest, he hated his mother for never fighting back or trying to get away. She was just as despicable. They were atrocious people, but Luke was worse than his worthless father and scared, useless mother. Both of them were gone, and only Luke knew where they were and how they had suffered.

As he thought about his life and who he was, Luke knew that he was his own special kind of monster. He wasn't recruited by the Matsui family, the largest Japanese Yakuza family in all of Australia. He recruited them. He made them, as the ridiculous American mob movies always put it, an offer they couldn't refuse. They had no choice but to let him in after they had seen what he could do, and that he would do to anyone. He didn't need them, but he wanted their resources. He wanted to bleed them dry and watch them suffer like his parents had, but first he would be a part of them and make them feel like he really was a Matsui.

They fell right into his hands, and by seventeen, Luke was in Japan and playing for the Seibu Lions of the Nippon Baseball League because the Matsuis had influence over so much of what took place in that city. Now he was where he needed to be to begin executing his plans. He had everything at his disposal, and he now knew what his—as cheesy as it sounded—destiny was. Now he sat there knowing that he was about to fulfill his promise and again he began to laugh. And the only thing that stopped him was the knock at the door.

Chapter 7

"You better have answers to what in the world is going on with the patients in this hospital, Harlan." This was just Josie's way of saying hello and that she missed him. Such a sweetheart.

"I'm great, Josie. Thanks for asking," Harlan responded. Barry tried to hold back a smile, but it was apparent that Josie did not find a bit of humor in Harlan's moment of standup comedy.

"First, it's Dr. Silver. Second, glad you can find humor today. I'm sure your patients' families find you hilarious during this happy time." Classic power play; don't use my first name, call me Doctor. Got to make sure everyone in the room knows just how important I am. This was going to be even worse than Harlan imagined.

"Excuse me, Dr. Silver. That was inappropriate. I will think before I speak now." Not Harlan's best work of keeping his thoughts to himself, but he tried. Not hard, but still he tried.

"All right, all right." Barry finally spoke up to get them back on target. "How about we all just sit down and talk about the matter at hand. Sound good?"

"Yes, let's talk." Now it was Josie's turn to appear calm, cool, and collected. Harlan knew this was an act. He was unsure if Barry had seen through her charade, her particular brand of bull crap, but he wished he had.

"Where would you like to start? What do you need to know that you don't already know from all your time out on the floor today?" Again, Harlan probably should bite down on his tongue harder. But there were a few people that just got his blood boiling and made it difficult for him to not speak his mind. Josie was at the top of that list.

Josie glared, took a deep breath, and said, "I will let that one slide because I know this has been a stressful day for you. But now, I need more details. I know that we have past patients being readmitted to the hospital. I know that it seems as if it is not related to their past illnesses, but I don't know why or what is causing the issue. What do you know?"

"That's pretty accurate, but there is a little bit more. Currently, seven of my own patients and an additional five patients have been admitted today so we can monitor them more closely tonight and run a few tests. We are testing everything possible to see what could have caused their conditions. We currently have no explanation as to why they are in an incredible amount of pain one second before it disappears as if it were only a horrible nightmare."

Harlan paused, waiting to see if they had anything they wanted to add. When it was clear he had an attentive audience, he continued, "There is one thing that ties them all together. Each of these twelve patients had appointments with their docs either yesterday or today. And all were required to have some sort of lab work done pre-visit. It seems like a crazy coincidence, but we are looking at all angles. Hopefully that will help us find an answer soon."

There was a long silence in the room as it appeared that Josie and Barry were trying to take in what they were hearing. Barry was the first to break the silence. "That is excellent work, Harlan. Really excellent. Looks like it's a good thing we keep such detailed medical records, isn't it? With the tests and this knowledge, I feel like this will be straightened out by tomorrow. What do you think, Dr. Silver?"

"I am impressed. Hopefully these tests will get to the heart of the matter quickly," Josie added. She seemed a bit taken aback, like she wasn't expecting Harlan to have a clue. He did though, and he could tell she was not all happy about it.

"We're good then?" Barry asked. "Good. Then I'm off to another exciting financial update. Great work, you two."

Both Barry and Harlan got up to leave, but before Harlan was barely out of his seat, Josie looked at him and said, "Can you stay a minute, Dr. Allred? I just want to go over a few more things."

Harlan knew he didn't have a choice. He wanted to leave, go straight to his car, drive home, not pass go and not even collect $200. He had no desire to stay with Josie alone to "just go over a few more things." But he reluctantly sat back down and waited to hear what in the world she had to say.

"Honestly, I really am impressed." Now it was Harlan's turn to be a bit taken aback. Was she complimenting him? Was there more praise to come? "I was convinced that you would come in here with no answer and be completely clueless like always, but not this time. Good work." There it was. The only compliment he was getting was a backhanded one. Better than nothing.

"Thanks. We, all the hospital staff, have worked hard on this today. We want our patients to get better and go home quickly."

"Good. Glad to hear that. And let's hope you can figure it out. Let's hope that you don't have too much to drink again and mess this whole thing up. Do you think you could go one night without drinking your weight in alcohol? You will find out what is wrong, and you will fix this mess. I will not let you, of all people, ruin my hospital and my reputation. Do you understand me?"

Harlan had had enough. He shot up from his chair and looked Josie straight in the eyes. "You listen to me, Josie." He made sure to emphasize and draw out her name. "I couldn't care less about your reputation. I couldn't care one red cent. This is not about you. This is about the patients. This is about little Stacy Montgomery and her father. This is about their lives. We, the doctors who actually see patients, will figure this out. Not for you, Josie. For the patients."

Harlan felt no need to explain to her that he was five months sober. He didn't feel the need to waste his breath talking to her anymore about himself or any of what was going on. He was done and had no desire to hear anything further come out of this sorry woman's mouth.

Chapter 8

Harlan walked away from his meeting with Josie. He could not believe the accusations and claims that had come from her mouth. He hated it even more when she called this "her hospital." This wasn't her hospital at all. Who cared about her reputation? Who was this woman, and what made her think she could say the things she said?

His head was spinning, and he could feel himself losing control. Just a few months ago, this kind of conversation would have taken Harlan directly to the closest watering hole to drown his sorrows until the bartender put the closed sign on the door and kicked him out. In fact, adding up all that had taken place today, he seemed to have the perfect excuse to jump right off the wagon again. Just one drink, and he would be transported away from all this stress for just a moment, and that sure sounded good.

But he knew better. He knew one drink wouldn't be just one drink, but most likely nine or ten. He couldn't contain himself. He was, to use a phrase often used in AA, completely powerless when it came to alcohol. He was weak, yes, but he was not going to give in this time. He had come too far in the past few months, and would not take even one step back.

Before he left for the day, Harlan decided he would stop by Stacy's room. He was sure that her father would be there sitting by her bedside, holding her hand. Harlan was positive that this was harder on Phil than Stacy. She would be the strong one in the room, giving them all, Harlan included, the strength to make her better.

The door for room 418, where Stacy was staying, was closed. Stacy always asked for this specific room when she had to stay for any length of time. Even though Harlan may have prayed to escape Clara's crazy conversations, he wasn't religious by any stretch of the imagination. But Stacy was. Even after all she had been through, she still believed in a higher being that would help her. For that reason, she always wanted room 418 because it reminded her of her favorite scripture—John 14:18. Because the hospital didn't have fourteen floors, she settled for 418 but always told Harlan she just pretended there was an extra one put on her door by an angel just for her.

During Stacy's third stay at the hospital after her accident, Harlan decided to look up this scripture to see why this little girl loved it so much. That night he went into the hospital's chapel, found a Bible, and flipped through until he came to the scripture. He was amazed by what he read.

"I will not leave you comfortless: I will come to you."

Harlan was dumbfounded that a girl who had lost so much loved this passage. How a girl who was in so much pain physically, emotionally, and especially spiritually could feel anything but anger was remarkable to Harlan. In fact, remarkable may be the best word in all the English language to describe Stacy.

The scene in Stacy's room was not exactly what Harlan had been expecting. Yes, her father was holding her hand as she lay in her bed. Yes, Phil was extremely distraught and looked at the end of his rope. But Stacy was not the pillar of strength and comfort he thought she would be. The feeling in the room was the same as when he had seen her earlier in the day. It felt completely devoid of hope.

For what seemed like the thousandth time that day, Harlan took a deep breath to clear his mind. He knew he could not show a sign of worry or weakness as he met with these two enormously important people.

As he walked in, Phil looked up at him with a look of sheer desperation. After Harlan checked on Stacy to make sure she was resting as comfortably as possible, he asked Phil to sit with him and talk for a moment.

Phil slowly got up and moved to the little couch on which he had slept so often the past four years. Here the two of them had spoken often about Stacy and her health. Harlan had given him both good news and bad news on that very couch. Because he currently had no definitive answers to give to Phil, Harlan was unsure about what kind of news he would be delivering today. He just hoped beyond all hope that whatever came out of his mouth would give Phil some sort of comfort. This good man and loving father deserved that.

"How has she been today, Phil? Any signs of improvement?"

"I don't know, Dr. Allred. I just don't know." Phil was on the verge of tears. He had been crying, that was obvious, but right now he was all dried up—like he wanted to cry, but he just couldn't get it out.

Harlan knew he would have to ask more direct questions to get answers. This was the toughest part of his job because he didn't always like the answers he got, but he needed the specifics to give them the help they required.

"Talk to me about how *she* is doing. How is she acting? How are her spirits, Phil?"

"She goes back and forth. One second she looks like she is about to be Stacy again. Happy. Smiling. Loving. Then before she can get there, the pain returns. And with that so does the look of horror in her eyes. I don't know, Dr. Allred. I just don't know."

Harlan needed a moment to take in Phil's description. Look of horror in her eyes? He did not think it was possible for Stacy to have that type of look. What in the world was inflicting her and all these other kids?

"And the pain she is in," Phil continued, "it's getting worse. When you saw her earlier it was as if it started from her toes and moved throughout her body. Now it just hits and hits her hard in every single part of her body. Both inside and out. It's unbearable. I never thought that anything would be unbearable for her."

"Phil, I want you to know how sorry I am. Words cannot describe how much I wish this were not happening." Harlan was telling the complete truth. How he wished they were not having this conversation, now or ever. But they were; this was the reality. He had to keep going. "Unfortunately, it is happening, and I do not have any clear answers for you right this moment."

If there was any hope in Phil before, it disappeared when Harlan told him that—like Harlan had opened a window and the wind had carried it away. Harlan knew he had only a moment to decide what to say to give him more hope and help him get through the night.

"But, we are already running tests and we have some ideas that could lead to answers soon. The lab will be working on this first thing, and you will be watched over closely by Clara tonight."

"Clara? She doesn't normally work nights, right? She is going to be here for Stacy?" Now there appeared to be some optimism in Phil's eyes. Clara did that for a lot of people.

"Yes, sir. She went home this afternoon to get some rest so that she could be here tonight to keep her eyes on you two. She even canceled some big important date for you. I didn't think that was possible!"

A little smile seemed to appear on Phil's face for a second. That was a welcome sight.

"There is one other thing I think you should know," Phil said, hesitating like he was mentally debating whether he should say anything at all. Harlan didn't like to push people, he wanted them to feel comfortable.

"Stacy's nightmares have become, um, clearer."

Stacy had been plagued by vivid and disturbing nightmares since the accident. She would live through the accident again, but in slow motion. She could see everything that happened to her mom perfectly. She would feel the pain of losing her all over again. It was always a horrible experience. Harlan wished he could at least take those away. Now they were clearer, and he wasn't sure if that was a good or bad thing.

"She's starting to see the other car. Not the one that hit them, but the one that swerved in front of them. And the driver. She is starting to visualize the driver. It's still fuzzy, but every day it's getting easier for her to see."

This was news. No one had seen the car that caused the accident. It had driven off without incident, and everyone was more focused on saving those that were left behind. How Harlan wished he could find that person and show him (or her) the damage that had been done; show them the lives they had ruined.

"Wow." That was all Harlan could think to say.

"That was my reaction when she first told me, too. Part of me wants to know, but another part just wants us to move on. You know what I mean?"

If Harlan were being honest, he didn't know what Phil meant at all. This person deserved to pay. But he nodded his head like he agreed, hoping that might comfort Phil a bit.

"Anyway. You will be at the game tonight, right? Your son coming with you again?" Phil knew of Harlan's love for the Mariners, and that lately Jack had been coming with him to more and more games.

"Yup. I'm on my way out now to go get ready and pick him up. But if you need anything, you know how to get in touch with me. Do not hesitate for one second."

"I know. But I want you to enjoy every moment with your son. You never know when it might all disappear." Phil looked back at Stacy with a longing for her safety and quick return home.

"Wise words, Phil. Very wise words. Now get some rest. Clara will be here soon, and I will see you in the morning. We are going to figure this out. And soon." But as those words of comfort left his mouth, Harlan was unsure if he believed them himself.

Chapter 9

Lucy watched Harlan as he finished up with Stacy and her father—admired, actually, was a better word for it. As a nurse, she had worked with a lot of doctors and most of them were incredible at taking care of their patients, but none did it quite like Harlan. His skill was only matched by his love for his patients and their families.

"How are they doing?" Lucy asked as Harlan walked out of the room.

"Oh, hey Lucy. Didn't see you there. They are ok. Not great. Hard to tell, actually."

"Anything that you need me to do for them tonight?"

"Just the normal great work you do, Lucy. Clara will be here to be with them and the others soon. I hope that works for you."

"Always helpful to have her here. She knows them best," Lucy said, attempting to hide her jealousy. What she wouldn't give to be Harlan's right-hand woman, his go-to nurse.

Another thing she admired about Harlan was how he wore his emotions on his sleeve. Many people have the false impression that doctors moved on easily and could just go onto the next case, but this wasn't true. Lucy had met very few doctors that did. Most would hide it and pretend all was well, but not Harlan.

Another thing she admired about Harlan.

Lucy clearly remembered him coming out of that very room a few years ago after rounding on a patient who was having a harder recovery than anyone expected. The little seven-year-old boy's surgery was supposed to routine, but there had been complications that were causing pain that no child should feel.

"Dr. Allred?" she had asked him as he walked by her desk. "Is everything all right with Curtis?"

He paused, looked at her, and just shook his head. He started to walk down the hall to check in on another patient, but he stopped and looked back at Lucy.

"Ya know what?" Harlan had said with a sad look in his eyes, the type of look a child has when their favorite toy goes missing or breaks in two. "I don't care what anyone says. This never gets easier."

"I completely agree, Doctor. It never does."

"If it ever does, if I ever get so hard-hearted that I just move on to the next patient and don't seem to care, then you have my permission to slap me as hard as you can in the face to get me back on track." A smile started to form on corner of his lips for a brief second before the sad look returned. “And if that doesn’t work, it’s time for me to find a whole new career. Probably in pharmaceutical sales. You don’t need a heart for that.”

Lucy had laughed a little as Harlan winked at her and took a deep breath to reset himself before going on to help the next patient.

Anyone watching could tell it hurt him to see his patients and their families struggle. He always used that hurt to work harder and find the solution. It always amazed her not just how much he cared, but how much he showed it.

“You enjoy your night with your son and don’t worry about us here. We’ve got this.”

“I know you do. They’re in good hands. But, don’t worry about them? Have we met? These are my patients. And that little girl in there? Stacy Montgomery? She’s special. Take care of her.”

Just another thing she admired about him—how candid he was with the nurses. Never making them feel like he was somehow better than they were.

Was admired even the right word at this point? She more than admired Harlan. She kind of felt pathetic thinking about it. And she felt great, too. If she wasn’t careful she was going to start twirling her hair and giggling like a high school girl.

“Thanks. We appreciate your faith in us. Now go. Enjoy some family time.”

"Will do," he said. He slowly walked away while Lucy admired, yeah admired, the view.

Chapter 10

This was the perfect opportunity for Harlan to learn how to do that whole compartmentalizing thing other people were so good at doing. He had had a horrible day at work, but he was going to leave that where it deserved to be left—at work. Tonight he would concentrate on enjoying a night at the ballpark with his son. Jack had a right to that.

Harlan was going to enjoy his night eating hot dogs, peanuts, and Cracker Jack with his son. He was going to compartmentalize the struggles of the day and watch history take place at the ball game. And, as the song they always sang during the seventh inning stretch goes, truly he didn't care if he ever got back.

Harlan was snapped out of his thoughts by the loud ring coming from his cell phone. He was sure that whenever it rang the people in the car next to him answered theirs, too, and he could not for the life of him figure out how to turn it down. Oh well. At least he would be able to hear it, even if he were on the top of the Space Needle and had left it at home.

As Harlan put his Bluetooth in his ear, he looked to see who the incoming call was from. He was afraid that it would be Barry wanting to talk about Harlan blowing up on Josie. He was worrying about the impending lecture when he finally saw the name flash across his screen. It wasn't Barry or anyone from the hospital for that matter. No, it was the love of his life. The one he let get away. It was Emily. And just looking at her name caused Harlan's heart to skip a beat. Cheesy? Sure, but he didn't care.

As Harlan was about to answer the phone, his mind was brought back to another day just like this one. It was his freshman year at the University of Washington and he was enjoying what many people longingly called the best years of their life. But this day was the most special of all those special days. It was the day he met Emily.

That fall day all those years ago, as Harlan was walking into a party, he noticed the most beautiful girl he had ever seen on her way out. The truth is, there was one thing that separated Emily from every other woman on campus. Since they were in Seattle, the normal college experience of the co-eds spending too much time trying to make themselves look perfect for the party by wearing short skirts and low-cut tops with not a hair out of place wasn't what happened there. The grunge look was without a doubt the thing, but not for Emily. She was wearing jeans and a Ken Griffey Jr. jersey. Perfection. Absolute and utter perfection.

She stole Harlan's heart that very moment. Here was a girl who came to a party in not just any jersey, but the jersey of the player who represented the future of all of baseball.

The only problem Harlan had was one simple fact: he was horrible with girls. Always had been, and he was certain he always would be. He wasn't some hideous troll who scared the girls away with just his horrible glance. Some, and by some Harlan meant his mom, might say he was quite the looker. So it wasn't so much that girls didn't like him. It was more that he turned into a bumbling fool every time that he tried to talk to any member of the fairer sex.

Actually, it was quite humorous for everyone around him, and they turned it into a game. His friends would attempt to set him up with girls just to see how he would mess it up. They called it "Harlan Bawl" because it usually ended with him crying, and the girl crying, too, either from horror or laughter. And now he was faced with the daunting task of trying to speak to and ask out the girl of his dreams. And all he could think was, "How will we both end of crying once I open my mouth?"

Harlan started out with his best pick up line. "Hi." She was hooked, he could tell. Mostly because she returned the favor with a line of her own.

"Hey." Wow. She was just as smooth. Could this girl get any more perfect?

Then something strange happened to Harlan. His throat didn't get dry, his thoughts didn't get all jumbled up, and when he started to talk, words flowed freely. It was amazing. If only his friends could see him now.

Once they started speaking he noticed more about her than just her choice of wardrobe. Harlan noticed her beautiful green eyes that would make the evergreen trees of western Washington pale in comparison. He finally saw her perfect, long blonde hair and her body, oh that body, that make-traffic-stop-from-Seattle-to-Tacoma body. Once Harlan realized just how gorgeous Emily was, he was glad he hadn't noticed earlier. He knew if he had, the likelihood that he would still be talking to her was slim to none. But he brushed that thought aside and turned his attention 100 percent to the world's one and only Perfect Ten.

Harlan and Emily sat on the porch until 2 a.m. just talking. They talked about Junior Griffey and debated whether the trade for some tall, lanky, mullet-haired pitcher was the ace the Mariners' staff had spent years searching for. They talked about their families, their ambitions, and how they were going to change the world. It's amazing how much you can learn about someone when you just listen, and every word Emily spoke was amazing to hear.

They both came from very loving, though quite different, homes. Growing up, while Harlan was an only child, Emily was number three of five—right smack dab in the middle. While Harlan got all the attention his parents had to give, Emily was that middle child that sometimes got lost in the shuffle, but she never let that bother her. She continued to work hard to accomplish every goal a teenage girl could possibly imagine. If Emily wanted something, anything at all, she would get it because she knew she could. Her family didn't have much money growing up only fifteen minutes from the Canadian border in the small town of Custer, Washington, but she felt privileged. For that reason, she wanted to be a high school guidance counselor in the most destitute and impoverished place she could find in Seattle. She was amazing. She was perfection. Absolute and utter perfection.

Before he answered, Harlan took another deep breath and reminded himself that Emily was not calling to re-confess her love for him and read him some long, sappy poem she had written about how she couldn't live without him. As much as Harlan wished that would be the case, he knew there was no way it would ever happen. He didn't deserve her. Never did. He just wished he hadn't screwed up so much that she had finally realized it.

"Hey, Emily. How goes it?" Harlan was still smooth after all these years.

"I'm good, Harlan. I hope that I'm not catching you at a bad time. Jack said you were going to have a busy day today, and I know how that can be for you." Just hearing her voice caused his heart to skip another beat. Too much of this and he was going to end up in the emergency room himself.

It wasn't just her voice, but the fact that her first worry continued to be making sure the other person was in the best position possible. She was never worried about life being inconvenient for her. Even after all Harlan had put her through, she still wanted to make sure all was right for him.

"Nope, now's great. Just on my way to come get Jack for the game." As he said that, Harlan became worried that was the reason she was calling him in the first place. Could Jack not go? Had something happened to change Emily's mind? Or maybe it was Jack who didn't want to go?

"I was hoping I would catch you before you got too close." Shoot. Emily was about to deliver the hammer and let Harlan know he would be alone that night again. Could anything go right today? "Jack is staying a little later at school today to help tutor some kids, so he is going to meet you at the park. Does that work for you?"

Harlan exhaled a little too loudly, because, by the gasp that Emily let out on the other end, he could tell he had surprised her. He was still coming, thank goodness. "Perfect. How's he getting there? The bus? He's not driving, is he?"

"Nope. He's not quite ready for that. He is, but I'm not. He's taking the bus. It's pretty much a straight shot for him from school. And don't worry, he'll be there about 6:30 so you two can grab some food and still be in your seats for the first pitch."

"Great. I will be waiting for him outside the gate we go in for each game," Harlan said, hoping that he could somehow drag this conversation out longer and they could talk forever. "Just have him call or text if he is running late."

"Will do. Have fun tonight. This is all he has been talking about for weeks. Thanks for being there for him. He deserves a dad."

And you deserve a good husband, Harlan thought as they hung up, *and I wish it were still me.*

Chapter 11

Because he didn't have to pick up Jack, Harlan got to Safeco, home of the Mariners, much earlier than he had planned. This worked for him because it gave him a few minutes to change into his Masterson jersey. Those few minutes meant he didn't have to go to the game wearing his shirt and tie. He hated when he had to do that.

It also gave him the time to do two more tasks as he waited outside the ballpark for Jack. The first was to worry, one of the things that Harlan did best. Worry. Worry about his patients. Worry about traffic. Worry about the starting lineup for the game. But most of all, worry about Jack as he traveled to the game. He knew that Jack could handle the bus ride just fine, but it still made Harlan pull out more and more hair each time he did it.

If Harlan had his way, Emily and the kids would be living in a much safer part of western Washington, but that was not what Emily wanted. Three years ago she had landed her dream job, high school guidance counselor, at Franklin High School right in the middle of Seattle, and she insisted that they live close to the school. She felt that there was no way that she could guide these kids through their tough and significant years if she lived in plush living conditions in some Seattle suburb.

Plus, she wanted to be in her kids' school. She felt it made the job mean even more. So she up and moved the kids to a small home right around the corner from the high school. It was not a dangerous area for Seattle, but it still made Harlan nervous. He felt justified in his worry because that was what he felt a good dad should do. And he probably wouldn't stop being concerned about Jack's traveling to the game until he saw him waving when he finally got there.

The second task Harlan did while he waited was check his Twitter account to see what news he could get about tonight's game. He typically listened to the radio as he drove, but he had been distracted by Emily's call and never even turned it on.

He unlocked his phone and opened his Twitter app to see what the people he followed—not stalked, followed—were talking about. Harlan didn't like to brag, but he had to have the most creative name on Twitter of anyone in the history of the social networking site: @DocAllred. He didn't like to reveal to people how he came up with this inspired and innovative name, but it involved a very expensive marketing firm and months and months of research. Either that, or he looked at his name tag at work.

First thing Harlan searched for was the Mariners' Twitter account because they would have posted the starting lineups before the game so anxious fans could know. After scrolling through his feed, he finally found the tweet, but he was confused by what he saw. Everything looked normal except for one glaring mistake. Next to the SS for the starting shortstop was Salmon, not Masterson.

Harlan tried to wipe away whatever had to be in his eyes that was making it difficult to read properly because there was no way that what he was seeing was real. But when he read the tweet again, it said the same thing. He looked through more of their tweets hoping that there would be a correction, but he found nothing. Masterson was really not starting.

As a fan, Harlan could understand this decision by the Mariners not to start their star today. It was the last game of the season. The playoffs would be starting in a few days, and they needed Masterson healthy. A fluke injury could happen at any moment, and they could not afford that if they wanted to bring home that World Series title.

But also as a fan, Harlan could not make sense of this decision at all. Today was the day the fans were going to experience history being made. Masterson's not playing would suck a lot of joy out of today's game. This must have been what it was like for the people of Mudville when Mighty Casey struck out.

Now Harlan had something else to worry about—how in the world was he going to break this news to Jack?

For Harlan, his biggest worry in life was that his kids would end up even slightly like him in any way. If they could just be 110 percent like their mother, they would have happy lives and would be well-adjusted members of society. Unfortunately, he knew, as did every other parent in the world, that was impossible. Whether on the nature or the nurture side of the argument, he had to admit that kids always seemed to get some of both their parents' characteristics. Bad and good.

For Jack, this meant he had a passion for his favorite sports teams. Actually, it was more like an obsession. It was a crazy, over-the-top, all-consuming obsession that Jack inherited from both his father and grandfather. It meant not being able to watch any sports highlight shows the morning after a loss. It meant that when his favorite player got hurt, he didn't go online for fear of reading another article about it. It meant pacing halls at night in frustration when his team lost any game, so for the Allred men it meant that most seasons they were, you guessed it, sleepless in Seattle. With that in mind, Harlan had to figure out how he would tell Jack the news so that it would not ruin their night together.

Harlan looked on his phone and noticed it was 6:15, which meant he only had fifteen minutes to formulate the perfect way to let Jack know about Masterson. He was never very good at this kind of stuff when it came to Jack and Leslie. He could tell a family that their child was not going to make it through the night in a way that would help them feel as much ease as they possibly could, but when he had to tell his children he was out of ice cream or their favorite team lost, he turned into a bumbling fool. He knew they would handle it just fine, but it didn't make it any easier for him. Strange how life works.

After thinking about it more, he finally realized that there was probably only one way to make sure he did this right the first time—call his dad. The great Dr. Alan Allred had years and years of practice breaking bad sports news to his own son, and he always seemed to have done it perfectly. He consistently knew exactly how to talk to Harlan even when he was being, as his father always so lovingly put it, a first-class moron.

Harlan pressed the speed dial for his dad and after two rings he picked up, but skipping his usual hello said, "No Masterson, I see." He always knew why Harlan was calling. He was either a physic or a genius. Or perhaps both.

"Not tonight, it seems. The guy plays the first one hundred and sixty-one games and now they sit him down? Crazy with what he is about to accomplish. You would think the Mariners would want him on the field for it."

"True. But you can't risk having him get injured just to put on a show. Unfortunate, still." Harlan was not surprised his dad had gone through the same thought process about Masterson sitting out. How does the saying go? Great minds think alike? Or maybe it's fanatical minds think alike. Either way, they were both on the same wavelength on this one. Harlan was right to call his dad.

"Jack is meeting me here in just a few minutes. He has been looking forward to this game—to see Masterson finish off the season on the field—for weeks. Seeing that he was lucky enough to have been born with the Allred Crazy Sports Fan Gene, how do I break this news to him?" Harlan felt like a little kid asking his dad to help him with some impossible math word problem about two trains driving toward each other at different speeds. Luckily, his dad always knew how to figure out those questions, too.

"Funny you ask. I was just thinking of calling you so I could break the news to you first."

"I think I am going to make it this time, but thanks, Dad," Harlan said through the laughter. "Honestly, I am concerned about Jack. What should I do for this one?"

"This might be a tough one, but I think I have something." *Thank goodness*, Harlan thought, because he still had nothing. "Do you remember what happened during the 1983 Seahawks season? It had to do with your sports idol at the time?"

Harlan pondered about this for a second and then remembered. "That was the year Chuck Knox decided to bench Jim Zorn in the middle of the season." Jim Zorn was Harlan's favorite football player as a kid—the quarterback from day one in the 1976 season when Seattle finally got an NFL team. He was not the world's best quarterback, or really a very good one at all, but he was fun to watch—a charismatic leader who loved to run around the field and sling the ball as hard as he could. Harlan loved that guy, and the day they decided to sit him down on the bench for good was not a happy one in Harlan's life.

"That's the one. You were just twelve, and he was all you talked about during the football season. Your room was covered in his posters and your handmade drawings from top to bottom, and I use the word drawings loosely. When you played football with your friends you always had to be quarterback and you played just like him. Running around like an animal, trying to make throws that weren't there. If I remember correctly, your neighborhood team won about as often as those Seahawks teams did." Alan laughed again, but not at Harlan. He was just laughing at another fatherhood memory that kept him going.

"You stuck with him when everyone was calling for anyone else in the world to start. You were so blinded by your love for Zorn, you could not see what everyone else could see. It was time to move on. I knew it, and you know what? Zorn probably did, too. But you wanted him to be wearing number ten for Seattle forever."

Alan paused for a moment, as if he was reliving the memory all over again. "I think it was the sixth or seventh game of the season, and it was just brutal. Zorn was a disaster. I woke up the next morning early, went out, picked up the paper, and turned right to the sports page. First thing I saw was a quote from Seattle's coach saying it was time to move on for good from Zorn. Do you know what my first thought was when I saw that?"

Harlan knew he'd thought about how his son would take the news.

"It was about you, son. Just like you right now, I only had a few minutes to come up with the perfect plan before you bounced down the stairs. I thought about shielding you from it, taking you out of school for the day so there was no way you would hear it. But I knew that wasn't an option. Eventually you would hear. Plus, your mom would never let me take you out of school for a whole day. So responsible, that woman. Do you remember what happened next?"

Harlan could tell Alan was hoping that this instance had stuck with him like it had for Alan; it had been a major bonding occasion in their lives. Harlan racked his brain for this memory. He wanted to remember for both his dad and for Jack. What was it? What did his dad do for him that day?

Sensing Harlan could not remember, Alan spoke up. "Honestly, I wouldn't expect you to. It was so small. Only the person who did it would probably remember. Before you came down the stairs, I got out a pair of scissors and cut the article out. Of course, I thought of just throwing it away, but instead I got out a piece of paper and glued the article to it. Then I placed it in a binder and put it on your chair at the table."

"I do remember that. I remember going to my seat and seeing the binder. I remember wondering what it was and you wordlessly telling me to open it up. I remember reading the article and hoping that there was more on another page saying that they were going to give Zorn one more start. I looked up at you, tears starting to form in my eyes, and you said that was just part of being a fan. The names on the back of the jersey change, but it's the name on the front of the jersey that matters most." Harlan smiled at that memory. How his dad knew exactly what to say and helped him get through the sports crisis of a twelve-year-old boy.

"That's the funny thing, Harlan. I didn't say anything at all. I just looked at you and let you work through it. You came to that conclusion yourself. I just chose to treat you like a man. And you responded. Like a man."

Harlan was unsure what to say as tears formed in his eyes once more. He fought them back and said the only thing he could think of. "Thanks, Dad."

"You're welcome, son. Even though you lost your way for a bit, you're a good dad. Give me a call tomorrow and let me know how it goes with you and Jack."

"Will do. How about instead we have breakfast together tomorrow? I plan on getting to the hospital at ten, so how about eight? I could use a little home-cooked meal at la Casa de Allred." Harlan didn't get to the old house often enough, and tomorrow seemed like the perfect time. He could use some doctor-to-doctor advice, too.

"It's officially on the schedule. I'll let your mom know. I am sure she will make something elaborate and special for you."

Harlan laughed. "I am sure she will. Tell her that her famous peanut butter and jelly sandwiches will do just fine, even for breakfast." Now Alan laughed, too.

"All right. Now go. Enjoy the game with Jack. Give him a hug from his old Grandpa."

As they hung up, Harlan smiled. He really was glad he called his dad. When he was young he always thought that his dad was Superman. As he got older, he started to realize that he was fortunate. His dad really was Superman.

Harlan continued to smile as he looked up to see Jack walking over from the bus. Game time. Time to be like the dad that Harlan had as a kid—that he still had today. Time to be the dad that his son deserved.

Chapter 12

Clara sat at the nurse's station on the fourth floor exhausted and beside herself, wishing she could be any place other than work. Not that she didn't love her job. She did more than words could describe, but this was the sort of night that made her wish she worked in a much less involved field, something where she could just clock in and clock out and not give a crap about what happened when she left through the door. Health care, especially nursing, was not that way at all.

And what about Marcus? She was supposed to be out with her firefighter tonight. Not to be selfish, but she could use another night out with her muscle-bound freak of nature. Luckily, he understood that Clara needed to be here, another thing that made him so great. He understood that she needed to be with her patients. Unlike her policeman, Dalton, whom she was with just last night. That dude was so needy.

Throughout her career, she'd heard people say not to get attached to patients. Whoever said or even thought that must be a moron. They'd obviously never worked in health care. And above all, they had never met Stacy.

Clara walked by Stacy's room and stuck her head in to see how everything was going. There was the little angel, resting like nothing was happening and she was just fine.

Over in the corner in his usual spot sat Stacy's dad. He, on the other hand, didn't look well. Clara couldn't see his face because it was buried in his hands, but she was sure if she could it would be the saddest thing she had ever seen. Drenched in tears. Just another long and difficult day for all of them.

Clara didn't want to stand in the door and stare. Even though it was her job to check in on them, she felt like she was invading their privacy. As if she were witnessing them struggle through a horrible nightmare without an invitation.

As Clara turned to walk back to the nurse's station, an ear-piercing scream came from right behind her. She turned and began to run into Stacy's room, but before she could even get close to Stacy, more screams came from the room next door. And almost like they had rehearsed it, all the patients began to scream out in agonizing pain. How could everything be so calm one second and then explode into a million pieces the next? Why had this been happening to these poor children all day?

It didn't matter how many years of training or how many decades of work nurses had put in, nothing could prepare them for this. Clara felt frozen to the ground, and it appeared all the nurses on duty had the same reaction. Fear gripped their hearts, and it was going to win.

Except Lucy. She was moving with the determination of a nurse possessed. The look on her face and confidence in her stride were things Clara often noticed Lucy had in situations like this.

Even with Lucy on the scene, Clara still wanted to call Harlan to get his advice. To get him to come to the hospital. But he was with his son, and there were more important things to life than work. Even if he would want to know, she couldn't do it.

Besides, there were other doctors around besides Harlan. None that she trusted as much, but still they were there. And they were good and could do this. Her biggest fear was who was available that night, who was on call. Who were the doctors that were rounding and could be there right away? As she realized her options, the fear once again took over and her heart sank.

There were only two choices: Dr. Alex James or Dr. Diana Baxter. Her hope was that one would get there first and take the lead in the disastrous situation. But, why would that be the case? It was never that easy.

"Clara! Get your fat butt moving and do something. Dr. Allred's not here to hold your hand tonight," Dr. James yelled out—his typical way of communicating—as he turned the corner. Perfect. Just the man she wanted to see.

Dr. James was the type of doctor that, if you didn't know him personally, you would want taking care of your children. He was a genius. More than that, he was a jerk. But because he was invaluable to what they were trying to do at the hospital—on top of the rumors he was shacking up with the CMO—no one said anything about it. Except Harlan.

While Harlan wasn't one for conflict—Clara was positive he avoided it at all costs—something about Alex caused Harlan to lose his cool.

Clara could clearly remember the day that Alex came storming around the corner, yelling and swearing at the top of his lungs about something one of the nurses didn't do correctly. It looked like a vein in Harlan's forehead was about to burst wide open, but he calmly walked over to Alex to remind him where they were, and that there were children around.

Alex smiled and said, with his face as close to Harlan's as he could possibly get without kissing him, "Did I hurt your feelings, Dr. Hero? Maybe if you had put as much thought into your marriage as you do into the way I talk, you would still have a family."

It went absolutely silent on the floor. No one could believe it. Alex just stood there with that ridiculous "worship me" smile on his face, and the only thing Harlan did was move a few inches closer until it looked like they were touching noses.

Harlan then whispered in Alex's ear something that only the two doctors could hear. The grin, that stupid grin, slowly disappeared off Alex's face. Harlan turned, with his veins still exploding, and slowly walked to his office.

Clara later asked Harlan what he said that seem to scare Alex into needing a diaper. Harlan just smiled and said something about not wanting her to think less of him. Then he winked at her and walked off.

Now, however, Clara had to work with the man. She didn't want to, but she knew she didn't have a choice. Especially when she heard the screams coming from Stacy's room again.

Chapter 13

"Dad! Hey!" Jack called out as he approached the gate where they would enter.

Harlan was unsure if Jack already knew that Masterson would not be starting tonight. He could have heard it on the radio during his bus ride or read it on his smartphone that everyone, including teenagers, had these days. Part of him hoped that Jack already knew. That would make his job much easier.

But the other part of him, the stronger part, was looking forward to the chance to help his son grow. This may be something small—getting over a beloved player not playing in one game—but it would still matter to Jack. And if it mattered to Jack, then it mattered to Harlan.

"Hey, Jack. Glad you made it. 6:30, right on the dot. You've got your grandmother's punctuality," Harlan said to Jack as he gave him a hug. "So, what are you most excited about for tonight's game?" he asked, hoping that Jack would spill that he already knew the not-so-happy news.

“I’m guessing you want me to say something cheesy like, to be able to spend time with my daddy!” Jack was laughing as he said this, probably knowing that Harlan would love to hear that. What dad wouldn’t? “I think you know the answer. We get to see history tonight, Dad. Masterson is going to finish the season over .400, and we get to be there to witness it. Pretty freakin’ awesome.”

Shoot. He hadn’t heard yet. Time to give him the news, and he finally knew how to do it. He would take a page out of his father’s playbook. He was going to treat Jack like a man.

“Can I see your phone for second?”

“Um, sure. I guess. What for?” Jack seemed puzzled but handed his new, sleek smartphone to him. Harlan unlocked the phone and found the starting lineups for tonight’s game and handed it back to his son. Jack scanned through the lineup once and then again. He then looked up at Harlan with a puzzled look in his eyes and then back down to his phone and scanned it one more time. Harlan could tell he was hoping beyond hope that he was reading it wrong.

“Why? Why wouldn’t they start Masterson tonight, of all nights?” Harlan wanted so badly to give him all the reasons why, but he knew that Jack needed to walk through this one on his own.

After what seemed like ten minutes, but was probably more like ten seconds, Jack appeared to have figured it out. “The playoffs are much more important than this game. What if he slips rounding first base and tears his

ACL or something? We would be lost. Plus, he will still end the season on top. I guess that means we have been witnessing history all year."

Awesome, Harlan thought. Pretty freakin' awesome. Not only did Jack get it, but he got it much better than Harlan had.

"Exactly, my man. Exactly. And they will probably bring him out at the end of the game for some sweet ceremony. Maybe there'll be some fireworks to go with it." Jack was a fan of fireworks, but who wasn't? Loud explosions and bright lights in the sky: that's how you know something special has happened in America.

"Awesome! Now let's go in or we won't get our food before the first pitch. Can't break tradition or something bad will happen tonight." Jack was not smiling when he said this and neither was Harlan. Superstitions for sports fans were serious business, and if they missed out on their pregame ritual, they both feared they would be the sole reason the whole season blew up in one night.

They got to their seats in plenty of time with all their food: peanuts, two hot dogs for each covered in ketchup and mustard, and a box of Cracker Jack to share. And to wash it down they got something healthy to balance out the heart attack they had just ordered—thirty-two ounce root beers. Nothing quite like father/son bonding time to ensure that you will both die at an early age.

By the end of the third inning, they had both polished off their hot dogs and were about done with their peanuts, too. It was usually about this time at every game that Jack, having the bladder of a pregnant woman, needed to head to the bathroom. And it was usually about this time Harlan would check his Twitter to see what everyone was saying about the game.

Tonight he was hoping to get some more news about Masterson and why he was out of the game. Maybe there would be something more about a planned ceremony for him after the game, too.

He scrolled through his Twitter feed and came across a tweet from @SamsoniteTimes—the Twitter handle for John Samson, one of the most respected sports journalists in the country—which made him take pause.

Hearing Masterson is not even at the game and hasn't been seen all day. Not surprising, if you ask me.

Not even at the game? Why in the world would Masterson not be there? And why wasn't this surprising to Samson? Harlan decided that drastic times called for drastic measures, so he was going to do something he rarely did—send out a tweet. He hit the reply button and sent a message hurling through cyberspace, hoping that Samson would respond.

@SamsoniteTimes Not surprising? Why do you say that? Seems like Masterson would want to be here for his big night.

He pressed send and waited. He figured that Samson got hundreds of tweets, so there was little chance he would even give Harlan's tweet the time of day. Just as the Mariners turned a huge double play to end the inning, Harlan's phone vibrated in his pocket. He would never get used to that strange feeling. Ever. But it got his attention, so he would live with it.

Harlan took his phone out of his pocket figuring it was an email, or maybe a text from Jack saying he was getting some more food, only to be surprised to see a tweet, directed to him, from @SamsoniteTimes. He read it, paused, and then read it again.

@DocAllred Hard to explain, but Masterson is a bad seed. I've never seen anything like him in all my years. Always all about him.

Bad seed? Nothing like him in all his years? Always about him? Masterson seemed like a solid, upstanding citizen who really cared about the fans. He thought about all those times Masterson visited the hospital and spent a great deal of time with the kids. He wouldn't only walk around and take photos for some sort of publicity stunt. No, he would sit and talk to each child. He'd find out why they were there and how long they had been there. He would talk to them about their dreams and how they would reach them once they got home. He would tell stories about his childhood in Australia with all the wild animals and the kids would eat it up. He was their hero. He was everyone's hero.

He didn't merely take time with kids, but he visited with the whole staff. In fact, Harlan remembered the time Masterson spent with different members of the hospital staff about nine months ago. Not just doctors or administrators either. It was everyone from a janitor mopping the floors to a CNA exhausted from a twelve-hour shift to a phlebotomist who needed a break from drawing blood from the sickest of the sick.

It was an amazing sight to see a star athlete take time like that. And now he was hearing that Masterson was some sort of villain from the mouth (or the fingers) of his favorite sports writer? He wasn't sure how to take this all in. He decided to see if he could find out anything further from Samson.

@SamsoniteTimes What makes you say that? Anything specific? Sounds different than the guy we all see each day. Really strange.

This time a response came less than a minute after Harlan sent his tweet.

@DocAllred He doesn't show it often or to many people, but I saw this other, dark side. Read tomorrow's article for more information.

Wow. Harlan wasn't often interested in gossip magazines or TV shows, but he was interested in this. He was interested in reading what Samson's article would say that would give more details into this dark side of Luke Masterson. He had never read an article by Samson that wasn't backed up by proof and 100 percent accurate. Samson wasn't some hack who wanted to dirty the reputation of any of Seattle's athletes to further his career. Whatever it was, Harlan guessed it was awful and factual.

As Harlan was about to get lost in this thought and what this all meant, Jack returned to his seat with some fries for them to share. They watched the rest of the game together, just enjoying the atmosphere. There were lots of high fives, jumping out of their seats at big hits, and hugs all around.

But there was no more talk of Masterson, and there was definitely no post-game ceremony to celebrate his season. It was, for almost everyone in attendance, anticlimactic.

But it wasn't just that for Harlan. Yes, it was a difficult game to witness because of what everyone was expecting. It was much more than that now for him. He guessed it was a difficult thing for him to know that come morning, when he opened his computer, Samson's article would prove everything he thought he knew about his and Jack's sports idol was a lie.

Harlan dropped Jack off at his mother's home after the game. As always, he got out of the car and gave his son a hug and let him know he loved him. Jack declared he loved him, too, words that meant more to Harlan than anything in the world, and thanked him for a "freakin' awesome night!"

"It's been a fun regular season, Dad. Seriously, I am so glad you've got season tickets," Jack said as he opened the house door. "Thanks for taking me so many games. Now just eleven more wins and Seattle gets that championship! So pumped about that!"

"Me, too. It will be tremendous to have front row seats for the whole thing. Well, not front row, exactly. But they are still pretty good."

"Front row, back row, box seat, I don't care. It's just been fantastic to finally spend more time with you, Daddy." Jack was smiling as he said it. It was a little sarcastic, alluding to their conversation before the game, but it also seemed sincere.

At least one thing went right for Harlan that day, because everything else was a disaster. Although he had no idea what to expect from tomorrow, he did know one thing. He was glad that this long, complicated, and heart-wrenching day was finally over. But when he finally pulled into his driveway, Harlan was no longer sure if his day was over after all. He looked up and saw the shadow of someone snooping around his front windows, and it made him freeze as fear ran through his veins.

Chapter 14

Harlan slowly got out of his car and tried to think back to all the cop shows he had watched throughout his life. How did they move gradually so the person they were tracking couldn't see them? Did they roll around on the ground to avoid detection? He was sure they did, but he was also unsure if that worked in real life. Plus, he didn't have a gun. He looked around for something, anything, he could use to protect himself from his would-be attacker. He had nothing. Seriously, nothing to use at all. He was done for, and he knew it. Turns out this day could get worse.

"Whatever you want, you can have it. Take my car, I don't care. Just please let me live," Harlan yelled out in hope that maybe this shadow would spare him.

"Wow. I haven't heard someone whine like that since I took the last pudding cup during lunch in the fifth grade," laughed Cole Panunzio, Harlan's best friend since they were seven years old. It was not some robber, here to take all of Harlan's valuables and end his life; it was Cole. Harlan, not for the first time in his life, felt like a fool. Maybe he should stop watching cop shows. Then he wouldn't let his imagination run wild with every tree branch breaking or creak he heard in his house late at night.

Harlan had met Cole during recess as they both were vying for the same swing when they were just first graders. To say that it was a "bromance" at first sight would be completely accurate.

Cole was an absolute genius. Harlan was a relatively smart guy himself, but Cole was always the smartest person in the room, and it usually wasn't close. This incredible intelligence was both a blessing and a curse for Cole. A blessing because school was easy for him; he could remember every single fact he heard and have a discussion with anyone about anything at any time.

It was a curse because Cole couldn't control it, and at times, it overpowered him. He would lose sight of what was important and for days at a time lock himself in his room, unable to face the pressures of all the expectations around him. For Harlan, this was difficult to watch because Cole always wanted to go at it alone, and too often this desire just made things worse.

During the fall of their junior year of high school, the majority of their class was in full prep mode for their upcoming SATs, the stupid standardized test that only tells you how well you test and not how smart you are. But because of its importance for getting into college, students and high schools still overemphasized its importance. And it wasn't any different at Everett High School, except all the pressure was squarely on Cole.

Everett High had never had a student obtain the perfect score of 1600 and everyone, seriously everyone, expected Cole to finally be their first. Harlan remembered thinking the pressure was stupid even then and Cole felt the exact same way, until Ms. Bridges, their AP American History teacher, changed everything about one month before they were to take the test.

"Who knows the main causes of the Civil War?" she asked while scanning the class for someone to raise their hand to volunteer. When no one did, she did what most teachers did to get an answer. She called on Cole.

"Sixteen hundred? What do you think?" Everyone in the class turned to Cole, who seemed to be oblivious to the fact that she was calling on him.

"Wait. Did you call on me?"

"I did, Cole. So, what were the main causes of the Civil War?"

Cole stared at her and said nothing.

"Well . . . what do you think, Cole? We would all love to hear your thoughts."

"Did you really just call me sixteen hundred?" He started to stand up, a little fear and anger coming through his voice. Harlan grabbed his arm, attempting to push Cole back into his seat.

"Why did you call me that? Why did you call me sixteen hundred?" His voice was getting close to shouting, something Cole hardly ever did. Especially to a teacher.

"Cole," Harlan said, once again trying to calm his friend down. "Don't worry about it. It's no big deal."

"No big deal? No big deal? Are you in on it, too?"

"I'm sorry this is upsetting you, Cole," Ms. Bridges said. "It's just what the teachers have been calling you lately."

"All the teachers? Are you freaking serious? Is that all I am to you idiots? A number? A perfect score? Something that will make you all look better?"

"No, not at . . ."

"It is," Cole said as he sat down, but now he sounded more like a wounded puppy than an attack dog whose perimeter had been breached just seconds before. "Whatever. If that's all you want, if that's all I am to you, that's what you'll get."

And then, like nothing had happened at all, Cole moved on. "Slavery was the reason. Lots of people have theories of what caused it, but, to me, they are wrong. It was completely about slavery."

For the next month Cole ate, drank, and slept the SATs. He would study all night, maybe sleep for two hours, go to school because he had to, and then head home to study the rest of the night. He never came to hang out anymore. He just studied.

When the day for the SAT finally came, the usual test-day calm Cole didn't show up. Cole was there but was replaced by a nervous and jittery version of himself that Harlan had never seen before.

About halfway through the verbal section, Cole leaped out of his chair, threw his fully sharpened number two pencils against the way, started swearing like a nurse (sailors have nothing on nurses), and stormed out of the classroom, went home without stopping and holed himself up in his room without looking back.

He stayed there for two weeks and would not let a soul enter. When he finally came out, he picked up life where it left off, before he was even thinking about the SATs, and went back to being Cole. It was like nothing had ever happened.

This incredible intelligence, this once-in-a-lifetime gift, was like the most amazing superpower and the world's most devastating kryptonite all at the same time.

Harlan snapped out of the memory of this childhood and gave his oldest and best friend a hug, "It was vanilla anyway. Who in the world wants vanilla pudding in the first place? You saved me from eating that disgusting crap," I should have known it was you. I could smell something rancid from a mile away."

"Same insults from when we were kids. Nice. Dude spends half his life in medical school and still spews his vicious comebacks like a prepubescent boy." It was true. Harlan turned into a little kid the moment they were around each other. It was like they were seven years old, vying for that swing once again. He loved that. It was such a needed escape from the real world.

"Well, get off my front step. You're lowering the property value the longer your sorry butt sits here." Yup, prepubescent boys and Harlan wouldn't have it any other way. "Need a place to stay, again? Plenty of room in this empty house for you." Although it had been a month or two since Cole had crashed at Harlan's place, it was still a normal occurrence, and a welcome one, too. It meant he was not alone, at least for one night.

"I was hoping we could both use your bed tonight. It's been a while since I've spooned with anyone. Probably even longer for you."

"That would be perfect. NOT. Wow, I just said not. Someone save me. How about you just sleep on the futon and keep your hands off me?" Harlan and Cole both chuckled. This was a necessary and enjoyable distraction. The perfect night for Cole to show up. "So, what brings you here this time? Apartment burn down? Rent money run out? Rat infestation? Come on, why am I so lucky to be graced with your presence?"

"I missed your face. Let's just leave it at that and move on. Sound like a plan?" Harlan sensed a bit of defensiveness in Cole's voice, which truthfully was quite rare, and decided to drop it. No reason to push this one further, because he knew it would eventually come out.

"Good plan. You are welcome here anytime and for however long you need. Make yourself at home but leave some food for me," Harlan said as he grabbed some of

Cole's stuff and put it in one of the downstairs bedrooms. "Speaking of food, I am going to my parents for breakfast tomorrow around 8:00. You're more than welcome to join us. They would love to see you."

"That could be a good time. I could use some of your mom's cooking. If I am up and your dad's not cooking, I'm there." This meant there was absolutely no way that Cole would make it in the morning. It was already after midnight, and Cole needed his beauty sleep.

"Perfect, buddy." As Harlan was about to go upstairs and get himself ready for bed, he realized that Cole's car was not out front. He was about to ask how he'd gotten there but remembered how adamant Cole was that they not talk about it further, so he let it go. "You need anything else before I turn in? It's been a long day and I could use some shut-eye."

"Nope. Just hoping all is well in your world. Saw that Masterson didn't play today and I know how much that stuff really matters to you. You surviving?"

"I'm actually handling it much better. Fourteen-year-old me is freaking out and breaking stuff all over the house. Forty-one-year-old me is, um, calm-ish. I will survive." He was telling the truth here. He would survive, though he was quite concerned about it. Especially considering what Samson had said in his tweets. "I did have a strange Twitter conversation with John Samson about tonight though."

"Twitter conversation? I am not sure how that whole thing works, but please spare me the nerdy details." Cole always mocked Harlan's use of social media. It was well-deserved; it was kind of a dorky obsession. "That being said, what did he say?"

Harlan filled Cole in on how Samson said Masterson was a bad seed with a dark side, and that there would be an article about it in the morning with more details. Cole seemed extremely interested in this development, and Harlan could tell that he was using his massive intellect to figure out a solution to this revelation before the article was released.

"What do you think?" Cole asked Harlan. "Does this have legs to it, or is it just some fluff piece to drive hits to their website?"

"No way it's a fluff piece. Samson is above that. There has to be something to it or he would never report it."

"True. I guess we will have to wait with bated breath to find out what the story has to say. I can hardly contain myself." Cole was a bit sarcastic with this remark as he exaggerated his interest in Masterson, but Harlan could tell he wanted to know. "Anything else going on in your world? I am guessing something else is weighing you down."

"Seriously, what makes you come to that conclusion? You reading my diary again?"

"Of course. I love all the juicy details about your late-night sleepovers and the girls you are going to ask to the prom. Come on now. You're going over quite early to your parents tomorrow, and I am guessing there is something you need to talk to them about. You can't hide this stuff from your bestest friend." The guy could read him like a book.

"All right, you got me. Stacy Montgomery is what is going on." Health privacy be damned, Cole knew all about Stacy. He knew how Harlan had saved her life yet felt he should have done more. No matter how many times Cole tried to explain to Harlan that he was a hero in all this, it fell on deaf ears.

"It's not just her, but she is, ya know, Stacy. She is the one that weighs most heavily on my mind. Today she came in for a visit and something had changed. When I was looking at her, all of the sudden, she started to scream out in incredible pain. And it only got worse, as though it were taking over her body."

Harlan explained the situation to Cole even though he hated reliving the details, and Cole understood that, so he just listened without uttering a word. "I couldn't help her at all. And then she stopped crying out and was calm again. It continued happening throughout the day. Twelve patients, seven of them mine. Twelve, Cole!"

There was a long pause, and Cole decided it was time he chimed in. "Have any clue what is going on? Can't be some crazy coincidence."

Harlan explained how all the patients had had appointments over the last few days with blood draws. They were all now admitted for the night, and tests were being run—every test that Harlan could think of that would give them an answer fast.

"Sounds like you've covered every angle. You still seem bothered though, bro."

"If I weren't, wouldn't you be surprised?" asked Harlan, always overthinking every situation. "Something just doesn't seem right about all this, like there is something more going on. I just can't put my finger on it."

"You will. You're the great and amazing Dr. Allred. Stop worrying and rest your pretty little head for the night. There is nothing you can do about it now anyway, except worry yourself to death."

"Sleep, schmeep. What fun is merely sleeping it off? I would rather sit up and stew it over. It's good for my heart and my mind, too. Helps you live longer, right? At least that is what four out of every five doctors say in a recent survey of all the industry's leaders."

"That must be why you and I are both pillars of health. Glad to know we were ahead of the curve on that one." If there really were such a survey or study, then they undoubtedly would be the healthiest people on the planet.

"How about we both get some sleep anyway," Cole stated. "You never know when a new study will come out proclaiming the exact opposite."

"True. We doctors always change our minds, don't we? It's part of the fun." Was there fun in being a doctor anymore? He always loved finding a way to help his patients. That was fun. And he was completely uncertain that with this case, this haunting case, he was going to have any fun at all.

Chapter 15

That night, despite all the stress and worry, Harlan was able to get some sleep. And he only knew it because he was jolted out of bed by the sound of his phone ringing. As he fumbled to pick it up, he noticed that the clock next to his bed said 5:23. Who in the world was calling him at this early hour? This better be good. No, it better be the most important phone call ever.

Afraid that he wouldn't get to the call in time, he didn't look at the caller ID and groggily answered, "This better be good news."

"Good to talk to you too, Harlan." It was Clara. This must be important. "Sorry for calling so early, but we need you to come in earlier than you were planning."

Shoot, Harlan thought, he was looking forward to breakfast with his parents. Luckily, they would understand that when duty calls, the doctor must answer.

"I can do that. Is everything all right? Did something more happen during the night?" Maybe he should have just skipped the game and stayed with his patients.

"Everything is, how do I put this, manageable. It's a lot like yesterday, but when the kids are in pain it's much worse than we've ever seen. We can give them the best support possible, but you need to come in. They need you."

Harlan was not sure how he felt about the word manageable. This was not what a doctor or a patient would want to hear at all. Clara was doing her best to not send Harlan into a frenzy, but that didn't stop him from being extremely distressed.

"I'll do my best to be there by 8:00, but it will probably be more like 8:30 with traffic. Hope that will be soon enough." Harlan was already taking off his clothes and heading to the shower, hoping that this head start would give him a few extra minutes, and he could get to the hospital earlier.

"Ok. Don't drive too fast to get here. You won't be any good to us if you are brought to another hospital on a stretcher." She was always so loving and tactful when it came to Harlan, but great advice still. *Don't die, Harlan, just don't die.* He would do everything in his power to take good ol' Clara's instructions.

Take them he did. Every time he started to speed up worrying he would be late, he would hear Clara telling him to take his foot off the peddle and take his time.

As he rolled into his spot, he thought about how just yesterday he had parked with all the optimism in the world, believing it would be the perfect day. Now, as he got out of his car and made his way inside, he was filled with doubt. He was amazed by how much could change in only twenty-four short hours.

Before entering the hospital, Harlan stopped to make sure he had on his best game face and realized he had not called his parents to let them know he would not be able to make it. He pulled out his phone. It was 7:50. He had made it in plenty of time and had a few minutes to make the call.

This time his mom, Rachael, answered the phone. It was always good to hear her calming voice. Harlan seemed to feel that way about a lot of people.

"Hello, honey. Are you getting close?" His mom sounded eager, like she had been looking forward to this for weeks. Even though they just set this up last night, she probably had been. Time to break his mother's heart. Again.

"Sadly, I've been called into the hospital. Emergency, you know how it goes." She knew better than anyone in the world. How many nights had she had to put dinner aside because Alan had a much later night than expected? How many times had she had to cancel her plans because something unanticipated had happened that needed Dr. Allred's attention? Too many to count. She understood all too well.

"Yes, I know how it goes. I was afraid that would happen. Everything ok at the hospital? Anything you can talk about?"

"Everything is, um, complicated. That is the best way to put it. Complicated. I don't have time to talk right now, but I want, no, I need to talk to you both about everything. Let's plan a meal soon. Would that work?" Harlan knew that she would say that would be fine, but she also wouldn't be holding her breath thinking it would be any time soon.

"Great. Call us when you have a break and we will save a space at the table for you."

"I'm really sorry, Mom. I was looking forward to this. I am truly sorry." Harlan was hoping that she genuinely knew how bad he felt. This was not how he wanted to start his day, and it was not at all how he wanted to start his mom's day.

"It's ok, Harlan. Come soon, and don't be a stranger," she said as they said goodbye.

Harlan felt his heart fall slightly out of his chest. His mom, like his dad, was a huge supporter of all things Harlan. Because of that, when Harlan messed up his life or did something else to let her down, it crushed her. She expected better from him. She was worthy of better from him. He would make it up to her because she deserved it. And he would make sure to do it as soon as possible.

Harlan made his way into the hospital and realized that in the rush, he hadn't had time to read Samson's article about Masterson. He wanted to simply open it up on his phone, but he knew he needed to be at his best, his very best, to deal with whatever revelations the article held. He could not afford to think about anything else whatsoever.

He took the elevator up to the fourth floor where Stacy and the rest of his patients had stayed the night. He tried to prepare himself for what would be behind those doors. He felt he had adequately done so as the doors opened, but he couldn't have been more wrong.

As he walked down the hall, the feeling was that of pure gloom and despondency, and when he opened the door to room 418, he was taken aback with complete dread and panic for what was waiting for him inside.

Chapter 16

The moment Harlan walked into Stacy's room, he knew he had made a mistake. He should have done what he always did before entering a patient's room—get information about what was going on. But he had been in a hurry and had lost sight of what was best for that moment.

If he had, then he would have been prepared for what was awaiting him. Instead, like he had done so often in his life, he didn't think before he acted, and now he was in the middle of something that he had no idea how to handle.

Crowded around Stacy's bed were Clara and two additional nurses who looked like all they were trying to do was comfort her, unsure if they could do anything more. On the couch sat Phil, tears streaming down his face and onto his lap. The room was filled with despair, and Harlan had yet to see the worst of it.

He slowly made his way over to Stacy's bed and made eye contact with Clara, trying to read her thoughts in hope that she had some sort of master plan that could be beamed to Harlan's brain, and they could find a solution right then and there. Instead, the look in Clara's eyes was that of a lost puppy; not only a lost puppy, but one that wasn't sure if it would ever be found.

"When I called you this morning, it wasn't this bad," Clara said as Harlan finally saw what was happening to Stacy. "She, and the rest of the patients, were in so much pain but we could control it with medication. Now, well, now it's like nothing I have ever seen."

And neither had Harlan. As if there were a line drawn down the middle of Stacy's body, the entire right side of her, from her toes all the way to the top of her head, looked like it had been pumped full of air. She was swollen, and her skin was scarlet red. Harlan was astounded and felt like he would pass out any moment from shock. Everything that he was seeing screamed the worst, most excruciating pain imaginable.

Everything except for the look on Stacy's face. It no longer showed worry or concern like it had the day before. Now, as Stacy looked up at Harlan and caught his gaze, the only look was that of comfort and hope. As if she knew, without any doubt, that this was just a passing moment and soon she would be outside playing with her friends again. Who was this amazing girl? And could she transfer some of that confidence to Harlan? He could use an ounce of that right now.

Then, without any warning at all, those reassuring eyes rolled back into her head and she began to shake with a fury that Harlan had never seen before. It seemed like the whole hospital was now moving under the weight of this fragile little girl's pain. Or maybe that was just how Harlan felt watching it take place. He took a deep breath and got to work, and boy, did he ever work.

During a crisis, Harlan felt like a world-class athlete in an important big-game situation. When everyone else was on edge, he entered a zone that no one else could penetrate no matter how hard they tried. It was like his mind went completely blank; not blank as if he didn't know what he was doing, but blank like the rest of the world wasn't there. He knew nothing else but how to save a person's life. All the doubts and fears that plagued his life were gone. Completely gone. And everyone knew it. Every nurse, every tech, every ward clerk, heck, even the dietary and environmental services (the politically correct way of saying janitorial crew) knew it. They either worked with him and did whatever he asked, or they rightly stayed out of his way.

Clara knew exactly what Harlan was like during these times. They were a team, moving in rhythm and perfectly in sync. Without fail, as Harlan was about to ask for something, an instrument or fifty cc's of some sort of medicine, Clara had it in his hands before the words were out of his mouth. And this time was no different.

Actually, it was different. It was more like they were in the middle of a perfect game. Every thought, every movement, every action was perfect. They were—and not just Harlan and Clara, but the whole medical team—

perfect. The color returned to her face. The swelling was almost completely gone. And her eyes, those ever-believing eyes, were back staring at Harlan and the rest of the team with what appeared to be a look of gratitude. They were going to beat this, and they were going to beat this now. Stacy and the other patients would be home in no time. They would be whole again.

Until it all unraveled with two outs in the bottom of the ninth. Just as it was all about to come together, it all collapsed again. Why was there always an until or a but or a maybe? Why couldn't those types of limiting words be removed from the dictionary and everything just work out for once? Why?

Right at that moment when Harlan felt he had finally saved little Stacy's life, her heart stopped. Completely stopped. And so did Harlan's. As the flatline screeched across the screen, taunting him and showing him that, once again, he had failed, his knees buckled, and if it hadn't been for Clara holding him up, he would have collapsed to the ground.

"Get with it. Get back in the game," Clara whispered to Harlan as she held him up. "You can't lose hope. Not now. Not ever. We've got this."

Harlan looked at her and nodded to show her he was back. Back as much as he could be. Back as much as he needed to be for Stacy. He began again to bark out orders. Helen, one of the nurses, pulled out a "miracle" drug for children they were researching at the hospital for this kind of life-threatening situation. It had been successful many times, so it made sense that Helen would want to use it now.

As she prepared to inject the medicine into Stacy's IV, Harlan felt strongly that they should not use it, as though a small voice in the back of his head was shouting a warning that would not go away, and there was no time to second-guess his instinct.

"Don't use that, Helen! Now is not the time." Helen stared blankly at him, like he had lost his mind. As she opened her mouth in protest, Clara stared a dagger right through her that Harlan was positive every person in the room felt, and Helen quickly put the medicine down.

"What she needs is something we know will work. Helen! Michael! Use the defibrillator! What are you waiting for? Now!" As they sprang into action, Harlan turned to Clara and quietly said, "And you, grab my hand. We are going to do something that I have no idea if it will work or not, but it's what Stacy would want us to do: say a prayer for her."

While they stood next to the bed with the rest of the crew hard at work, they did just that. They did something Harlan was positive he hadn't done in over twenty years. A quick plea for help. A quick plea for strength to help Stacy. A quick acknowledgment that they couldn't do it all by themselves, and this God Stacy so adamantly believed in would pick up what they couldn't and add the needed push to get Stacy back where she belonged.

Moments after they ended their prayer, Helen yelled clear and Michael sent a shock through that little helpless body one more time. Harlan watched, just as he had hundreds of times before, the little body in front of him jolt under the electricity pulsing through her. This act would always amaze and terrify him. The person, an incredible man of science, who came up with this unbelievable idea to pulse electricity through a dying person's body, was a genius of the highest order.

The next few seconds felt like days, but as they were about to give up all hope, the monitor next to her bed started to beep, those beautiful beeps that meant life was back in the room. Call it a miracle or call it science, Harlan didn't care at this point. Stacy wasn't dead. She wasn't better, no, but at least she wasn't dead.

Chapter 17

Harlan slumped down in the chair in his office after another incredibly long day. He could not understand how he could possibly survive, either mentally or physically, any more days like the last few.

His patients were suffering pain that he could not explain. *His* patients. Yes, other doctors' patients were having the same horrific issues, but the majority spent time with him. He had spent most of that day trying to remedy similar episodes like Stacy's that so many of his patients were experiencing.

Every time he, or the other doctors and staff for that matter, got close and felt they were turning a corner, the world would stop and everything would once again go wrong. No, he didn't lose a single patient; they always came back from the brink of death, but he was, once again, a failure. A massive failure. And he was a failure in something he had spent close to ten years studying and training to become. Come on, Harlan. Snap out of it and figure this out.

Through all the commotion today, he had forgotten about what had happened the night before at the long-awaited baseball game. Now, it was extremely unimportant that Luke Masterson hadn't shown up for the last game of the season. People think that while doctors are at work, they are completely focused on work. But they need distractions too. Something to keep them sane. He decided that meant it was time to finally read John Samson's article about Luke and his dark side.

As Harlan picked up his phone to find the article, he noticed he had missed an incredible amount of phone calls, emails, and texts. Sure, it had been a few hours since he'd had his phone, but this seemed excessive. What had he missed? Had something happened to Jack or Leslie?

Was everything ok? It had to be, Harlan reasoned with himself. If it were something serious, something that was life-threatening or involved the health of his family, they would have called the hospital and tracked him down. It must have been messages from his adoring fan club. Yeah, that was it.

As he scrolled through his phone Harlan noticed that the calls and texts were almost 100 percent from three people: his dad, his son, and his best friend. They hadn't left any voice messages, but their texts all pretty much relayed the same message, although in different lingo according to the age of the sender.

"Harlan! (Or Dad! or Son!) Have you heard about John Samson?"

"Where are you? Call me as soon as you can!"

"Dude! (Or Son! or Dad! or Stud! Ok, not that one.) Your Twitter conversation with Samson from last night is all over the Internet and the news!"

What in the world were they talking about? What could have happened to a sports writer that had even Cole freaking out? And the little Twitter conversation he had with Samson was all over the World Wide Web? That was not only strange, but it sounded ridiculous. Now Harlan really needed to read that article and find out what was causing all this insanity.

Quickly, Harlan opened a browser and went to the sports section of the Seattle Times website hoping he wouldn't have to look far to find what he was looking for. He didn't, but it wasn't what he expected. Not in the slightest. There, right as he opened the page, was a headline that made his knees buckle underneath him: TIMES WRITER, JOHN SAMSON, FOUND DEAD.

Found? Dead? What? Where was he found? Dead? How could this be? He just tweeted with him less than twenty-four hours ago. How had he died? He wasn't that old, was he? And why was Harlan getting so worked up and depressed by the death of someone he didn't even know? Yes, he had been reading his articles for as long as he could remember, so Samson had strangely become a huge part of his life and now the life of his son. But did that give him any reason to freak out the way he was right now? No, but it just seemed so surreal and hard to wrap his head around.

As he sat there going through all these questions and crazy scenarios, Harlan came to the realization that he could probably get answers to these questions if he would just read the article that was opened on the screen right in front of him. Using that sound and complex logic, he did just that.

"Being ever the quintessential newspaper man, John Samson always went back to the office after any game had ended to write his report or his article for the next day's paper. He often said he never felt like writing while sitting at the game because he was sure he would miss some sort of magical moment. He wanted time to reflect and take it all in, and it always showed in the work he delivered day in and day out. Last night was no different and all of us at the Seattle Times wish it had been. Around 3 a.m. a member of our cleaning staff found our beloved colleague dead in front of his computer. While it is early in the investigation, the police believe that foul play was involved and are currently ruling this a homicide."

A homicide? Harlan blinked hard and read that last word again, but it didn't change. It still amazingly said homicide. Sure, someone who works in the media makes enemies, but Samson didn't really seem the type to do something so horrible, so slanderous, to warrant something like this happening to him. He couldn't wrap his head around this or anything that was going on right now.

Harlan continued to read the article that, up until the very end, was mostly a eulogy of the life of John Samson. The last paragraph was a plea for anyone who had any information, but it had a little twist that made Harlan glad he was reading it while he was sitting down.

"The police believe the article Samson was planning on writing that night may have a connection to these tragic events. If anyone knows anything more about this or has any other credible leads, they are asked to reach out as soon as possible."

Like a tornado sweeping a trailer park and not missing a single home, Harlan was blown away by what he read. He knew what Samson was going to write about, and he wondered if he was the only one who knew, which meant he needed to do his civic duty and take this to the police.

But it was such a convoluted theory that he couldn't really see the purpose of wasting the police's time with it. Come on now, why would an article about an athlete being a bad seed cause someone to murder Samson? It seemed like a stretch, a plausible one he guessed, but a stretch nonetheless. Maybe he really should call the police to give them the information he had just to get them off this strange tangent and back in the right direction to find Samson's killer. Yup, that seemed like a good idea.

As he was about to close the browser on his phone so he could use it for what it was made for, Harlan noticed a headline on the bottom of the article about Samson: SAMSON'S TWITTER EXCHANGE SPARKS CONCERN.

Harlan clicked on the link and, while he waited for the article to open, he remembered the texts he had just gotten that said his Twitter conversation with Samson was all over the Internet. Is this what the article was about? Once again, Harlan's now increasingly fragile heart skipped a few beats as he thought what this simple social media site had gotten him into. He couldn't believe that this had anything to do with him. This had to just be some sort of coincidence, but since he started going to AA, he no longer believed in coincidences.

At almost every meeting he went to something would happen, something would be said, someone would do something that seemed like a coincidence. This would always lead someone to say, "There are no coincidences in AA." Everyone would laugh but only for a second, because after a while they had all begun to really believe this was true, that, religious or not, everything happened for a reason. This was no different.

At the same time, Samson probably engaged in hundreds of Twitter conversations each week. This story could be talking about any of those. He just needed to calm down and apply the logic he had used with the earlier article—read the story and maybe get some answers to all the questions bouncing around in his head instead of speculating for hours and driving himself mad.

"This morning we all woke up to the horrible and saddening news that John Samson was found dead at his computer. As the police continue their investigation, they currently believe that the article Samson planned to write may have led to his death. The question on everyone's mind is if he never actually wrote the article, how could the police come to this conclusion? The answer is Twitter. That's right, it was a Twitter exchange that Samson had with the user @DocAllred during last night's Mariners game that led them in this direction.

"Around the fourth inning Samson sent out this tweet in regards to Luke Masterson, the Mariners star, who was nowhere to be seen last night:

Hearing Masterson is not even at the game and hasn't been seen all day. Not surprising, if you ask me.

"This tweet seemed to surprise many and led to over 5,000 retweets from all over the country and hundreds of responses from Twitter users wondering what Samson meant. As is his custom, he only responded to one person's tweet, which led to the discussion in question."

And there it was. Printed on the screen in front of Harlan. His Twitter conversation with Samson. Why? Why did this matter? Harlan continued to read, hoping for an answer.

"As anyone can see, Samson tells the Twitter user that Masterson is not what everyone thinks he is, and that tomorrow he would be printing an article that would explain what he meant. From this simple exchange the police see a motive for someone to go after Samson to shut him up. Initially, many expressed skepticism that this exchange would have anything to do with what the death of Samson as negative articles are written about athletes often.

That was until one last tweet that Samson sent at 1:30 am was released by the Seattle Police Department.

@DocAllred Help me.

"That's it. Samson pleads with what is believed to be a random Twitter user to help him moments before he was murdered. This addition, this very simple addition, has changed my mind. There is something that was going to be in that article that caused this to happen to Samson. The police are asking anyone . . ."

At that point Harlan's head started spinning, and the words on the page followed the same pattern. He put down his phone in hopes that it would stop him from passing out. It didn't help. The article may have answered the questions he was asking himself before he read it, but it added many more.

He did not remember seeing any additional tweets from Samson, but he was in a rush that morning and had not checked his Twitter account at all. Why, seriously why, in the name of all that is good and holy, would Samson tweet him for help? There was nothing logical about it at all. Aside from reading his articles every morning for years, he didn't know the man from Adam.

He opened his Twitter account and went to his notifications to see if he could find this tweet pleading for his help, and at first, he couldn't. That was because his "mentions" were filled with tweets from people he didn't know but had seen his exchange with Samson.

He found one from someone named @ cheesedancer2001 (what kind of name is that, and were there already 2000 cheese dancers out there?) that said **why didn't you help him, bro?** He clicked on it, and it expanded to show the whole thread. There it was, plain as day. The tweet, **@DocAllred Help me**, was staring him right in the face. And as he read it his head began to spin again, and he wasn't sure it would ever stop as long as he lived.

Harlan rested his head for a moment on his desk, and that moment gave him some clarity. He needed to call the police. He needed to let them know that it truly was just some simple Twitter conversation. He needed to help them try and apply some logic to the whole situation. Samson was probably just looking at their conversation when the attack happened and that was the only way he could reach out for help. It wouldn't take any more time than sending a text. They were overthinking this, and if anyone could identify overthinking, it was Harlan. He would call them and let them know to move on to an actual theory. That seemed like the best plan.

Once again, Harlan went to use his phone as a phone. When he went to push the button to open the phone (another thing he would never get over, just how much work it was to get into the phone on his phone) he saw a red little one on the corner. When he cleared out all his missed calls from earlier he must have missed the notification of an actual voice message.

Curious, he went to his voice mail and saw that it was from a blocked number. He made the choice not to let this linger and to listen to the message now from what was probably a telemarketer or pharmaceutical rep. He clicked the play button and listened.

"Well hello, Doc Allred. It appears that you and I have a mutual friend. Or should I say, HAD a mutual friend. Your life, if it hasn't already, is about to become more exciting, and, dare I say, fun. Stay prepared for what comes next. And don't say a word about this to anyone. We wouldn't want your boy Jack to suffer like your patients."

Harlan listened again. And then again. And then one more time. The message stayed the same. Some insane madman, whose voice he felt he maybe had heard before but could not place, was using these tweets and connecting Harlan to John Samson.

He was being pulled into some world he had no desire to be in. And if he told anyone, his son would suffer. *Suffer. Like your patients.* All because he had replied to some stupid tweet about some stupid athlete. Such a simple, insignificant action had flipped his life upside down. Who was this stranger, this voice, and how did he know so much about him? He had to ask again, what in the world was going on?

As he pondered this question so much his brain felt like it would explode, he thought that maybe his Twitter conversation with Samson really did play a role in his untimely death. Once again, what he learned in AA was dead on. There really were no such things as coincidences.

Right as Harlan finished listening to the message for what felt like the five-hundredth time, his office phone rang and snapped him out of his trance. Time to get back to work, he guessed. But he wasn't sure how that was even possible. He wasn't sure there was any way he could give his patients the attention they needed now.

Before he picked up the phone, he glanced at the caller ID to see the call was coming from Barry. Great. For the second time in just two days, the big boss of the hospital was looking for him. Now what had he done? What else could possibly be added to his already overflowing plate? Please let this be a call filled with praise.

"Hey, Barry. How may I help you?" he said in his best 'there is absolutely nothing wrong and I love my life' voice.

"Harlan. It's Barry, um, but you already knew that 'cause you, um, said my name. I'm sorry to interrupt what I'm sure has been a hectic day, but do you have a minute for me?"

Harlan wanted to say, "No! I don't have even a second for you! My patients are dying and I don't know why! I'm being dragged into the reason a sports writer, who I've never met, was murdered! And now someone is leaving me messages threatening me and my family! So, sorry, I don't have time for you or anyone!" Harlan knew it wouldn't be fair to take his frustrations out on Barry, especially because Barry sounded so out of it. He sounded completely off his game. He sounded how Harlan felt. He was never this way. Barry was always so cool and calm under pressure, and it unnerved Harlan even more.

Instead of unraveling, Harlan mustered every ounce of self-control in his body and responded, "Yeah, of course I do. What do you need?"

"Great," Barry replied with what sounded like ever-increasing trepidation in his voice. "Why don't you come up to my office? The, um, police are here and they would like to speak to you right away."

Chapter 18

The room was disheveled and dusty, Grimy was the best way to explain it. There was no way that it was Luke's apartment. In fact, he had no idea where he was waking up or how in the world he got there. He wiped the sleep out of his obviously drugged eyes so that he could get a better look at his surroundings. He sat up and before even taking an inventory of the room, he was stunned by the fact that his arms and legs were not tied together.

Whoever had taken him yesterday, and he was confident that he knew the idiots who were behind this, were at least smart enough to know that tying him down was of no use. He would get free, and they knew it.

Luke scanned the room, hoping to get evidence and maybe some sort of weapon that would get him out of his current predicament. He saw that there was just one window and by the looks of the sliver of light coming through, it was most likely around 8:00 in the morning. Unbelievable.

He had been here all night. He had missed his night in the bright lights of the sporting elite. His opportunity to shine was taken from him by someone's shortsighted decision and attempt to send him a message. That someone, and all those involved, would pay a hefty price for their lapse in judgment. They had just added more fuel to his already white-hot fire.

Why is it everyone he had ever met was an unconditional imbecile who couldn't think their way out of a paper bag? Good thing the world had one intellectual being. To be perfectly honest, everyone should bow down in gratitude to Luke for saving them from their idiocy.

Next, he noticed that the room was almost completely empty. He had slept the night on the floor, which would explain why his right shoulder was a bit stiff. Good thing he recovered quickly from that kind of stuff. There was no couch for him to move to, no flat-screen plasma TV mounted to the wall, or even a kitchen table. Whoever spent their time in this hole had no place to eat or enjoy anything at all. It did, however, have two chairs.

The first chair was just a few feet behind Luke and it did not look like an inviting place for him to rest his behind. It resembled something you would see in an elementary school, bolted to a desk, but the wood was cracked with splinters shooting from every possible angle. Not exactly what he remembered from his school days.

The second chair appeared more like a place that Luke deserved to sit down and rest. It was one of those incredible black reclining leather seats with all the massage options one could dream off. But it was obviously it wasn't for him. It was obvious because staring back at him, sitting in the seat Luke wanted as his own, were the eyes of someone that was not there for small talk nor to be his friend. No, the eyes were that of a cold-blooded enforcer with nothing to lose and so much to gain. Luke knew those eyes all too well. He had worked with the man that they belonged to on many occasions in the past. Those eyes belonged to Kenji, or as most people knew him, The Master. Kenji—Luke had no desire to play into his head games and call him by some silly nickname—was the Matsui's first line of both offense and defense.

Generally, when most people sat across the room from The Master, their bodies filled with fear and their pants filled with their own waste. Luke was not most people. The only emotion that filled Luke's entire frame was joy because he knew that he had the Matsuis right where he wanted them.

"Sit down, Luke." Kenji spoke first, trying to let Luke know that he was in charge of this situation. This was going to be more fun than Luke first thought. Overconfidence was always the best way to be the one to lose.

"Where would you like me to sit, sir? On the floor? Or do I get the privilege of sitting in that comfortable wood chair behind me?" Luke wanted to come off as both a terrified child and a sarcastic jerk. He hoped this impression was coming across as he spoke to the "scary" Master.

"Sit down now. And keep your trap shut until I tell you to open it again." Luke was not surprised by Kenji's attempt to intimidate, but he was astonished that he was dense enough to try this with Luke. Kenji had never struck him as an idiot. Yes, he was an enforcer for a crime family, but he was not like any other enforcer for any other family in the world.

Typically when the Matsuis needed information from one of their targets, they sent two people to push the prey to the edge. One was the brains of the operation—the one who spoke, the one with the ability to extract the information by pushing every conceivable button using only words. The other was the brawn—the strength, the intimidating force in the room that, if the words didn't work, if the person was thick enough not to give up what the Matsuis desired, he would make him. And it would be done by any means possible.

Kenji, however, was a one-man show. When they needed anything big and needed it fast, he was sent in and no one accompanied him because he could do both tasks better than anyone. He was the best at his business of psychological and physical pain and suffering. And here he sat across from Luke thinking that he could outsmart him. It wouldn't be too long until he knew that this would likely be his last opportunity to threaten and terrorize anyone again.

Luke decided that his best course of action would be to play along with Kenji. Tone it down and take instructions. So he stood up and slowly moved over and took his seat.

It turned out to be an even more painful place to sit than to admire. The splinters, though small, covered the entire area of the chair's seat and they seemed to be glued to the legs and the handles. It didn't matter which way he tried to sit, something was piercing his skin. This was a different kind of the Matsui's torture chairs that Luke had never before seen. It was impressive, Luke thought, very impressive.

"That's better. Now slide your chair a bit closer to me." Luke did as he was told, but he wasn't sure how much longer he could take this game. *Get on with it Kenji*, Luke thought. *Let's talk about why you have brought me to this party.*

"Sorry you had to miss your big moment last night," Kenji said with a little smile coming from the corners of his mouth. He wasn't sorry now, that was clear, but he would be sorry soon. "I know how much that meant to you. We were all ready for your big night in front of the whole world. I mean, you of all people deserve an ego boost to help you get over your low feelings of self-worth."

This was a different side of Kenji that Luke had never seen. He was always so serious, both while working and when he was off the clock. He must have something special in store for their time together. Something that was making him giddy just thinking about it.

Since it appeared that Kenji was waiting for Luke to share his thoughts, he decided it must be time to open his trap. "It's no big deal, mate. I'll still get my day. I am sure that whatever brought me here in the middle of all this is for the greater good of the family. That is what matters most to me. I just—"

"That sounds like you," Kenji interrupted before Luke could go on. "Always putting everyone else's concerns before your own. Lovable Luke, that's what we all like to call you."

"I didn't know you had a pet name for me. That's cute. This whole time I thought we were just co-workers, but it turns out you have always thought of me as much, much more."

"You have always been my favorite, you should know that, but I was just waiting for the right time to confess that to you." This was strange to hear, which was making Luke a little uncomfortable. What was going through the genius brute's mind? What did he think he had on Luke that would get him to give them what they were after? And how long was he going to drag this out? He couldn't imagine it would be that much longer. He was right.

"Now, let's cut all this lovey dovey crap and move to the heart of the matter." It was business time for Kenji. He shifted in his chair, so that every part of his body seemed to be staring right at Luke. "You know why you're here. You know why you and I are together in this decrepit apartment in the middle of Seattle."

"Of course I know." Even though each movement he made in his chair caused more pain to pierce through his body, Luke moved so that he was facing his counterpart completely. But unlike Kenji, who sat up straight with both arms resting on his knees, Luke slouched over a bit and kept his right hand in his pocket. This seemed like an unorthodox and possibly even stupid way to prepare oneself for the chance on an attack, but Luke knew a few things that Kenji didn't. And he decided to reveal one of those things to him right then.

"But I also know that you have no authorization to seriously harm me in any way." Luke knew Kenji was shocked because the usually unflappable demeanor on his calm face flinched for a split second. Not wanting to give up how much joy this brought Luke, he kept his smile on the inside as he continued to burst Kenji's bubble. "You see, I know that your specific orders are to get what you need from me while threatening to break every bone in my body, or maybe feed me my own fingers—my personal favorite technique of yours, by the way. Always a crowd pleaser."

"What makes you think that would be true? What makes you think that I don't get the satisfaction of being the one to finally cause you excruciating amounts of pain?"

"Good question. I guess since you're asking me questions that means you should start calling me The Master now. Sounds like a good plan, don't you think?" The anger in Kenji's face was beginning to show. It looked like every vein would soon burst wide open like a backed up, rusty old pipe. "Let me tell you why I know what you were certain I did not know. Ready? Good. I know you thought you had me fooled when you didn't tie me up, because I know how you like to work. You feel it is some sort of dishonor to inflict pain on someone who's tied up.

You want to feel like you gave him a chance to get away or defend himself. I guess whatever helps you sleep at night, my pupil. Do I have this right so far, mate?"

Kenji said nothing, but he didn't need to. Luke was right. He was always right. "But even that wasn't going to fool me, the new Master. Want to know why? Because you all need me too much. You need me to keep playing baseball to give you a way into furthering your empire in the US of A. Yes, the Matsuis are big shots in Japan, but you're just small potatoes here. And I know nobody is happy with being a small fish in this massive pond. Without me you all will get chewed up and spit out by some family that's larger and has more control here. You know it. The person who sent you here knows it. And I know it. You can't touch me because I am the most vital person in the whole operation."

Luke decided now it was ok to show Kenji how much he was enjoying this, so he gave him his most toothy smile and let out one loud laugh.

"You may be right, but you really have no idea what you are doing, do you? You have no idea that by not cooperating with the plans that were made when we first recruited you, you are going to hurt everything we have all worked for."

Luke laughed again, but not just one loud laugh this time. He let this one last a little longer. "Let me stop you right there before you make an absolute fool of yourself. The Matsuis recruited me? Is that the fairy tale they've told you? That's rich, so very rich. Do you have a moment so you can learn something else from your Master? Why don't you sit back, relax, maybe pop some popcorn? What I am about to tell you will be better than any movie you have ever seen in your life."

Just as Luke was about to go on, Kenji interjected. "How about instead of telling me some story that you think I don't know, you start talking about what I need to know?"

Kenji was now standing up, with his arms across his chest. The look in his eyes was no longer that of shock or anger, it was that of someone who was about to go to work and get his job done right the first time. "You are so incredibly full of yourself. You think you know every move. You think you are always one step ahead of every person in every room. That may be the case most of the time, Luke, but not this time. No, my friend, not this time at all."

Luke stayed motionless while listening to Kenji. He didn't get up and try to match the intensity of his counterpart. No, he just sat there, not moving a muscle. Not even his eyes twitched. He didn't want to miss a second of Kenji's speech.

"You should know how this works even though I am not allowed to harm one hair on your precious little body. You should know that I know something that will push you to the edge. That I know something that will make your skin crawl with fear. You should know that once I let you in on my little secret you will spill everything, and then you will be begging me to kill you so you don't have to think about your pathetic life anymore."

Luke knew his methods, and he knew that whatever came out of Kenji's mouth next wouldn't be the emotionally damning words that would send Luke into some life-ending tailspin. He knew because nothing could do that to Luke. Nothing mattered to Luke at all. He was stunned, truly stunned, that Kenji and the rest of the Matsuis didn't know that fact. It turned out he had overestimated all of them.

"All right. Go ahead and tell me my deep dark secret. Spill your guts so that I can be so terrified I will finally want to spill mine," Luke told him through his widening smile. He was interested in what horror they thought they had dug up.

"I know what you did to your parents, and I know where to find them. And if you choose not to tell me every last bit of what I need to know, I won't lay a finger on you. But I will lay all my fingers on them and, in the process, expose you to the entire world for what you are. The bright lights dim quickly once it turns out their hero has no regard for the lives of his family." Kenji, still standing, thinking that he had landed the blow that would finally get to Luke, relaxed a bit. Not his finest decision.

"Ouch. You've got me. Whatever shall I do?" Luke grabbed at his heart with his left hand to demonstrate just how much this hurt. He was acting, obviously, but he was surprised that Kenji knew anything about his parents. This was an interesting development indeed.

"But I have a few more secrets for you, too. You ready?"

Before Kenji had time to react, Luke shot up from his chair and slammed his left hand into Kenji's neck. Luke felt an explosion as Kenji's voice box collapsed inside his throat, making it temporally impossible for him to make any sound, let alone call for help. Before Kenji hit the ground, Luke's right hand burst out of his pocket and smashed into the middle of Kenji's face, breaking his nose and spraying blood all over the room.

As Kenji lay on the ground writhing in pain, Luke leaned in close. "Here is my second secret. You forgot to check the inner pocket of my pants, and by neglecting that, you left me with this." Luke placed a razor thin and extraordinarily sharp blade, now covered in blood from Kenji's nose, right in front of his blood-caked eye. This razor was always with Luke. He always had it hidden in case a situation like this one arose. Just another thing that the Matsuis had overlooked.

"Look closely. Look really closely because I want you to see the tiny blade that was your demise, and here's the thing," Luke said as he got closer to Kenji's face. "I am not done with you yet."

Luke flung Kenji onto his stomach, making sure that his face slammed into Luke's chair on his way down. Then he pulled up the pant legs of Kenji's high-priced suit pants and began to cut. Not his pants, his legs.

"You see, I do know how this works," Luke heartlessly explained as his blade ripped through Kenji's Achilles tendon. Kenji was still unable to scream out in pain, allowing him to hear the loud pops of his tendons severing as Luke slashed through his legs.

"They trust your abilities and because you like to work solo, no one is watching this place at all. Based on the time that you and I have been talking, in about ten minutes the rest of your crew will be here to transport me back to my apartment if I have given in or somewhere worse if I haven't. And I need those precious minutes to get out of this place and get where I need to be. So, I am going to make sure I get that necessary time by making certain you can't leave for help or follow me."

After Luke finished with both legs of what used to be The Master, he flipped Kenji onto his back and continued, "One of two things will happen to you. Either by the time your associates arrive you will have bled out and all they will find is a dead man lying on the floor. Or they will come just in time to save your life, only to discover you let me get away without acquiring any information, and then they will kill you. I guess there really is only one outcome: you will leave this place in a bag."

Luke began to laugh again as he saw the look of throbbing pain on Kenji's face. He was enjoying this, every second of it, but he felt at least he owed the bloody, pathetic, weeping mess on the floor something he could tell the Matsuis so his pain and anguish would not be completely in vain.

"How about this? Before I go, I'll give you something. Something that you can share with your buddies when they show up to get their worthless hands on me. This is the last secret. Ready?"

Luke leaned over and plunged his razor as deep into Kenji's neck as he possibly could, listening closely so he could hear the flesh rip away from his body. As he slowly, painfully, pulled it back out again, he whispered into Kenji's blood-filled ears to emphasize what he was saying. And Kenji got the message—he got it loud and clear. This would never end. Luke had made it that way. No one would ever find out what was wrong with the kids.

Chapter 19

Harlan hung up the phone and his mind began to race with fear.

Before he even got the chance to go and talk the cops down from their ridiculous theory, they show up at his place of work. And was it about this whole deal with John Samson? It had to be. What else could it be? But what did they think he would know? He was just some middle-aged dude who sent a few tweets to a sports writer who was murdered a few hours later.

Of course, for some reason, that guy who was murdered asked Harlan for help right before his life met its untimely end. Was he suddenly a person of interest? How could he be? But, was he?

All at once, Harlan was frozen with fear. He couldn't move. His thoughts were jumbled up inside his head, and he wanted to hide under his desk or maybe behind a bottle one more time. He wasn't sure what he should do. The person on the message told him not to say a word to anyone. Not a soul. Or Jack would . . . he couldn't even think about it. He was trapped and confused.

At some point in everyone's life, he or she comes to a crossroads. Harlan always felt depending on which way you choose, which path you take, your life will go in a certain direction that will decide who you are and what you will become.

Harlan, like most people, had many of these roads diverging moments in his life and because he rarely took that road less traveled by he was where he was today. A divorced, recovering alcoholic whose patients were dying, whose family was being threatened by a lunatic who somehow believed that he had something to do with a story a newspaper writer was going to write. And to top it all off, the police were waiting for him in the CEO's office, and he wasn't supposed to be talking to them. *Well when you put it that way*, Harlan thought, *my life really doesn't sound all that bad*.

Harlan felt this was another one of those crossroads moments, when the roads were really diverging and he would have a chance to do something great. The problem was, he didn't know which way to go. He didn't know the right path to take. This had been an issue for him whenever he experienced moments like this. It was as if a road block was set up in front of each path that made it impossible to see what lay ahead. He would have to guess and probably, once again, guess wrong.

This time he needed to decide, and it appeared that he needed to decide quickly, what he should tell the police. He had two ways he could go on this. One, he could tell them everything he knew. Everything. This meant playing the message from the unknown caller, even though whoever it was made it clear he should tell no one.

The other option was to do what he originally had planned to do, which was to convince them they were following a false idea. It was just a simple Twitter exchange and the only reason Samson had sent Harlan the "help me" tweet was because he had to have been looking at his account at the very moment everything went down. But that was before he received the message. Then it was the truth. Now he wasn't so sure.

Before he could settle on a decision, his cell phone rang. Harlan was terrified merely to look at it—this stupid contraption had given him nothing but grief today. Right now he was wishing Alexander Graham Bell had never been born.

He stole a quick glance and saw Cole's name on his caller ID. Harlan exhaled, glad it wasn't some unknown number again. While Cole was not a fountain of moral judgment or advice, he would still be helpful in this situation, though probably not on the phone. This person was probably listening to all his phone calls. Or was he just being paranoid? He didn't care at this point. He needed to be as cryptic as possible. Say something only Cole would understand and then fill him in later.

"Who this be?" Harlan, not wanting to show that anything was wrong, answered with his normal, very adult greeting he always used when Cole called.

"It be yo' momma." And Cole kept it going. It be yo' momma. If anyone was listening Harlan hoped the first seven words of this conversation would stop them from thinking he was any sort of threat to them.

"Where have you been?" Cole continued. "I've been trying to reach you all day. You had to have heard the news about . . ."

"Yup." Harlan quickly cut him off, not wanting John Samson's name to be said. "Heard all about it. Crazy."

"Just crazy? Aren't you freaking out right now?! With everything that happened yesterday? And, dude! Your name is all over the place! Your Twitter conversation is, too! What is going on, bro?"

So much for playing it cool. Harlan still couldn't tell him what was going on though. He couldn't risk it. He needed to get him off the phone fast, both for Harlan's sake (the police were upstairs waiting) and Cole's, too. He was officially worried whoever these people were would now find a way to track Cole down. Harlan really needed to breathe, and maybe it was time to finally stop watching all those cop shows.

"I'm ok. It's been so busy here, I haven't had much time to think about it."

Cole started to say something, probably something in disbelief, but before he could continue, Harlan cut him off again. "Sorry to cut this short. I've got to get back to work. Duty calls and all. Meet me at the hole tonight at 7:30."

This was perfect because no one would be able to figure out what he was talking about. They would most likely believe they were going to meet at The Hole, a dive bar downtown. But that's not what he meant. The hole was what they called Cole's first apartment after he dropped out of college, because, and the reason was just too creative, it was a whole pile of crap. They were ever so clever.

"Um. All right. Sounds good, I guess," Cole responded sounding completely confused. "Smell ya later, bro."

"Not if I smell you first!"

And with that, even though they discussed nothing at all, even though no advice was given, Harlan knew exactly what he needed to do next.

Chapter 20

Harlan made his way to administration feeling like he was about to do what was best for everyone involved. It may not be smart, but he needed to do what he needed to do, and it didn't matter what anyone else thought.

Unfortunately, there was one last obstacle before he made it to Barry's office. Standing outside her office, obviously waiting for Harlan to pass, was Josie. Not exactly who Harlan wanted to see at this exact moment, or any moment for that matter.

"This is not what I remember the walk of shame looking like in college," Josie said as she shot a happy grin in Harlan's direction.

Before Harlan could stop himself, he opened his mouth and the words flowed right out. "From what I've heard, you haven't stopped having walks of shame since college."

The look on Josie's face was enough to tell Harlan he better keep walking as a meeting with the cops would probably be more fun. But there was no way that Josie was just going to let him by without getting in a few choice words of her own.

"You arrogant idiot. You pompous fool. The police are waiting down in Barry's office for you. For you! And you have the audacity to insult me?"

"Wow. Big words, Josie. Someone has been studying the dictionary, and then taking the words she learned and looking them up in a thesaurus. Amazing! Astounding! Astonishing!" Harlan knew this wasn't the smartest strategy, but something about cops waiting for him behind the CEO's door gave him more confidence than he had felt in a long time. It helped him to be even less mature.

"Harlan, are you drunk right now? Listen to yourself. Do you know who you are talking to? You may have Barry fooled, but I see right through you."

"And what do you see? Do you see someone who hasn't touched alcohol for almost six months? Do you see a doctor who has done more work in the last nine hours than you've done in your whole life? I'm no saint, Josie. I know that. But get off my back." Harlan began again to walk toward Barry's office, but before he was two steps away Josie grabbed his arm and glared hard into Harlan's eyes.

"Listen to me. No matter what happens in there, I will personally ensure that this all ends poorly for you."

Harlan pried his arm away from her, surprised by her strength, and returned her glare. "I'm shaking in my boots,

Dr. Silver. Can't you tell? Now excuse me, I need to finish my walk of shame." Harlan turned, smiled, and finally made his way to his destination.

The door to Barry's office wasn't open, so Harlan knocked. As he did, butterflies swarmed his stomach, and he began to doubt himself. Was he doing the right thing? Had he really thought through every factor before making his decision? Had he really contemplated how this would affect the lives of others?

At this point it no longer mattered, because Barry opened the door and ushered Harlan in. The doubts he had, no matter how strong they were or how endless they seemed, had to be tabled. Now it was go time.

Harlan wasn't sure what he expected to see, but this clearly wasn't it. He thought that maybe a couple of cops in their blues would be there wanting to chat and check in to make sure that all was well in Harlan's world. At least, that was what he hoped it would be. Instead, sitting in Barry's office were two police officers in plain dress. These were detectives. They were here to do a full investigation of the matter. Harlan felt this was getting out of hand, although he realized he probably should have expected this to be the case. Who else would be sent during a murder investigation?

Before he could extend his hand and introduce himself, one of the detectives—a short, comb-over-sporting stump of a man—stood up and started the process. It was obvious he was the lead, the senior on the case.

"Dr. Allred. Thank you for taking the time out of what I am sure has been a busy day to come talk to us," Detective Stumpy (Harlan had decided that this is what he would call him, no matter his actual name) said with a tone in which Harlan detected a strong undertone of sarcasm. "I am Detective Rick Mancuso, and this is my partner, Detective Selena Rodriguez."

Selena Rodriguez stood up and faced Harlan. It was like the whole world stopped for a quick second. As she stretched out her hand, it was all he could do to keep his eyes from popping right out of his head. Maybe it was, once again, those cop shows that skewed Harlan's reality, but Rodriguez was not at all what he'd expected. It was usually the Assistant District Attorney who was the sexy, show-stopping one, and if there was a female cop, she usually had a face and body for radio. But this was not the case with Ms. Detective Foxy. Not at all. She was tall, with long brown hair which she had up in a very business-like (but oh so amazing) ponytail and the body of a Greek goddess. She was going to be distracting, to say the least.

As Harlan looked at the two detectives he felt for a second that he was being set up. There was no way that Stumpy and Foxy were an actual team. Stumpy and Foxy sounded like a horrible kid's TV show that he would be stuck watching on a Saturday morning. There had to be hidden cameras somewhere.

"Please, call me Harlan," he said as he shook their hands. "You are not here for an appointment. No need to be formal. What can I do for you today?"

He knew that he should probably make eye contact with both of them equally, but he was finding it impossible to pry his gaze away from Rodriguez. This really was going to be hard. Harder than he could have imagined.

Barry cleared his throat, hoping this would get Harlan back to Stumpy's questions, and fortunately it did. Thank goodness for that. "Well Harlan, I am sure that you are aware of everything that has happened over the past day with the Seattle Times writer John Samson."

"Yes, Stu—um, Detective Mancuso. Such an awful tragedy to happen to an important person in our city."

"No need for you to be formal either. Just call me Mancuso. Then you are aware that because of some, what are they called? Twits . . ."

"It's tweets, Rick." Rodriguez jumped in to help her partner. When she spoke, even three little words, Harlan heard angels sing. He needed to snap out of it. This had to be their shtick, using Rodriguez's beauty to confuse doofuses like Harlan.

"Yeah, that's right. Tweets. I don't think I will ever get used to all this technological mumbo jumbo. Anyway, because of some tweets, there is a lot of thought that it was some article he was going to write that got him killed. And because he was tweeting with you, you might know something about it."

This was the moment where Harlan officially hit the crossroads and he was glad that he had already decided what to do, because if he hadn't been prepared, he would have been completely lost.

"Yup. I have read all about that. And, personally, the whole thing makes no sense to me, and I cannot figure out why anyone would think I have anything to do with it. I just sent him a few questions, and he answered. That is all." Harlan had decided the best thing to do, the only thing to do, was not give them all the details. His reason for this was plain and simple. Jack. He had to protect Jack.

Detective Stumpy looked long and hard at Harlan, and Harlan noticed that Rodriguez and Barry were doing the same thing. Did they know something about the voice message somehow already? Was it obvious he was lying to them or at least leaving something out? This is what happens when you lie, Harlan thought. You get paranoid and start thinking of worst-case scenarios, even more than normal. But he still knew that he couldn't say anything. He absolutely couldn't.

This time it was Rodriguez who spoke to Harlan and, while he still heard angels when she spoke, they had more of an edge to them than before. "It does seem like a crazy idea, until you factor in that last tweet he sent you not too long before he was murdered. Why would he ask you, some random keyboard warrior, for help?" She was tough and direct. No skirting around the issue at hand. On TV, one detective always played it tough and the other was either overly kind or acted aloof. These two just went straight at it with no hesitation. They were going to figure this situation out quickly.

"That baffles me too, especially because I am just your normal, average keyboard warrior. The only thing that I can think of is that he was on his Twitter account right before everything happened to him, and that was the fastest or maybe only way to communicate with anyone."

Harlan nailed it. It was almost word for word (he ad-libbed the keyboard warrior part) what he had rehearsed in his head over and over again as he was on his way up to meet them. It sounded perfect. From the looks on Rodriguez's and Stumpy's faces though, maybe it was too perfect. Maybe too rehearsed. Maybe he had made the wrong decision and taken the wrong path. No, he once again reminded himself, this was for Jack.

"We thought that, too," Rodriguez said, but with a look questioning the validity of what Harlan was saying. Like she, too, believed that what he said was too perfect and too rehearsed.

"Here's the thing." Stumpy, obviously feeling left out of the conversation, decided it was time for him to jump in and do some detecting, too. "He sent you that tweet early this morning, and this story has been going on all day. Why haven't you brought this to our attention? Why did we have to come to you?"

Harlan had an answer, an honest answer, for this one already, but he was starting to feel the heat. Once you start lying, simply telling the truth can be hard. He was sure that no matter what he said, it wouldn't be credible because of the lies he had already told. He knew how everything else would sound moving forward.

"Um, well, that's a good, um, question." Harlan was already fumbling with his words. Where was the confident person from just a few minutes ago when Josie confronted him? He needed to pull himself together and remember why he was doing what he was doing. "Because of an emergency here at work, I did not check my phone—aside from a call to my parents when I got to work—my email, my texts, or anything on the Internet until about twenty to thirty minutes ago. It wasn't until then that I even knew anything was going on."

He sounded a bit more confident than when he first started, but it was almost like he was trying to convince everyone in the room, including himself, that what he was saying was true. Had he taken the wrong path? Maybe he had overthought this whole situation. No, he thought. No, he hadn't. The voice on the message was clear. If he told anyone, anyone at all, Jack would suffer like his patients. It was hard enough to watch Stacy go through this, but Jack, too? Especially if he could prevent it from happening. Jack's life and the life of his daughter were worth lying for, and they mattered more to him than finding the killer of some writer.

"Interesting. Very interesting," Stumpy (Harlan really loved this nickname more and more) said as he and Rodriguez exchanged glances. Those glances terrified Harlan. Did they know more? Or were they just trying to throw him off his game?

"Well, thank you for taking time for us today," Rodriguez said to both Harlan and Barry. "If you think of anything, anything at all, that may be good for us to know, please do not hesitate to give us a call." She handed

Harlan her card with her number circled on it. Great. The first time in who knows how long that he had gotten a girl's number and it had nothing to do with his rugged good looks and undeniable charm.

"In the meantime, please don't leave the area. We might need to stop by and speak to you again."

Even though Harlan knew he should probably agree and say thank you, he could not understand this order from the cops to stay put. "Not to overstep my bounds, but why shouldn't I leave the area? I have told you all I know. I have to stick around because of some 'twit' I sent?"

"Why?" Stumpy said. "Because I don't like your attitude. Because I think you are lying or at least not telling me something. Because . . ."

Before he could keep going, Rodriguez stepped in. "Because this is just protocol. You have a connection, even if it's in some obscure way, to a victim of a murder. That connection is from seconds before he was killed. Because of this we may need your help later, and we need you close for that."

Harlan wasn't sure what to believe—what the real reason was that they wanted him to stick around—but he knew one thing. He would believe anything this angel detective (another horrible sounding TV show) had to say. Sure, he wasn't thinking with his head right now, but what she had to say was better anyway, so he went with that.

"Sounds good," Harlan said as he shook both their hands, probably holding onto Rodriguez's for a little too long and Stumpy's for much too short. "You know where to find me."

"Would you like me to show you out?" Barry spoke up for the first time. Harlan had almost forgotten he was there. "Or do you know your way?"

"We've got it. Thank you," Rodriguez said as they walked out the door and down the hallway. Once again, Harlan gazed too long as they made their way out. But this time, especially with that view, he didn't care who saw him.

Harlan was about to leave, too, but before he could, Barry placed his hand on his shoulder. "Can you stay for just one second? I promise it will be fast."

Even though Harlan wanted to go and check on his patients one last time before he left to meet with Cole, he knew he should stay behind to talk. With all the insanity going on right now, it was amazing how calm Barry was. Harlan needed that. This would be helpful.

"I know that this has been a traumatizing few days for you, with everything that has happened. It's been nonstop. But I just wanted to ask and make sure that you're not hiding anything and are completely telling the truth about everything that is going on here. Is there anything more you need to address?"

Harlan would have been shocked had this come from anyone else, but not Barry. It was obvious, as always, that he was asking these questions because he genuinely cared. There were no accusations in his tone at all.

"I am telling you, and everyone, everything I know. I promise. This is the whole story."

"Great. I believe you, Harlan. Now go get some rest. You've earned it."

Harlan left Barry's office frustrated with himself for lying to one of the few people left in the world that still trusted him.

Chapter 21

Luke walked slowly through downtown Seattle, careful to make sure he wouldn't be recognized. That would be disastrous to his image and would make it more difficult to finish off his work. He had gone into some hipster dive because none of those freaks would have any idea who he was, bought some ironic hipster hat, and wore it low enough that no one would be able to pick him out of the crowd.

He was beyond understanding at this point. He could not even fathom what had led the Matsuis to act so irrationally and try to take him out, the only reason they were finally going to make some noise in the greatest market for crime in the world. He knew they could be shortsighted and rash, but this was a whole new level of idiocy.

What Luke could not afford to do, however, was dwell on what took place. He had to consider what his next steps would be, then come up with a plan of action, and fast.

He was still feeling a little of the aftereffects of the drugs that had been injected into his body, so his normally sharp mind was feeling a bit groggy and rundown. Usually in a situation like this, or any situation really, he could come up with a plan in seconds. But not right now. Right now it would probably take him a few minutes. Tops. Yes, that was fast for most, but for Luke it was infuriatingly slow.

First things first, he needed to check in to make sure his plans were still working as well as they had been the last time he checked. He had to ensure that the Matsuis hadn't found a way to screw this up. Second, he felt it prudent to make a visit to those who were responsible for his night locked away in some dump.

As he thought about how he would do both of these things quickly, the fog lifted from his mind, and it became incredibly clear he could accomplish both easily and in one fell swoop. *This is going to be enjoyable*, Luke thought. More enjoyable than if things had gone according to his original plan.

Luke heard footsteps right behind and turned to confront whoever was dumb enough to be following him. But no one was there. He kept walking and heard them again, but this time there was laughing and talking. It sounded like, but it couldn't be, his parents. He quickly turned again and there was nothing. Not a single person. He was losing it, and he couldn't do that. He needed to stay focused.

Luke walked toward his destination, and in those moments he allowed himself to get distracted by his own thoughts, letting his guard down as a man peeled away from his family and eagerly approached him with a knowing look. Some crazed sports fan had recognized him, and now Luke had to act fast to put an end to this threat.

He darted down an alley hoping this stupid man would follow and, true to form of someone desperate for the attention of the famous, he did. Luke reached into this pocket to make sure his blade was still there. It was, and that was not good for the approaching stranger.

As the man turned the corner, Luke took a step back, unsure of what he was seeing. Kenji? How could Kenji be following him? If he wasn't already dead, there was no way he could walk. Luke had seen to that.

"Excuse me, sir? Can you help us for a second? We can't seem to find, and this is embarrassing to even say, the Space Needle. Can you point us in the right direction?"

Luckily, before Luke could do something stupid, the man's questions snapped him out of it. It wasn't Kenji, it was a stupid tourist. A stupid tourist who had no idea who Luke was.

"No worries. Sometimes it's like finding a needle in a haystack if you are just a visitor," he said as they both laughed at Luke's best attempt at a dad joke.

He quickly gave the man directions and moved on. As he walked, he had to take pause for moment—it was happening again. The confusion. The hallucinations. The doubt that had plagued him for so long and allowed his father to prey on him. He had to snap out of it. There was too much at stake, and his next target deserved Luke at his best. And his best they would get.

Chapter 22

After what was an emotionally draining conversation—it really is amazing what lying will do to a person—Harlan didn't want to do anything else at all. But he knew he had to keep moving, keep pushing forward, keep searching for answers. Answers to what was going on with his patients and answers for why so many seemed to think he was involved in the murder of John Samson. He had to figure all this out, and he wouldn't stop until he did.

He went straight back to the fourth floor and rounded on his patients once more for the day. All, at least on the surface, seemed well. They were all resting and appeared to be comfortable. This was a good and welcome sign.

But all their tests, especially their blood work, told a different story. Each patient had a high white blood cell count, which made sense to Harlan and the other doctors. They were all struggling to fight off any infection that came their way. But, and this was a big but, it still didn't tell why they were acting and suffering the way they were. It made no sense at all.

Harlan decided to take one last look at the test results to see if anything stood out. Nothing. Nothing stood out at all. Everything seemed normal. It was as if nothing were wrong at all.

Just as he was about to put everything away and leave to meet Cole, something caught his eye. It was small, and the report barely mentioned it, but he still couldn't believe he had missed it. Halfway through the third page of Stacy's tests results was written, "Unidentifiable substance found at high levels." Six simple words that may hold the key to what was going on. Six simple words that no one had seen or thought were important before. Why hadn't they seen them?

Thinking that maybe they were just in Stacy's chart, so they hadn't caused any alarm, Harlan decided to look through the test results of the other patients for similar language. And there it was. In each patient record were those simple words: "Unidentifiable substance found at high levels."

Harlan rushed out of his office, found Lucy, and showed her the report.

"I don't know what this means, but I need you to put in an order to the lab to have them run every test imaginable to find out what this undetectable substance is. We need to see if we can identify it right away."

"I'm right on it, Dr. Allred," Lucy said while she opened her computer and began to put the orders in. "I'll call the lab once I've put in the orders and make sure they put a rush on it."

"Perfect and fantastic idea. I need to head out, but call me once you get the results, or if anything else happens. This is exciting, Lucy. Very exciting. We will figure this out."

To punctuate his excitement, Harlan gave Lucy a huge high five as he turned and rushed out the door to meet Cole at the hole.

***

Just as Harlan reached his car, his phone let out the loud musical sound notifying him of one of those pesky text messages. He looked down and saw it came from a strange number he didn't recognize with a simple but strange message.

"In 30 seconds, a phone in your glove compartment will ring. Answer it."

A phone in his glove compartment? How? What? Who? All sorts of questions swirled around his now very crowded brain, but before he could even attempt to answer them a ring came from inside his glove compartment. Just as the text promised.

With a great deal of hesitation, Harlan opened the compartment and found an old-school flip phone. And with even more fear, just as he was instructed, he answered it.

"Hello. Who is this?"

"Oh, Harlan. That's cute. There is no chance you'll ever get that answer from me." It was the same voice on the voicemail from earlier, only this time it was a little more distorted. A little harder to pinpoint any distinguishing characteristics.

"Fine. Then what do you want from me?" Harlan was terrified, and he wasn't sure if his voice showed that. He hoped it didn't.

"What do I want from you? An excellent question. The answer to that will come over time." Of course it would. Why would this become easy now?

"Then why are you calling me on some phone you somehow got into my car? What do you want?"

"It's simple. I want to commend you on how you handled your meeting with those idiot detectives. I thought you would give in when that stunning specimen started making eyes at you. I've underestimated you. Very impressive."

"How do you know . . . What is going on?" Harlan asked, but now any confidence in his voice was gone. The only thing left was fear. This person, this evil person, knew his every move.

"Don't you worry about that at all. You've got too much on your plate to be concerned with how I know things, what with everything that is happening to your patients and what could very well happen to Jack. Or even your little Leslie if you don't always do what you are told to do."

Harlan could no longer find words. They were dried up. He sat there in stunned silence.

"Soon I will have more for you, but for now keep this phone close by and answer it every time I call. I will not be contacting you on your cell phone anymore. You never know who will be listening," the voice said with a hint of a smile. "We'll talk again soon. One last thing. Enjoy your meeting with your buddy Cole at the hole."

Chapter 23

Without any thought to where he was going, Harlan made his way to Cole's old apartment in the Rainier Valley section of Seattle. While it was only about twenty minutes from where Harlan went to college, it was a far cry from the part of town he now called home. It was an area that was getting better, but back then, it was riddled with crime and not exactly the safest place for some kid to get an apartment by himself.

Harlan always thought that was why Cole chose to live there, because everyone told him he couldn't and he wanted to prove he could. Because, and Harlan always thought this was the most real reason of them all, he could get away from the places (home and school) that made him feel like a failure.

Even though it had been years since he had been to the hole, it was a familiar place that Harlan had gone to hundreds of times during those days. For that reason, even when his thoughts were somewhere else completely, Harlan could drive there without any thought at all.

Harlan looked at the clock on his dashboard and saw it was only 7:15 which, under normal circumstances, meant he was fifteen minutes early, but since he was waiting for Cole he was on Cole Standard Time. Great. Now he had anywhere between thirty minutes and four days sitting and waiting. Just what he needed.

What he needed now was a way to distract himself for a few minutes (or hours) so that he didn't go any more insane than he already was. At first, he couldn't think of a single thing. He didn't want to turn on the radio knowing all he would hear would be endless commentaries on Luke Masterson and John Samson. None of those would help. The same could be said for going on Twitter or Facebook or any site on the Internet. He felt at a loss.

Then he remembered he had missed calls and text messages from both his dad and Jack. Maybe he should call them back. Yes, they would want to talk about everything that was going on, but talking to them would help. Just hearing their voices would help.

Before he could decide who to call first, his phone rang. At first Harlan was terrified that it was the unknown caller again, until he realized it wasn't coming from his new phone. Thankful, Harlan looked at his caller ID and saw it was Emily. Two calls in two days. This was quite unexpected.

"Hey, Emily. How goes it?" Harlan didn't want to deviate from this smooth line from the day before. That's what made him such a catch.

"Where have you been?" Wow. She didn't say hello or ask how he was doing. She just went right into it. This was very unlike her. "Your son has been worried sick!"

"I've had a very busy day, Emily. Nonstop since the moment I woke up."

"So busy that you couldn't call or text your son back? How long does it even take to send a text anyway? You couldn't do that for him?"

"I hadn't even seen that he, or anyone for that matter, had tried to contact me until maybe an hour ago. And I was just about to call him when you called."

"Likely story, Harlan. How many times did you use that crap excuse on me? Too many to count. And while it drove me crazy, it's much worse that you're using it on your son. I actually believed you had changed."

He had changed. He really had. This wasn't an excuse. It was the truth, but he knew it didn't matter what he said at this point. To Emily everything would be a lie, an excuse. Everything. And he couldn't tell her the whole truth, about the cops and some stranger thinking he may know something about Samson's murder or even been involved in some way. About Jack and the threats on his life. About how his patients were suffering, dying, and he didn't know why. Not only would she not believe him, she might shut him out again. Jack and Leslie would be gone forever.

"I understand why you think I'm lying and making some sort of ridiculous excuse. I get it. I deserve it. But this time I'm not. My day has been more difficult than I can explain."

"Why can't you explain it? Too hard to come up with a believable lie on the spot?"

"Because you would never believe the truth. I don't even believe it myself, and I am living it."

There was dead silence on the other end. Harlan was afraid she had hung up, once again fed up with him, and this time never to return.

"Emily? You there? I'm sorry. I'm sorry for all I've put you through. You have every right to be angry and not believe me. But, please believe me this time. I did not plan to leave Jack hanging. I have had no time until now."

"Ok, Harlan. Ok. Whatever you say. Call or text him. Just do something. For once, do something." Before he could say anything more, she hung up without saying goodbye. And, once again, Harlan was stuck, sitting in his car, alone. Stuck wallowing in his own self-doubt and lifetime of mistakes.

Chapter 24

Harlan attempted to snap out of his pity party. How many times had he tried to do that lately? It was pathetic how often he sat and sulked over his problems. Who didn't have problems? Maybe he needed to put on a pair of big girl panties and get over it.

Only he couldn't. He couldn't just move on. The only woman he'd ever loved, the only woman who'd ever mattered, told him he was a waste of space. Do something. For once in your pathetic, sad, worthless life, do something. Where had it all gone wrong? When had he reached this point of no return with her where she went from seeing him as the man of her dreams to what she saw now?

There was no answer to these questions. He had tried to answer them thousands of times and each time he came up empty. Why would tonight be any different?

He needed to move on from this for now. Right now. There were too many other issues to think about than how he had wrecked his marriage. Wasn't Harlan just a bundle of joy and good thoughts? Who wouldn't want to spend more time with him?

Before he forgot, Harlan sent Jack a quick text. The last thing he needed was another lecture or a son who wasn't speaking to him again.

"Sorry I didn't respond earlier. Crazy day. And crazy about Samson too. I'll call you first thing tomorrow. Love you and all that other mushy stuff."

Harlan sent it, hoping it was good enough. And before he could stress about it any longer his phone made the familiar beep again and there was a response.

"No worries. I know how life can be for you. U da best. That mushy enough for you?"

"Perfect amount of mushy! Talk to you tomorrow."

Thank goodness Jack was still cool with his dad. He guessed that meant he still wanted to spend time with him.

Speaking of time, Harlan looked at his clock—7:46. Cole was late. Not late late. But late still. Harlan thought about giving him a call to check in, but then he saw a cab pull up in front of the hole, and Cole jumped out. Harlan had forgotten that Cole didn't have his car with him when he showed up at his house the night before. That was still a story he needed to hear. But, again, something for another day.

Cole slid into the passenger's side of Harlan's car, ready to roll.

"What's cooking, good looking?"

"Oh, the normal everyday stuff. All my patients are dying. Some random Twitter conversation I had is all over the Internet. And Emily just ripped me a new one. And chicken. There might be some chicken cooking, too."

"Screw her, man. Your ex–old lady is off her rocker."

Harlan had never heard Cole talk about Emily that way before. He hadn't said anything nice about her for quite a while either, but he never ventured into full on insults.

"What's that supposed to mean? And where in the world did that come from?"

"Just forget it. You place her on such a ridiculously high pedestal that it won't matter what I say anyway. You won't hear it. You'll never see what everyone else sees when it comes to the way she has treated you. Let's just move on."

"Move on? I am just supposed to move on from that? Nope. How about you explain yourself?"

"Harlan, come on. Let's not do this. You've got enough on your plate. Let's talk about what we came here to talk about."

Harlan had no desire to do that. He wanted to hear all that Cole had to say. He wanted the whole story and he wanted it now.

But, he hated to admit this, Cole was right. There were too many other things going on. It didn't mean they wouldn't come back to this soon, but it meant that they would table it for now.

"Fine. Let's move on. How about we go for a nice walk on this crisp autumn night in Seattle?"

"Here? You sure? If I get scared will you hold my hand and tell me everything will be ok?"

"Of course, my dear. I shall keepeth you safeth."

They both got out of the car and started walking. Harlan wasn't sure if his car was bugged, too, and hoped that maybe they could have a more in-depth conversation without that hanging over his head.

"So, what's up? You were so cryptic on the phone earlier. You've got me intrigued."

"Things are a little more complicated than a Twitter conversation being all over the Internet. And by a little, I mean a lot."

Harlan was unsure, even though he felt safe away from his car, how much he should tell Cole. For some reason he felt the need to tell him everything. He needed to tell someone. Someone who would believe all that had happened. Someone who would believe his crazy theories and help him figure out a way to make things right again. And that person, the only person, was Cole.

So, he spilt it all, doing his best to explain all that had transpired that day, all the while looking over his shoulder to see if they were being followed and nervously checking his new cell to make sure he hadn't missed a call. He told Cole about the message, the visit from the cops (he even took time to give some details about detective Foxy. Men.) and the phone call he received right before he left to meet Cole. And the whole time he told this crazy story, Cole didn't interrupt. He didn't speak or even look like he wanted to, until it was obvious Harlan was finished.

"If I didn't know you and know you don't have the imagination to come up with something like this, I wouldn't believe a word you're saying."

"Seriously. If I brought this up at AA, they would all think I'd started drinking again. I think I just might start anyway. That way I don't have to think about it all the time."

"So, what are we going to do about all this?"

This was exactly what Harlan needed at this moment, the reason he told Cole everything. No judgment. Just help.

"I have no idea where to start. And this isn't everything. Remember what I told you about all that's going on at the hospital? It's getting worse. I've screwed this up, too. Just another thing to add to my long list of failures."

"Shut up, Harlan. I'm getting sick of this self-loathing. I'm tired of your thinking everyone else succeeds and all you do is fail. Just, shut up." So much for no judgment.

"Your kindness really helps right now. Thanks."

"You're welcome. I don't even care if you're being sarcastic. You need to hear it."

"What do you mean by that? First the crap about Emily? And now this? What are you trying to get at?"

Cole gestured for Harlan to sit down next to him on a nearby bench, as if to say the cliché line, "You're going to want to sit down for this."

When it became obvious that Harlan had no desire to join him, Cole said with a look of genuine concern, "Come on, Harlan. You're going to want to sit down for this." He still wouldn't sit down. He didn't care how much it pained Cole to say a line only used in movies and horrible books. He would hear this standing up.

"Do you remember when we were about eleven and Rebecca Lawrence broke her foot in gym?"

"Yeah. But I don't know what that has to do with what's going on right now."

"Do you remember how it happened?"

"Vaguely. We were playing some weird game, something no one would actually play in the real world. Just gym class. What was it?"

"Mat ball. It was like soccer, but you threw the ball and tried to get it to a teammate standing on a mat. Honestly, it was nothing like soccer. It wasn't like anything. I don't know what it was."

Cole was trying to get Harlan to laugh or at least smile. Once he realized it wasn't going to work, he moved on.

"Rebecca was on the other team, and she was being crazy. Running around. Pushing people and knocking them over. You know, doing what kids do."

"That's right. She was like that a lot, wasn't she? I wonder what she is up to now."

"Ultimate fighting. And pretty good, too. But, do you remember what happened during the game?"

Harlan had no clue. He didn't have Cole's memory of all things useful and useless.

"Fine. I'll tell you. So, she's running around, acting crazy. You've got the ball, and you're about to pass to someone when she charges right at you, trips over your foot, and crashes to the ground."

"That's right. Oh man, I felt so bad about that. She may have been crazy, but she didn't deserve my breaking her foot."

"That's it! That's what I'm talking about."

"What's what you're talking about?"

"You didn't break her foot, Harlan. Rebecca broke her foot. You didn't stick your foot out and trip her on purpose. She tripped over you. She did it to herself. And yet you took the blame. In fact, you still take the blame for it today."

There was silence for what seemed like eternity. Silence as Harlan tried to take in what Cole was trying to say. When it was obvious that Cole couldn't take the silence anymore, he broke it.

"But that's just a basic example. Something I'm sure could just be brushed to the side as you just being a kid. But it's not that at all."

Harlan still didn't know what to say or how to react. He reluctantly sat down next to Cole and waited for more.

"Look, Harlan. You've been my best friend forever. But this has got to stop. Your ongoing relationship with Emily. The way you take the blame for me. It's ridiculous."

"What do you mean? That's the second time you've said something about Emily tonight. And take the blame for you? No more vague responses. Explain yourself."

Cole took a deep breath and stared off into the distance, like he was formulating the right words to say.

"Here's the thing. You're probably not going to like what I tell you. Not at all. And I may talk for a long time because I've been stewing over this for longer than I can remember. So, please stop me if you feel the need to slow me down."

Harlan nodded his head, but he wasn't sure he would be able to talk much more tonight. He would try. In fact, he might even need to defend himself.

"Emily. You have always been a sucker for her. And I get it. But, man, you're a fool. Riddle me this. Why did she leave you?"

"Because I was never around. Because I'm an alcoholic who would've rather been at the bar than at home with my family or watching my kids play sports.

Because I missed everything and stopped showing them I care. Because I failed her."

"Same answer you've been giving since it happened, but it's not true. I know because I watched the whole painful thing happen. The whole thing."

"And I lived it, so I know what I did. I know what I caused. I know it was all me, and I know it's true."

"Come on now. She could have slept with another man, and you would have found a way to blame it in yourself. 'If I only had taken out the garbage when she asked. He probably takes the garbage out right away. He's so much better than me.' I know it and you know it."

"But that's not what happened. Not at all."

"No, it's not. But your version isn't exactly what happened either. When did everything start to go south for you?"

"After Stacy's accident. After I couldn't save her."

"First, you did save her. She's alive. You did amazing work. Just another example of what we are talking about. Second, where was Emily after that? Did she help you at all as you struggled?"

Harlan thought for a moment about this. He had never thought about this before. It had never crossed his mind.

"She didn't help you at all. She just dismissed it, like you needed to move on. Do you remember when she didn't get that job with the high school in Everett? I know you do. She was devastated. And you were there for her every step of the way when that happened. But when you needed her, she shut you out. It was so frustrating to watch."

"But, the drinking. I couldn't stop drinking. Even before that, I was at the bar all the time. Not home enough, off at some stupid bar."

"Before that? No, you weren't. Sometimes you would go out and come home late, but who doesn't do that? I could hardly ever get you to go and hang with the boys. Maybe once a month. As for your drinking after the accident? That was stupid and idiotic. That's on you and there is no excuse."

"So, you agree with me. I screwed up my marriage. She left because of me."

"You're not listening to me at all. Listen to the words I'm saying. All the words. Stop hearing what you want to hear."

Harlan began to stand up to walk away from all that Cole was throwing at him, but before he got up, Cole grabbed him by his arm and forced him back down.

"You're not going anywhere," Cole said with more force than Harlan could ever remember. "We aren't done here. Got it?" Harlan got it and decided it was best not to get up again.

"And how about me?" Cole continued. "How you always look past my stupidity. I'm a mess. An absolute mess."

"No, you're not. Sure, you've made a few mistakes, but you're not a mess."

"A few mistakes? That's laughable. I almost didn't get into college 'cause I blew things off. Then once I did, I flunked out."

"You dropped out. That's a big difference."

"No, I flunked out. But that's not how you remember it. I one hundred percent flunked out."

"Do you know why I remember it that way? Because I feel like it's my fault. I should have done more to get you to class. More to help you."

"Holy cow, dude. Are you even listening to yourself? You are ridiculous. With all this self-loathing and guilt, no wonder you became an alcoholic."

Just as Harlan was about to fight back, his phone rang. Again. Both Luke and Cole jumped at the noise, bringing them out of their intense conversation. And because he had two phones now, he didn't know which one to answer. He hoped against hope that is was his own phone. Although that phone hadn't been too lucky lately either.

Harlan fumbled through his pockets until he found both and looked to see which one it was. It was his phone. He could almost breathe again. It was the hospital. Maybe it was Lucy or Clara with good news.

"This is Harlan."

"Hi, Dr. Allred. It's Lucy."

"Please tell me you're calling with something good. Give me something to actually cheer about today."

"Not exactly. I guess it depends on what your definition of good news is. The lab ran more specific tests and what they saw before isn't there anymore. They think it was just a reaction to whatever is going on, but nothing to be worried about."

"Nothing to be worried about? Are they kidding? Something is there, then it's gone and they think that's fine? Really? Put an order in to run the tests again."

"I've already asked for that, and they have run everything they can. There is nothing left to do."

"I don't buy it. There has to be something to this. Has to be."

"What would you like me to do? I honestly am at a loss, Doctor. They won't listen to me on this."

"Nothing. You've been great. Fantastic work. I will be there later tonight to see what more can be done. You just keep running the show."

"Thanks. That means a lot. And I will do just that."

"Wait. Before you go, how are the kids all doing? Are they resting?"

"Right now they seem pretty well. Do you want me to keep you updated?"

"That would be perfect. And maybe call Clara. Two excellent nurses putting their heads together is better than one lug-headed doctor."

Lucy let out a little laugh. "Sounds like a good idea. Thank you for your support. We will figure this out."

"I'm sure we will. Let me know if you come up with anything. See you later."

Harlan hung up, wishing that what Lucy said would be true. He had said it over and over the last few days, too: *we will figure this out*. The longer this went on, the more dead ends they hit, the more he felt they never would.

"That's not your good news face. What's up?" Cole said, breaking Harlan out of his deep thoughts.

"Work. It's not looking great. But we're not done with your lecture. I want to hear it all."

"I didn't set out to lecture you, but if that's how you feel about it let's keep it going, young man."

This time, Harlan did crack a smile. But he ended it quickly, hoping Cole didn't see. Plus, he wasn't sure he had any right to smile right now.

"There's that smile I love. So good to see it make an appearance," Cole said using the same sing-song voice Harlan's mother used when they were kids. The impression was uncanny.

"Here's the thing, Harlan: you're an idiot. You have done stupid things, but you forget to see others are part of the problem. Or the whole problem. You take the blame for everyone, every time."

"That's not true. Emily. The divorce. It was my fault. All of it was my fault."

"You're exhausting. Listen closely now. Listen to what I've been trying to get you to hear. You got yourself lost after Stacy's accident. You took all the blame for someone not paying attention and causing the accident. You took all the blame for her mother's death, even though she went to a completely different hospital. You took all the blame even though you saved Stacy's life. Do you see the insanity in this?"

"When you put it that way, I guess I do."

"Good. So, you lost your way and spiraled out of control and weren't there as much as you should have been for your family. There is no denying that."

"See? I'm right about my marriage. You're saying I'm right. You're agreeing with me."

"Don't interrupt me, because I'm not agreeing with you. You had a part to play in the end of your marriage. But, and I'm going to ask this question again, where was Emily after the accident when you started to struggle?"

"Like you said earlier, she wasn't really there at all."

"She didn't try to help you get over it. Not even a bit. She gave up before you gave up. But you were too blind to see it."

"I, um, guess you're right. Where was she?"

"Not where you needed her. You both played a role. Truthfully, you both played the same role. You both gave up on you, when you needed both of you the most."

Harlan sat in silence and looked past Cole into the darkness. The look on his face told the story of a man that was actually seeing the light for the first time.

"Do you get it? Do you see what I'm trying to say to you?"

And Harlan did. He finally got it. He finally understood what Cole was trying to tell him and didn't know what to do with it. But he at least got it. Got that maybe, just maybe, he wasn't to blame for everything. Maybe he wasn't the complete failure he had always felt he was. He was still, as Cole had so gently put it, stupid and idiotic. But maybe he wasn't the lost cause he had often felt he was.

"Yeah. I'm with you. I'm with you on this."

"That's my boy," Cole said as he ruffled Harlan's hair, this time mimicking Harlan's dad. Again, the impression was uncanny.

"Let me say," Cole said with a little smile starting to show, "I really appreciate your looking past my stupidity and foolishness. I wish you didn't blame yourself for my mistakes. I mean, come on, how could the times I've done things such as becoming a street pharmacist who produced his own goods be your fault?"

"Wait. What did you say?"

"You knew all about that, didn't you? About my recent past?"

"Yeah. Yeah, I did. But I'd forgotten you were making it. Do you still have your chemistry set? Please tell me you do."

"I do, but I don't use it, and I'm not going to bust it out. I do a lot of things for you, but one of those things is not turning you into another type of addict."

"No, that's not it. Not for that. Come with me. I think I've come up with a way to finally use that brain of yours for good."

Chapter 25

For the second time that day, Luke found himself in a dark room in the middle of Seattle. This time, however, it was his choice he was there. This time he was not sitting in some chair made for torture, but in a comfortable chair worthy of him. In fact, this one sure looked a lot like the chair Kenji was sitting in when he met his untimely demise. He was also sitting behind a large, beautiful mahogany desk that was covered with incredible decorations from all around the world. He could get used to sitting in a place like this and all the unbelievable things he could do with this kind of power. Too bad it was all wasted on the person who used it. Such a pathetic use of resources, if you asked him.

As he sat there, basking in the ease with which he had made his way into what should have been a highly secure building, he smiled. He had been doing a lot of smiling lately. Maybe it was to make up for all the lost time, the lack of opportunities to smile in his life. Just another thing he could blame on his waste of a father.

Regardless, he could not stop smiling. Right now, the cause for this moment of contentment was thinking of the look that would come on his guest's face when she entered the room, turned on the light, and saw him sitting at her desk, in her chair. Yes, he knew that it was not his office, so he was technically her guest. But he was no one's guest. Everyone was his guest, no matter the situation, or where they were. End of story.

He pictured the look on her face as a combination of surprise, shock, horror, and then superficial excitement to see him. Oh the joys of being Luke Masterson and having the ability to control every situation.

At last Luke heard the door unlock and slowly open. He could hear his visitor fumble around as she searched for the light switch. Finally she found it and began to walk in, head down buried in some boring paperwork. As she got closer to her desk, she looked up and saw Luke, smiling directly at her. The look on her face did not disappoint at all. It began with a look of "I am going to crap my pants" shock, and then quickly evolved into "I already crapped my pants" horror. But before she could reach the fake excitement stage, Luke began what was going to be a fun conversation. At least for him.

"Well hello, Dr. Josie Silver. Or would you rather I call you by the name that brought you this undeserved position, Joserin Matsui?"

Josie cringed in fear as she heard her real name, obviously terrified that someone might hear it.

"Luke!" Josie said, obviously trying to make it look like she was excited to see him. "What a pleasant surprise. After you didn't show up to your game last night, I was so worried. We have all been so worried." She slowly walked toward Luke with her arms wide open to give him some sort of concerned, motherly hug.

Luke's arm shot out, and not to give Josie a hug. Quickly and with minimal force because he did not want to kill her just yet, he pushed her away and right into one of the other chairs in her office.

"Shut up, Josie. Shut. Up!" Luke could feel his anger beginning to boil over and knew that all would unravel rapidly if he gave into it.

Very few things enraged Luke like lying. It reminded him of his mother and her constant lies. "Today will be better. Just you wait and see." "He loves us both so much. He doesn't mean it." "You have no idea how bad he feels after. He won't ever do it again." Every time someone lied to him he could hear his mother's voice lying to him. Not protecting him. Protecting his father instead. And every time he wanted to hurt that liar, just like he hurt his mother. Every single time.

Anger was another part of his past that he had worked so hard to control. It was his inability to master his incredible anger and his bouts of depression and delusion that had made his youth so difficult. For so long, Luke had allowed these traits to dominate his entire life and control his actions. But not anymore.

Now every decision he made, every action he took, everything he did was with a cool head. And on the rare occasion he felt himself spinning out of control, he had learned how to get himself to back away. It was one of many things that he had learned during his time in Japan, and all those things made the lives of those who crossed him more challenging.

Right now, though, he was finding this self-control increasingly more difficult. After all the Matsuis had put him through, after all their shortsighted decisions, he did not feel the ability to control himself quite as quickly anymore. Knowing he needed to do something, Luke paused, caught his breath, felt a little more in control and continued.

"I'm sorry for my little, unnecessary, outburst," Luke said with a measure of calmness. "That was not why I came here to see you. I just wanted to talk. Catch up. See how things are going. It's been way too long." Sadly, because of his mother, lying was never difficult for Luke; it came naturally. But this felt uncomfortable and forced. The angrier he became the harder it was to lie. He wanted to yell and make her feel the pain he had felt that very morning.

"Really? Oh, um, good. Your being here, out of nowhere, surprised me. Quite a bit, actually. Plus, I have been concerned since you didn't show up last night. I could not imagine you, of all people, not being there for something like that."

She just kept lying. She had to be. It made no sense if she wasn't. Why would she be concerned about him and wonder where he was? She was the reason he missed his game. She may not have been there, but she put him there. She called the shots for the family in Seattle, and she knew Luke knew that. Did she think he was a fool? Did she think he didn't know how things worked? The arrogance of these people was maddening.

Something was gnawing at Luke though. Something was off. At the moment, everything about Josie—her speech, her body language, everything—told him that she was telling the truth. And that made him even more concerned. And angry. He was not sure controlling it would be possible, but he needed to try. There was too much left to do, and as much as he hated to admit it, he needed Josie to do it.

"I'm not going to lie, I'm a bit confused." Luke didn't want to sit around and talk about the weather. He wanted this to be quick.

"Confused about what? Why wouldn't I be worried about you?"

"Because you've never been worried about anyone. Ever. Why would you start now?"

"Come on, Luke. Of course, I'm not actually concerned about you. I used the wrong words before. I'm concerned about losing what you bring to the table. What you know.

What you can do." At least she was being honest now. It did make sense as to why everything pointed toward her telling the truth before. She was. Except for one thing.

"What I still don't understand is why you were concerned in any way at all. You knew where I was last night. Why pretend that?"

"I'm not pretending anything at all. I have no idea where you were." Her words may have sounded sincere, but this time her body language gave her away. She was looking right at him, but it wasn't natural; it was forced. He could tell by her stiffened posture. And there was one more thing. As she spoke, she couldn't stop licking her lips. She was still doing it now.

With that, Luke had had enough. He slowly stood up and walked over to where Josie sat. He looked at her and began to laugh. Josie, relaxing a bit now, began to laugh, too. Just as she thought all was well, that he believed her lies, he quickly reached down, grabbed her by the waist and slammed her hard against the wall.

"Why are you lying to me? I'm not a fool. You can't lie to me!" Josie looked terrified, like she knew death was coming for her. "Speak, Joserin. Say something. Just be careful not to dig your grave any deeper."

"Please, Luke. Put me down. Please." She sounded pathetic and this made Luke's whole body fill with joy. He loved this feeling of absolute control.

"No. I will not. Not until you tell me the truth. Don't you dare lie to me again."

“I had no choice. No choice.”

Luke cut her off. “Stop lying to me. Aren’t you the Matsui calling the shots around here? No choice? That’s ridiculous.”

“You don’t understand. There’s another. Another with more power, more control. He threatened me with things no one else would know.”

“Who is this person? I need to know now.”

“I don’t know. I’ve never seen him. Just heard his voice. Seen his shadow. Felt his presence slowly creeping into every facet of my life. I don’t know anything more than that.”

She was telling the truth now. She had no reason to lie. But he wasn’t ready to put her down just yet. “He? What did he threaten you with?”

“He knew things about my past that no one else knows. He knew everything about my daughter and my son. About where they are.” She stammered with guilty emotion. “What, what, what I did to them. Or what I didn’t do for them.”

“And how does this faceless voice get in touch with you? How does he contact you?”

“It’s never the same. Ever. Sometimes it’s a message on my phone. Then it’s an untraceable email. Then he just shows up, like I said before, in the shadows.”

Luke was intrigued by this voice that was terrorizing Josie and running the show on this little operation. At least running the Matsui side, but he still did not have any control over him. Luke wanted to meet this person, this voice.

"Nice to hear some honesty. I'm glad there is still some honor among thieves. And, being a man of honor myself, I'm going to let you down like I promised."

"Thank you, Luke," Josie said as he slowly and carefully placed her back down on the ground. He didn't want to hurt her anymore. He would need her to find this new adversary.

Luke turned and headed back toward Josie's desk. This time, however, he did not make the same mistake that he made the previous day: the mistake of relaxing. The mistake of thinking that all was well and nothing bad would happen at that exact moment in time. And it was a good thing, too.

Out of the corner of his eye he saw Josie lunge in his direction. In the split second that he had, Luke reached out and grabbed her by the arm before she could connect the backside of his head with what appeared to be a solid stone paperweight that could have done some serious damage.

Luke pushed gently, because that was all it took to cause excruciating pain, on a pressure point on her left bicep. Just another trick he learned and then perfected during his time in Japan. Josie's hand flew open, and she dropped her weapon to the floor as tears filled her eyes.

"Josie, Josie, Josie. I've always known you to be stupid and rash, but a fool? I thought better of you."

"I'm so sorry, Luke. I needed to keep you here. I can't let you go. You're the only way he will leave me alone."

"You do need me, I know you do. It's good to hear you say that. But you won't be able to keep me here, not on your life."

"Please, stay. Don't you want to meet this voice? The person who has done all this to you?" Josie was trying to appeal to Luke's ego. She obviously felt she knew how his twisted mind worked.

"Of course I do. But not on your terms. And certainly not on his. We will meet when I am ready. When I say so."

"Then you need me to help you. I'll do anything. Please, just don't kill me"

"I love hearing you grovel at my feet. It's very becoming. And please don't worry your pathetic little head. I'm not going to kill you, but not because I need your help."

Josie let out a sigh of relief, thinking this meeting was over. That she had survived.

"But, my dear Joserin." Luke whispered in her ear. "That doesn't mean you will leave here unscathed."

Before Josie could even attempt to wriggle free from his grasp, Luke tightened his grip and began to twist until he heard a loud, explosive crack come from her arm. It wasn't only the sound that helped Luke know it was not just a break, but a complete fracture of her humerus bone, it was the feeling. That sensation, the exhilarating sensation, of feeling something that was once solid and strong snap in your grasp. That feeling of strength, of power, of dominance. Oh, that feeling of complete and absolute control of another person's ability to function. There was nothing in the world that Luke loved or craved more. Nothing.

Josie attempted to scream out in pain, but the pain was so intense nothing came out. She just stood there, still locked in Luke's grip, with her mouth wide open and her eyes pleading with him to stop.

"Just a simple reminder who you are dealing with," he said as he let her go, not onto the comfort of her overstuffed chairs, but onto the hardwood office floor. "And another reminder never to mess with me again." Luke bent over and grabbed her arm with such violent force that her broken bone ripped through her flesh.

"My goodness, Josie. That sure looks painful. Maybe you can find a doctor, a real doctor, to help you."

Josie just stared at Luke with an expression that simply asked why? Why are you doing this? So, Luke answered her look.

"You have earned this treatment. This pain. Without me, you are nothing. Yet, you forgot and tried to sell me out to some voice in the shadows." For good measure, he stomped on her already disfigured arm as he began to walk out.

"And when I want something, when I'm ready to meet this fool, I will contact you."

Without giving Josie another glance or thought, Luke slowly and confidently made his way out the front door of the hospital.

Chapter 26

"Are you sure this will work?" Cole asked as they pulled up in front of Seattle Children's.

"Nope. But it's all I've got."

"So then what do you need from me?"

"Right now? Nothing. Just wait in the car, and I'll be back in a few."

"Got it. But don't keep me waiting too long. You know how much I miss you when you're away."

"Shut it," Harlan said as he opened the door to get out.

Before Harlan went into the hospital he stopped, took another deep breath, and made sure he knew what he was doing. Made sure he was doing what was right for the patients and not just for himself. And he decided it was his only choice. Something more, something deeper, was going on. And this was the only way he could get to the bottom of it.

As Harlan walked into the hospital, Barry was walking out. It wasn't unusual to see Barry leaving the hospital late, as he often stayed later just to go around and make sure the night staff knew they mattered. Just another thing Harlan liked and appreciated about this administrator.

"Harlan! Fancy meeting you here. Why are you walking into work so late on a school night?"

"Just trying to wrap my head around what's going on here, ya know? I have some thoughts, and I couldn't wait until morning to check them out."

"Good. This is puzzling for sure. I'm glad you're working so hard on it."

"It's important to me. They're important to me," Harlan said pointing inside to where the patients were resting.

"I know. It's what makes you so good. But don't stay too late. Check out what you need to, then get some rest. Lots of good to do tomorrow, too."

"Sounds good. And you get some of that, what did you call it? Rest? Whatever that is, it sounds nice. You deserve to get some, too."

They both offered each other an exhausted smile and went in their separate directions.

Harlan made his way to his office to meet with Clara. On the way to the hospital he had called her to see if she could come help him with his new plan. And, even though she was on a date with the flavor of the month, she dropped everything when she heard it was to help Stacy.

He thought that he would probably have a few minutes to wait in his office before Clara arrived, but as he opened the door, there she was waiting for him and already in her scrubs. She was geared up and ready to do this thing. Whatever it was. Harlan hoped that after she heard the plan she would still be on board.

"I'm not sure how you find the time to be late for a last-second meeting, but you've found a way."

"Did I set a time? I wasn't aware of that. Sorry about breaking up your date tonight. I hope he wasn't too disappointed."

"What else would he be? But he knows, as they all do, that's how it's gonna work if you're gonna be with me. And complaining about it won't help, because your number will just return to the queue, and it could be months until you get with this again."

Her confidence was both incredible and nauseating. Right now, he needed it though and was glad to have it.

"But enough about where I was. Let's talk about where I am now. What's on tap?"

"First off, please hear me out before you shoot it down and run to get my license revoked. Can you at least do that?"

"You're funny, Dr. Allred. Nothing you could suggest could be that crazy. Give me your best shot."

"Ok. Good." But before he could start to explain the events of the day to Clara, the phone that the voice had given him began to ring. Once again, Harlan froze as he stared at it.

"What is that? Why do you have two phones?"

"I, um. It's, um . . . I'll explain later. But I have to take this," Harlan said as he picked it up and answered it.

"Hello?"

"Good. It brings me so much joy that you are smart enough not to ignore my calls. How was your rendezvous with Cole? I assume you didn't tell him anything. And do not lie."

Harlan was happy that for once his paranoia paid off, and this voice did not overhear his conversation with Cole.

"I didn't say a word. We were just hanging out. Nothing to even worry about."

"Good. Good. Keep this up and all will end up better for you than planned."

"What do you want? Why are you calling me again?"

"Why so angry, Harlan? Just relax. This call was a just a test to make sure you were still on board and not straying. You passed. Congrats."

"How can I stray when if I do you will hurt my family? You've got me on a pretty tight leash, don't you think?"

"That's the idea. But you'd be amazed by the amount of times people still don't follow the rules. People always think they can win, even when the odds are dead set against them. Human nature is a fascinating thing."

"I'm sure you just love using that against people, you sick piece of crap. Is your stupid test over for now? Because I have something to get to."

"It almost is. One last thing before I let you go. Sometime tonight, bordering on early morning, your two new friends, the detectives you met earlier today, will stop by your place to talk to you more about Samson and maybe a few other things. If you're smart, and I think we've already proven you are, you will follow my instructions to the letter."

"What instructions? And how do you even know they will stop by? What else could they possibly want from me?"

"Such silly questions. I think I've proven to you that I know what is going on all the time. As far as the instructions, a few minutes before they come you will receive a series of texts from me. Memorize them and execute them perfectly. Then we will be in the home stretch."

"Fine. Whatever you say. Can I go now? Or do you still have more?"

"We are done for now. And, Harlan. Don't stay too late at the hospital working tonight. I wouldn't want you to be too groggy for your bright and early morning."

And once again, the voice was gone, and Harlan was left wondering why he was involved in this in the first place. But he didn't have time to sit and wonder. He had work to do.

Chapter 27

"Harlan, what is going on? Someone is threatening your family? Care to explain?"

"I would love to answer your questions right now, but we don't have time." Clara opened her mouth to protest, but Harlan cut her off. "No. Not now. Stacy and the others need us. Let me catch you up quickly before I tell you our next steps."

"All right. But we will be discussing this later."

"I know we will. But first, here's what we are dealing with." Harlan explained to Clara what was going on with the blood tests. What he had discovered about an unidentifiable substance in the blood work. How he had Lucy request the lab run more tests which came back with nothing at all. Then how the lab didn't think it was strange. And how they were not going to run any more tests, and they were stuck once again.

"That's where we are. And it all confuses me more because we have never had this issue with the lab. Ever.

It strengthens my theory that something more is going on. It gives me even more resolve that what I'm about to suggest is the only way to go."

"Lay it on me. I'm ready to do whatever it takes."

"Since I don't feel we are going to get answers here, we need to do it ourselves. You know my friend Cole?"

"Yes, I do. How could I not? You never shut up about him."

"True. He has a bit of a checkered past—beyond just doing drugs, he maybe even distributed the ones he made himself. And while he is no longer involved in that world anymore, he still has all the equipment necessary to engage in those activities."

"That was the longest I've ever heard someone take to say my friend is not only a former drug dealer but maker of said drugs—who may be out, but could end up back in. Not that I've ever heard anyone say that before."

"It's a delicate situation for me. Still hard for me to say. But we are going to use this—his intelligence and our medical knowledge—to our advantage. We need to get a sample of Stacy's blood. Then . . ."

"Then you want to take that sample to Cole's and use his equipment to figure it out ourselves? Are you serious?"

"As a heart attack. Crazy enough for you?"

"Crazier than anything I've ever heard. Especially coming from you."

"Well? What do you say, Clara?"

"What do I say? Do you even know me? I'm in. Whatever it takes. But, and there is a big but to this, now that I'm in, I'm in the whole way. I'm not just here to draw blood and then leave."

"As much as I don't want to drag you any more into this than I have to, this is deeper and messier than you can ever know, I know you won't give in until I say yes. Plus, we don't have time right now for any sort of argument. So, yes. You're all the way in."

"Glad you know me well enough to concede a fight you could never win."

"Momma ain't raise no fool. But, enough of that, let's get to work."

"Wait. We can't just run out there and do it. Don't you think it will be suspicious that a nurse who is not supposed to be here is drawing blood on Dr. Allred's favorite patient?"

"Excellent point. Then what do you think? How do we go about this?"

"We need a distraction. Something simple. I will only need a few minutes. And it's going to involve Lucy and the very well-known fact that she's got the hots for you."

"That's ridiculous and you know it."

"You're blushing. I get why. She is a hottie with a killer body. And it is true, so we are going to need you to take advantage of that."

"What? You want me to seduce her? Have you ever seen me try and talk to women? That takes me more than a few minutes. It usually takes me an eternity."

"That's what I'm planning on. The attempt alone should give me all the time I need."

Harlan left his office first and went over to the nurse's station on the fourth floor. Clara would follow a few minutes later and then text Harlan when she had drawn the blood and the coast was clear. If all went well, they would be on their way to Cole's place in fifteen minutes, and he wouldn't have to do a thing other than be a bumbling fool.

"Lucy. How's everything going? Everyone doing . . . all right?"

"Oh, hey Dr. Allred. I'm glad you came back. We could always use you around here." She was flirting with him. Awesome. How had he never noticed? *I guess it's time for a game of Harlan Bawl.*

"You look exhausted and worn out. Why don't you and I go to the break room? I hear they have the best coffee in all of Seattle. My treat?"

"That sounds like perfection," she said with a girlish grin. Either he had gotten better at this, or she was so into him it didn't matter what he said.

"Great. You lead the way."

As they walked over, Harlan sent an already written text to Clara letting her know the coast was clear. It was a very clever and inventive text that said, "The coast is clear." He was a creative genius.

As they walked in and Harlan went to pour some coffee, Lucy gently closed the door and slowly pulled down the shade to the window next to the door. Then, to Harlan's surprise, he heard a faint click that meant she had locked the door. Harlan's hands began to tremble, and he was afraid he would spill the coffee all over the place. At this pace he needed Clara to be quicker than they originally planned.

"Um, so, you didn't answer my original question. How is everyone doing?"

"They're fine. Resting. Improving. But we are in the break room. Let's take a break from work for a second." Lucy was now standing right next to Harlan. Way too close. Unless, of course, she was about to give him some sort of invasive exam.

"Yeah. Let's do that. Let's, um, talk. Sitting down. Let's sit. Yeah. That would be nice."

Harlan quickly made his way over to the table and sat in a chair with no other chairs right next to it, hoping she would sit across from him. But of course she didn't. She grabbed the nearest chair and pulled it as close as she possibly could without actually sitting in the same seat as Harlan.

"Tell me a little more about yourself. Where are you from?" Harlan said, trying to make this conversation as bland as possible. "How big is your family? Do they live close by? Why is your hand on my leg?

"Come on, Harlan. We both know why you invited me here. I see the way you look at me. Stealing glances. Watching me closely as I walk away. It's just you and me now."

This was not going according to plan. This wasn't supposed to be happening. Where on God's green earth was Clara?

"How about this? You don't have to say a word. Neither of us do."

Lucy leaned in, and before he could do anything about it, her lips were on his. And as beautiful as she was and as amazing as this felt, Harlan hated it. It felt dirty and wrong. It reeked of a doctor taking advantage of a nurse. And in some way, it was. But not like that. It was so he could get what he needed to fix his patients. So he let it go on for a few seconds and then he gently pulled away.

"Wow, Lucy. That was really, um, nice. But, it doesn't feel right doing this here. We may be in the break room, but we are still at work."

"Everyone does it, but I guess you didn't know that." Lucy scooted back a little bit, like she felt what they were doing was wrong.

Now Harlan didn't know what to do. It was never supposed to get this far. Just as he was thinking of standing up and running out of there, his phone sang the beautiful sound of a text.

"Sorry. I need to get this. My daughter has been sick, and my ex-wife has been looking for advice all night." Best lie he'd ever told.

"Done. Meet me in the parking lot. But you should probably put your clothes back on first. ;)"

"I'm sorry. I've got to go. She, my daughter, is getting worse. Let's, um, do this again sometime. But, not here. Some place nicer. With actual coffee," Harlan said as he opened the door and walked out. He looked back and, although he saw a frustrated look on Lucy's face, he could see that the last thing he said made her happy, too. He still had it. Or she was just extremely lonely. Probably that.

Harlan rounded the corner of the nurse's station and felt he was in the clear when standing in his way, with that smug smile on his face, was Dr. James. Just what the doctor would never order.

He tried to walk around his colleague, but Dr. James was having none of it. "What are you doing here on your night off, Dr. Perfecto? And where are you going in such a hurry?"

"Pretty sure I don't answer to you, Alex. Please move so I can go."

"I don't think so. Not until you answer my questions. They're not that hard now," Alex said as he put his arm around Harlan. This made it impossible for Harlan to move and would make it look like Alex was being friendly with him. Harlan hated when he did this.

"Does a doctor ever actually have a night off?" Harlan asked while removing Alex's arm from his shoulder. "I'm checking on my patients. What else would I be doing here? And now I'm heading to . . ." All of the sudden, Harlan couldn't think of anything to say. Where was he heading so fast that would be believable? And why did he care what Alex thought anyway?

"Can't come up with a lie quick enough? Seeing that you don't answer to me, kind of strange that you feel the need to come up with a lie for me anyway. Makes ya wonder."

"Shut it. Why do you care so much? Did Josie put you up this? I didn't think you two had enough time for talking." Harlan was going to just walk off and not deal with it, but he remembered what he told Lucy and decided this might go further if more than one person had heard the same story. "But if you have to know, my daughter is sick."

"Your daughter, huh? I'd be sorry to hear that if I knew there was any way your family would ever call you for help."

Harlan wanted to say something biting back, but he knew that it would start an argument he didn't have time for, so he tried to calmly walk by and get out the door. Alex quickly slid over and grabbed Harlan by the shoulders in a grip that said he meant business. Harlan tightened up, having no idea what to expect.

Just as it seemed that Alex was going to bash Harlan's head in, he loosened his grip and let him go. Maybe he realized where they were and thought better of it. Harlan was just waiting for him to say, "You and me! Outside! Now!" At least if he did that, Harlan would have something to laugh about.

Instead, Alex got close to Harlan and, with a knowing look, said, "You would be smart not to mess with me, Harlan. You've got enough crap to deal with right now without making me even more of an enemy. I know how you work. For once, keep your head down and do what you're supposed to."

Alex walked off, and Harlan wanted to chase after him. What did Alex know about what Harlan had to deal with? Keep his head down? Who was this idiot, and what gave him the confidence to talk to Harlan like that? But, again, he didn't have time for anything more.

He needed to get outside to meet Cole and Clara without any more distractions. Harlan quickly, but not wanting to bring more attention to himself, carefully, made his way to the lobby. As he did, he noticed someone calmly leaving the hospital at the same time. This event, by itself, was quite normal. People obviously came and went from the hospital all day and night. It was the who that made him look longer than normal.

There, walking right toward him, was Luke Masterson.

Chapter 28

Alex hated Harlan in ways he couldn't really explain. He hated the way he never called him Dr. James. He hated that his quality and patient satisfaction numbers were always so much better than his. He hated that Harlan always had the best financial numbers every single month. He hated, and this may have been the thing he hated the most, how everyone loved Harlan. They treated him like he walked on water and could do no wrong. Alex didn't get it, and it drove him mad.

Alex was a helluva doctor. He knew it and so did everyone else, but they rarely acknowledged it. How often had he been the one that had been there to save the day or give the patients the comfort and care they needed when they needed it? Yet, no one ever said anything. Not to him, at least.

The second Harlan did something even remotely good, something he was supposed to do, they would throw him a party. All hail Dr. Allred. King of the freakin' world.

These last few days had been the icing on the cake. Here they were with all these patients suffering. And, while most of the doctors had at least one patient dealing with this disease, the overwhelming majority were in Harlan's care. Despite this—and this made Alex want to punch a hole through the wall or bash Harlan's head in—everyone was praising Harlan for his work. Barry was calling Harlan down to talk about the situation. The nurses were going to Harlan for advice.

On top of that, Harlan was coming in while Alex was on call, "just to check on his patients." Couldn't Harlan show some trust and let Alex do his work? Nope. He had to come in and be seen, so that every single health-care worker would sit around and talk about how dedicated and hardworking Dr. Allred is. Then they would stare at Alex through the corner of their eyes while they whispered about him. How he never came in on his days off. How he didn't spend extra time with the families of the patients. How he would never be as amazing as Dr. Allred, the magnificent.

Alex often asked himself what if he had been at the hospital the night that little Stacy girl was wheeled in on her last breath. First of all, she would be walking just fine today. Harlan was too slow and indecisive. He always had been and always would be.

Second of all, and this was the most important part to Alex, people would have started to praise him instead. That's when it all really started for Harlan, and when it should have happened for Alex. But it didn't. And still today, with all that was going on, everyone still fell over themselves trying to be the first in line to brownnose Harlan.

He shouldn't be surprised, and he guessed he wasn't, but it still made his blood boil. So much so that he had to grab whatever blood pressure meds he was on this month and take a handful. As a doctor, he should probably know what he was taking, but he didn't care. As long as it kept his heart from exploding, he would take it like candy.

Once the meds brought his heart back to normal, Alex smiled. As frustrating as the last few days—the last few years, truthfully—had been, it would soon be over. Once Alex saved the day, and he was the only one who could, everyone would finally love and worship the right person. And as the cherry on top, when the truth came out about everyone's beloved, perfect Dr. Allred, he would be gone for good. And the fountains of praise would be for Dr. James alone. Every last drop.

Chapter 29

Harlan stopped and stared. He rubbed his eyes hard to get anything out that was causing him to hallucinate. It made no sense. But he was certain Luke Masterson was walking out of the hospital. Right next to him.

Harlan wanted to follow him. He wanted to say something, but he was afraid of two things. First, that it wasn't really him, and he would be caught looking like a fool. That had stopped Harlan from doing a lot of things in his life. For better and for worse.

The second thing that stopped him was the blood sample that was waiting to be tested. That had to come first. Still, he couldn't help but stop and stare. And he obviously stared for too long, because Luke turned and stared right back. And there was something in his gaze, something different that Harlan had never seen before in anyone. Something dark.

Harlan looked away as fast as he could but it was too late. Luke had seen Harlan looking at him, and it appeared that he knew that Harlan recognized him.

"Can I do something for you?" Luke asked, but without a hint of an Australian accent. Maybe this wasn't Luke Masterson. Maybe Harlan was indeed a fool.

"No. Sorry. It's been a long day for me. At first glance you looked like someone familiar."

"I get that a lot. I've got one of those faces."

"I guess you do. But now that I've got a closer look, I was way off. You're not him at all." Harlan was lying. The American accent truly wasn't that close and did not hide the fact that Harlan knew it was Luke. There was no denying it. But he had to try. He had to lie, and he hoped it was convincing.

"No worries. I get it. Just be careful not to stare so much at people. Didn't your mother tell you it's not polite to stare?" Luke said as he stepped close enough to Harlan that they were almost eye to eye.

"She, um, did. I apologize. I just have a lot going on and you caught me, or who I thought you were, caught me off guard. Again, I'm very sorry."

"Apology accepted. Let's just forget it. And it's nice to meet you, Dr. Allred," Luke said as he jabbed his finger into the name badge on Harlan's chest. "Thank you for all you do for the children and the families of this city." He reached out and grabbed Harlan's hand with a grip so tight, Harlan thought his hand might explode.

"Thanks, I appreciate it. I don't think I caught your name." But before Luke could answer, he turned and was gone. And for what seemed like the thousandth time in just the past few days, Harlan was left confused and afraid.

***

"What took you so long?" Clara asked Harlan as he approached her in the parking lot. "I was beginning to think Lucy had you preoccupied."

"No, no, it's nothing like that."

"What is it then, Harlan? You look like you saw a ghost."

"Something like that. Something very much like that."

"Well? What happened? Come on," Clara said after enough silence for her to know he wasn't going to say anything more. "What's going on?"

"It's just. I, um. I don't know how to explain it. And, I don't really want to try to tell the story twice. Can we wait until we are in the car with Cole?"

"Sure. But you're not driving. Not with that lost look on your face."

"Whatever. Let's go find Cole."

Harlan was completely silent while he lay in the back seat of Clara's Mercedes Benz as they drove to Cole's apartment in downtown Seattle. In fact, the only thing he said was insisting they take Clara's car. Call it paranoia. He didn't care.

Both Cole and Clara stayed quiet, too, as if they knew it wasn't wise to ask Harlan anything at all. It stayed that way until Harlan broke the silence.

"I saw Luke Masterson. He was walking outside the hospital at the same time I was."

"Is that why you're acting this way? Starstruck? It's gotta be exciting to be so close to your real-life crush," Cole said as he and Clara exchanged smiles.

"It's not like that at all. It was strange. Not just strange. Terrifying. He pretended he was someone else. He had a completely fake American accent. And the look in his eyes. It was cold. I guess I might even say it was evil. I don't know."

"That is strange. Crazy strange."

"Come off it, you two," Clara said. "He's a celebrity. He was probably just trying to avoid crazed fans, especially because he's been missing."

"Good call. Plus, you're probably just seeing those things because of everything going on and with what Samson said in those tweets to you. The mind can play tricks like that."

Harlan thought about that for a moment. "I guess that makes sense. Maybe it wasn't even him. I don't know what's going on anymore."

"True. So, how was it?" Clara asked while giving Harlan some odd wink like he knew what she was talking about.

"How was what? Meeting Masterson? I already told you that."

"Really? You know what I mean. How was your alone time with Lucy McHotty Pants? Did you get some action?"

"Hold up," Cole said with a shocked look on his face. "Who's this Lucy? And are you blushing? Are you some sort of teenage girl?"

"I did what I had to do to make sure Clara got the sample. That's all."

"That's all? Give me a break. And speaking of breaks, is that where you took her? To the infamous break room?" Clara said with an ever-widening smile.

"Am I the only one who doesn't know what goes on in that room? Have you used it for more than taking a break from work?"

"Me? That's funny. Do I look like I need to use the break room to get some? Puh-lease."

"So spill it, buddy. How did you distract this McHotty Pants? I'm guessing you probably made her cry? Game is probably still on point."

"If it will shut you two up I'll tell you. I tried as hard as I could to play Harlan Bawl, but she wasn't having it. She wanted this." Harlan did his best impression of Vanna White and showcased his face. "So, she got some."

"You hooked up with a nurse at work? Well, well, well. Dr. Allred has joined the hospital's mile high club," Clara said, giving Harlan that wink once again.

"It wasn't like that. She kissed me. I didn't stop it because I was trying to give you time to get what you needed."

"And because you liked it, too. Don't lie."

"That too," Harlan said with a sheepish grin. "At the same time, I didn't. It felt dirty and wrong. Plus . . ." Harlan stopped talking and stared out the window with a look that was faraway.

"Plus what?" Cole said. "Don't leave us hanging."

Harlan waited a moment, unsure if he should really say what was on his mind. But he knew he could trust these two people, both to understand and to make fun of him relentlessly for it.

"It was the first time I've had any contact like that with a woman since Emily. I wish it weren't, but it was."

The car went silent. Cole and Clara exchanged quick glances, like they were trying to figure out which way to go with this one. And it was Cole who made the first move.

"First contact with a woman? Did you just say contact? Can you not use grown-up words, like 'action'? Come on, say it. It's the first time you've gotten any action from a lady in a long time."

"Wow. You sure haven't lost your incredible wit. Hilarious," Harlan said with a grin and a bit of a chuckle. It was amazing how Cole could always find a way to get him to do that even in the darkest of times. "Although, I did walk right into that."

"Yes, you did. You always make it so easy for my incredible wit to reveal itself."

Harlan was happy, not because of the conversation, but because it was finally over. And it wasn't because Cole and Clara didn't have any more to say on the subject, but because they were pulling up in front of Cole's apartment.

As they got out of Clara's car, Harlan noticed something parked on the side of the road.

"I thought your car was missing, Cole. It looks fine to me."

Cole did a double take once he noticed that his car actually was where it should be. He had a look of disbelief, like he never thought he would see it again.

"Good. She brought it back."

"She?" Harlan said. "She? You're not saying that June's back, are you?"

"Back and better than ever, my friend. She showed up a few days ago needing some help. So . . ."

"So you gave in, thinking this time she had changed."

"Guilty as charged. As always."

"What are you two talking about?" Clara interrupted their conversation.

"June is Cole's multiple-time lover. She shows up unannounced and sweeps Cole off his tiny little feet with promises of never leaving him again. Then she runs away after she's sucked him dry. It never changes."

"That is absolutely not true. My feet aren't tiny."

The three of them walked toward Cole's apartment to get down to business. But just as they were about to walk through the doors, just as Harlan was going to go do something that he loved, just as he was going to get hands-on for the second time in the last few hours (albeit in a very different, but equally enjoyable way), his phones rang. Both of them. At the same exact moment. One from his new best friend and the other from the hospital. Both calls he needed to take. Both calls of immeasurable importance. Cole and Clara stared at Harlan while he stared at his phones, unsure of what he was going to do.

Chapter 30

Luke kicked himself. He had let his guard down. He had allowed himself to celebrate his victory over Josie which almost got him caught by some guy, some doctor. Some doctor who looked familiar, and whose name sounded familiar, too. There was something about him that rubbed Luke the wrong way. But he didn't have time to worry about that now.

Who was this voice in the shadows? Why was Josie, who never seemed afraid of anything and had the backing of some pretty horrifying people herself, terrified of this person she had never seen? It made no sense to Luke. He needed to focus his attention, all his attention, on finding out who this person was and putting an end to whatever he was trying to do.

At this point, Luke's anger was bordering on out of control. He was sick of all the people he was forced to surround himself with and their inability to keep pace with him. Every single time in every situation, they proved they didn't have the brain power to get things done right. Maybe they were doing things right in their worlds, but not in his. And his world was always right.

Now he was in the unusual situation of being a step behind someone. Some voice. Some shadow. And this made his blood boil.

Luke headed toward a seat in the dark parking structure. He needed to sit for one second and think. He needed to figure out how to get that step back and then get ahead.

He didn't make it to his seat before his head began to spin with an uncontrollable rage he hadn't experienced since he had felt trapped by his parents. He had successfully kept this rage dormant for years. But now it was back, and he could not stop it. He wasn't sure he wanted to.

His parents. Hadn't Kenji said he knew what Luke had done to his parents? How could he? No one knew. No one would ever know. They couldn't. He wouldn't allow it.

Then why had he said it? Was it just a way to get Luke to give Kenji what he wanted? Just another trick of The Master? It wasn't like Kenji to lie. He always used the truth to get what he wanted. That meant he knew, and he probably wasn't the only one.

Luke needed to sit down. He needed to regroup, to clear his mind. But no matter how hard he tried, he couldn't. He could see his parents, their helpless bodies trapped. He could hear them. He could actually hear them.

"Luke. You're a failure. A loser. Did you think you could always keep us hidden? Did you think no one would figure out where we were?" Luke's father said to him. It was a sound he hadn't heard for years and one he knew he would never hear again. So, why was he hearing it now?

"What are you doing here? How, how did you get out?"

"It was simple, honey." Now his mother was here, too. "That nice Japanese man came and let us out. He said you missed us."

"No, he didn't. You can be so stupid. I can see where Luke gets it from."

"You shut up! Both of you shut up. You can't be here. I killed you. I left you both to suffer and rot. I killed you both!"

Luke was yelling. Without even noticing, he picked up a stray backpack that someone had accidentally left behind and smashed it against the wall where his parents were standing. But no one was there. He was alone. His parents were not there. They were gone just as quickly as they had come.

Why was this happening to him again? Everything he had worked for was slipping through his once-tight grasp. He was letting Josie and Kenji win. He was letting his idiot parents win. And it was all because of some stupid voice. Some voice had stepped in and ruined everything he had been working for.

That was it. The voice. He had caused the problems. He was the one Luke needed to be focused on. No one else mattered anymore. Once he found this voice, once he tracked him down, he would make him pay. Then his plan, the plan he had worked on for so long, would continue until it was finished.

Chapter 31

Harlan looked at each phone trying to figure out which one to answer. Both were important. Both needed his attention now. Neither could wait.

"Answer the phone!" Clara yelled at Harlan, snapping him out of his current state of confusion.

"Which one? Which one do I answer?"

"You've got to answer the one from the dude threatening your family. That's obvious," Cole said, and Clara agreed.

"But what about the hospital? The patients?"

"Here. I'll do you."

"You'll do what?"

"Give me your phone. I'll do my impression of you. You kiss one girl and your mind goes straight to the gutter, you pervert. The hospital will never know the difference."

"Right. Good call," Harlan said as he handed his phone to Cole and flipped open his new phone of doom.

"What now?"

"Your mother must be so proud of your manners. And what took you so long to answer your phone? I was beginning to think you had decided to become foolish."

"Why does it matter? I answered. What do you want?"

"I want to know why you're not home yet. The cops will be there soon and your not being there would be a failed test. All it takes is one failure, and Jack is mine."

"Soon? You said it wouldn't be until later tonight. If you know everything, then why didn't you tell me the time earlier?"

"I'm telling you now. A simple thank you is all you need to say."

"I'm positive you'll never hear those words come out of my mouth."

"Harlan, Harlan, Harlan. Your lack of gratitude is disturbing. Have I steered you in the wrong direction yet?"

"My lack of gratitude? For what? I'm supposed to be grateful to some person whose holding me hostage by threatening to harm my children? Are you insane?"

"I'm completely sane. Completely in control. And it would be important for you not to forget that and listen to everything I tell you. Go home. Now. And wait for my instructions. Follow them perfectly."

"Fine. I'll go. But this needs to be it. This has got to be it."

"Oh, good Doctor. We are just getting started. And you're about to find out this is much worse than you can imagine."

"What is that supposed to mean? How can this possibly get worse?" Harlan yelled into the phone. But it was to no one, because once again the voice was gone.

"I can't do this anymore," Harlan said as he slumped down to the pavement. "I just can't."

Clara sat down next to Harlan and put her arm around him. "Can't do what anymore? What did he say?"

"I have to go home now. The cops will be there soon, and I have to do what he says or . . ." Harlan trailed off because he just couldn't say Jack's name and what might be done to him. "I can't be this guy's puppet. I can't."

"You look more like a Muppet to me anyway," Cole said as he sat down on the other side of Harlan.

"Thanks, I think. Either way, I don't want to be controlled by anyone. I let alcohol do that for too long. I can't let that happen again."

"Then don't. You can still follow his instructions just enough that he thinks you're in his control. Keep Jack safe but do it your way," Cole said.

"How? How do I do that?"

"Honestly, I don't know exactly. But I know, we know, that you'll figure it out. Now go home."

"Wait. First tell me what the hospital said. Provided they bought you pretending to be me."

"They bought it. I'm that good. I believe it was your McHotty Pants who called. And she does sound like she has some hot pants."

"Get on with it. What did she say?"

"Mostly she was checking in. She was worried about your daughter, but don't you worry, I kept your lie going. Also, I guess the patients aren't having the best of nights. They've started throwing up all over with serious muscle twitching. She wanted advice."

"Great. What did you tell her? Nothing stupid, I hope."

"Me? Say something stupid? Have I ever? Don't answer that. I told her only basic stuff she probably already knew. Keep them hydrated. Give them some meds for pain. Call the on-call doctor. And I will, or you will, be in later once your daughter is stable. That good enough, Doctor?"

"Actually, that is pretty good. Either you've been watching a lot of medical shows or I've rubbed off on you," Harlan said with a little unexpected grin. "Clara, will you call Lucy in a few minutes? Tell her I asked you to check in while I'm busy."

"You got it. Do you want us to wait to test the blood until you get back?"

"No. Please start it now. Do everything you can to find out what is in there now. I'll call once I'm done with the cops."

"Will do. Wait." Cole ran inside his apartment and came back before Harlan even really noticed he was gone. "Take this."

"Another phone? You think I need another phone?"

"A phone that your voice friend doesn't know about. One that's safe for us to talk on. Got it?"

"Got it. Good thinking, buddy. Good to see you using that brain again."

"One last thing though," Cole said with a smile as Harlan began to drive off in Clara's car. "I think you've got a date with Lucy this Saturday. You can thank me later, buddy."

Chapter 32

"Who were you talking to?" Dr. James barked at Lucy as he turned the corner. He terrified her, absolutely terrified her. And the fact that she was talking to Dr. Allred made her even more terrified. Dr. James would go through the roof if he found out. He always did. She decided the best thing to do would be to just rip the Band-Aid off and tell the truth.

"Dr. Allred. He asked me to update him on his patients throughout the night, so I did." Lucy braced herself for the inevitable barrage of insults and profanity. Instead there was silence. Silence and a smile.

"It was Dr. Allred, huh? Then why were you blushing when you got off the phone?"

Now it was time for Lucy to be silent, but there was no smile. She sat and stared at Dr. James in disbelief.

"Have you and the doctor been fooling around, Lucy? Well, well, well. Isn't this a pleasing bit of news?"

"You're a moron." Lucy couldn't believe that left her mouth, but as frightening as the consequences might be, it felt good. "You think because I was blushing, Dr. Allred and I are hooking up? Seriously? He just paid me a compliment about my work. Something you should try doing every once in a while."

"Don't you call me a moron. You may call me doctor. Only ever doctor. Got it? Now get back to work," Dr. James said as he stormed off and out of sight.

This had to be the strangest night of Lucy's career, and that interaction made it even stranger. Nothing was going smoothly, and nothing made sense. First Dr. Allred showed up and invited her to the break room and acted like he didn't know what the staff often used it for. Then he ran off when it was starting to get good. She was also sure she saw Clara sneaking around the floor, too. And now, Dr. Allred was asking her out on a date? Something didn't add up. Although she didn't really care, seeing that she got a date out of it.

Truthfully, the thing that threw her most for a loop was the lack of help from the lab. Especially from Rex, the lab tech, who would always go the extra mile for Lucy. Actually, he would go that extra mile for anyone.

But not this time. This time he nervously, more nervously than normal, said that was all he could do, and there was nothing there. Even when she brought up the fact, the indisputable fact, that something was there before, Rex told her it was a mistake and to let him get back to work. It was strange, and it just didn't make sense.

Lucy pulled out two different results. The first read, "Unidentifiable substance found at high levels." Clear as day. But the second read, "Normal." That was it. All levels were normal. Nothing unidentifiable found. Nothing. How could that be?

She was determined to figure this out, to get to the bottom of it. For the patients, of course, but for Dr. Allred, too. She could use some more praise from him. She looked closer at the two reports. There had to be something there, even something small.

And there it was. Something small and seemingly insignificant, but Lucy felt it had to be something. The first report, the one that got their hopes up, had been run by Leah Purser, another lab tech at the hospital. The second was by Rex. Had he changed it? Had Rex changed the results?

She wasn't sure that it was the smartest thing to do, but she decided to confront Rex. This didn't seem like him at all, but it would explain why he had been more nervous and even snapped at her. That really wasn't like him.

Because it was late, outside of Rex being there, the lab was empty. As Lucy walked in she saw him sitting at one of the desks with his head in his hands. She figured he was just tired, resting his head for a moment, until she saw what looked like a tear fall between his hands to the floor.

"Rex?" Lucy gently tried to get his attention. She didn't really want to disturb him, but this was important.

When he didn't look up, she said his name again, a little louder. "Rex? Everything ok?"

Rex looked up at her with tears streaming down his face. It looked like he had been walking outside without an umbrella during a hurricane. When he saw it was her, he attempted to wipe the tears away like nothing had happened. But there was nothing he could do to hide his tear-soaked face.

"Oh. Hey, Lucy. What can I do you for?" Rex said, trying to sound casual.

"What's going on, Rex? Is something wrong?"

"No. No. Everything is good. Just a busy week. And my wife's been sick, real sick. It takes its toll." He had a wife? Lucy had no idea. "But it's nothing to worry about. And you didn't come down here to listen to my life story. What's up?"

Lucy felt guilty moving forward, but she wasn't sure what else she could do for him right now besides let him know how sorry she was. So, she at least did that, before accusing him of falsifying a medical document. Nice, Lucy. Nice.

"I'm so sorry to hear about your wife, truly. If there is ever anything I can do, let me know." Rex seemed to smile when she said that. Maybe this wouldn't be so bad after all.

"There is one thing though. It's about the labs from the kids on the fourth floor. There are a few strange things that I need your help with."

She showed him the two reports, pointing out the two big differences. The most recent being that Rex had put a different result in than the first lab run by another tech. Lucy wasn't sure what she expected to have happen. Maybe he would point the finger at Leah. Or say it was just a lab error the first time. Or maybe he would fess up and this would all be over.

But none of those things, or anything Lucy could have ever imagined, happened. The second Rex realized what Lucy was saying it was as if a switch in his mind was turned off and no one was home. His eyes glazed over, and he blankly stared right at Lucy.

"No, no, no. This can't be. It can't. No." Rex was mumbling like a crazy person. He kept mumbling and started to walk toward Lucy. "What have you done? What have you done?"

What was he talking about? The vacant look in his eyes never wavered as he got closer. What was he going to do to her?

"What, what do you mean? I haven't done anything. What are you doing?"

This momentarily snapped Rex out of it, and the vacant look left. "Not you. Me. What have I done, Lucy? What have I done?" A tear slowly rolled down his cheek. Lucy wanted to comfort him and tell him it would be ok.

But before she could, Rex reached his hand into a drawer, pulled out a gun, and pointed it in Lucy's direction. Lucy couldn't move. Her life was over, and there was nothing she could do.

"Please. Please don't. Please, Rex. Don't shoot me," Lucy pled, but his gun didn't move. It stayed pointed at Lucy.

Finally, Rex smiled a bit and looked at Lucy. "You've always been my favorite," he said with a gleam of hope in his eyes. Perhaps he would spare her life.

"Please do one thing for me. Tell my wife I loved her. Tell her it was all for her." And before Lucy could even react, Rex calmly placed the gun inside his mouth and pulled the trigger.

Chapter 33

As Harlan drove to his home, it began to rain. Of course it would. Harlan was terrified of being late and this rain, even though it was normal and expected in Seattle for nine months of the year, always slowed him down—especially since the night of the accident which had brought Stacy into his life.

The rain and everything going on with Stacy made it impossible for Harlan not to think of that night. The more he thought about it, the more he thought about his earlier discussion with Cole. He had always blamed himself completely for his divorce, but now he wasn't so sure. In fact, that night when he came home, everything was different. Everything had changed.

That night he got home around 11:00 after performing the surgery on Stacy. Right before he left they had gotten word that Stacy's mom hadn't made it. In a few hours Stacy would wake up and would eventually be told the news. The weight of it all pushed down on his body until he wanted to collapse. He knew he wasn't supposed to take these tragedies to heart, but he had always struggled with this, and this case was even harder. As he walked in, all he wanted was a shoulder to cry on and some reassurance that everything would work out, that he wasn't to blame. He needed Emily to be Emily.

But he didn't get any of that. He found Emily sitting on the couch reading some cheesy romance novel, like he had so many times before when he was running later than usual. Only this time, she didn't look up and give him a kiss. No, this time she just stared right past her book and right through him.

"Where the hell have you been?" Emily said with an icy calmness. This caught Harlan off guard. Emily was not one to wear her emotions on her sleeve and especially not one to use any type of four letter word, no matter the situation. Unless she had one too many, and that was as rare as ice water in, well, Hell.

"At the hospital. There was a horrible accident, and a little girl came in, and I was there to perform her surgery, and it was . . ." He was rambling on and the tears were starting to flow. If Harlan thought that this would change Emily's attitude toward him, he was sorely mistaken.

"How come whenever you come home, you don't ask me how my day as been? How come when you're going to be late, you don't call?" She still wasn't yelling. Her voice was quiet, just above a whisper. And she still wasn't looking at him, even when Harlan tried to move into her line of vision. She would ever so slightly move her eyes.

"I do ask. At least I try to." Guilt was running through his veins. Did he never do these things? "And I couldn't call you. I was in surgery. I'm sorry. I should have . . ."

"Should have what? Called me after? Wow. What a novel idea."

"I know. I got distracted by what happened. You should have seen her. And her mother."

"What about her mother, Harlan? What about the mother of your children?"

Where was this was coming from? Had he screwed up so much without even realizing it? He knew he wasn't the perfect husband and father, but he had tried to be better. To be there.

"She died. She died at another hospital and this little girl doesn't even know. She's going to wake up soon, and then she will find out. She'll find out that because some idiot wasn't paying attention while they were driving, she no longer has a mother."

He thought his explanation was the right thing to do. But he was clueless, as he so often was, when it came to emotional conversation. Clueless about how to hear cues for what was important.

She didn't yell at him. He wished she would. She didn't even talk to him. She just got up, grabbed her glass of water, and went upstairs. When he heard her get to their room, the door closed and the lock clicked. She had wordlessly made it clear he wasn't welcome near her that night, that he wasn't welcome in the room that they had promised to share forever.

Harlan sat down, stunned, unsure of his next move. Should he follow her up there? No, she had locked the door. She didn't want that.

Even though he had much bigger issues to deal with, Harlan's stomach had screamed at him. So, he did what any intelligent person would do in this situation. He opened the fridge in hopes of some leftovers. And there were some, but that's not what caught his attention.

In the middle of the first shelf was a new six-pack of beer that he was sure he had not bought. This was odd in and of itself because Emily hardly ever bought any alcohol but wine. What made it even stranger was that three of them were already gone. Emily had been drinking that night. And it was Harlan's actions that had led her to it. He had failed the most important person in his life. He had never felt lower at any moment.

Harlan grabbed one of the three remaining beers and turned on the TV. He wanted to watch some sports and hopefully get some distraction from the day he was having, but the channel was on the news and the story of the car accident was staring him in the face. Mocking him. Just another reminder of his failures that night.

He didn't hear much of the news report, except a few choice sentences. "No one knows what caused the car to be in the Montgomery's lane . . ." "The little girl involved in the crash was rushed to Seattle Children's Hospital . . ." "Although there were eye witnesses, it appears the rain made it difficult for anyone to get a clear view of the car as the driver sped off . . ." "We just received the sad news that the girl's mother, Linda Montgomery, has passed away."

Harlan shut off the TV, grabbed another beer, and began to cry.

Just as Harlan was about to be swept away into the dark abyss of this memory, his new phone let out a series of beeps. One after another. He didn't have to look to know what they were. His instructions. The instructions that he had to follow 100 percent or who knew what would happen next.

His throat burned as a scream built up. He yearned to open his window and toss this stupid phone out onto the road and watch it explode—to speed over to Emily's house and take them all away from this danger. But he knew that would never work. This voice knew everything. He probably had someone constantly watching Emily and the kids, ready to take them, to hurt them, to ruin Harlan's life even more at any moment. The only way this would end would be if he ended it. If he found the cure. If he took away whatever leverage this person had over him, this would go away.

He wanted to read the texts, but ever since the accident he pledged he would never read or send a text while driving again. Before he could pull over to check, Cole's loaner phone rang and he was happy to see that he recognized the number—it looked like Clara was calling. Maybe they had already figured it out.

"Hey. Please tell me something good."

"You've got beautiful eyes. I could look into them all day." Cole. Of course it was. Clara would never say such a thing to him.

"Tell me something I don't already know. Like, how things are going?"

"We are working on it. I'm thinking of all sorts of things it could be, ya know? So many possibilities. You have any thoughts?"

"If I did, we wouldn't have stolen a patient's blood to test with your chemistry set."

"When you put it that way, it makes it sound like what we did was illegal. Or at least immoral."

"I'm not sure what it was. Actually, I know exactly what it was—illegal, and I could lose my license, but it still feels like the only option. Something we had to do."

"Who needs a license to practice medicine anyway? You could be a street doctor. Traveling the streets of Seattle. Saving lives for free. A real-life superhero of the people. I like that idea."

"Wow. That really is a wonderful idea." Harlan hoped that his sarcasm was coming on thick. Sometimes he had to for Cole to get it.

"Shut your mouth. Moving on to the real reason I called. How you holding up? You almost there?"

"Yeah. Just about. Hard to concentrate on what's ahead. But I've got this. I hope."

"You do. We just wanted to check in and remind you that you do, in fact, "got this", my brother. You do." Harlan needed to hear that. He was a man in his forties and yet he still needed daily affirmations from his best friend. And he didn't care.

"Aww, thanks buddy. You make me feel so good about myself."

"That's the idea. Now go get 'em and call us when you're done."

"Will do," Harlan said as he hung up the phone and turned onto his street. He expected to see one of two things. Either one unmarked police car with the detectives waiting for him or nothing. Instead, sitting right in front of his house, were not only the detectives but two more police cars with the boys in blue. Waiting for him. And he had no idea why. Why would they need so many people just for him?

Chapter 34

Harlan kept driving past the chaos in front of his house, hoping no one would recognize him. He was glad he wasn't driving his car right now. He pulled into a side street a few blocks past his home. He needed to think and figure this all out. Was it just yesterday that he woke up with all the optimism in the world? How could life have changed so quickly?

Harlan let all the anger, fear, frustration, and worry he had been holding in for the last few years finally come out. He was sick of pretending he was strong. He just couldn't do that anymore, be that person.

He violently slammed his fists into the steering wheel of the car. Normally, the fact that he was in someone else's car would have stopped him, but not tonight. Not at this moment. He was sure that Clara would understand. Or maybe not. This was her baby he was driving. And now abusing.

After he had severely beaten this inanimate object, he felt a little better. The issues were still there, but he felt he could face them better without all that pent-up rage.

Right now Harlan wanted to talk to his parents. He wanted some reassurance that all would be ok. Once again, he knew he was not a child anymore, and it was probably time he grew up a bit, but he could still use their guidance. They would never stop being his parents, no matter how old he got.

He could even hear his mother say something like, "As long as you did what you knew was right, it doesn't matter what people are saying." Then his father would say something sarcastic, but helpful. And he would feel much better. He would know they believed in him, so no matter what happened next, he could do it. He really did need a lot people backing him to accomplish most tasks. Just another thing he had never grown out of but hoped one day he could.

Plus, Harlan reasoned with himself, he was sure they were worried. He had been all over the news earlier for his Twitter exchange with John Samson. His dad had even texted him about it, but Harlan had not reached out yet. He wasn't always the best communicator, but they would still be concerned they hadn't heard from him. He really would be performing a service by calling them. Yup, this would be more for them than him.

As he attempted to call them, he noticed it was close to midnight. His mom had never been a great sleeper, while his dad had always fallen asleep before his head hit the pillow. Even if there was a chance his mom was up, pacing the floors, eating leftover dessert as she worried about Harlan, it was still too late. He would call them first thing in the morning. He had to.

Harlan began to drive back toward his house when the phone let out a loud beep letting him know he had a new text. The instructions. He had forgotten about the instructions. Truthfully, Harlan had decided he wasn't going to follow them. He didn't care what the voice had to say. He was going to do this his way. Even if he wasn't so sure he knew what his way was.

As a surgeon, he always had a plan before going in for any procedure, even ones performed in an emergency. He needed to make sure his team was on the same page, and everyone was prepared for what they were about to do. Sometimes, the plan didn't matter. Unforeseen difficulties arose. Chaos happened. And, if there was one thing Harlan had learned since finishing medical school, it was that you can't plan for chaos. The most successful sports teams knew it, and so did the most successful people.

Now he was about to enter chaos, and there was not a set of instructions in the world that could prepare him for what lay ahead. Still, he was curious. So he opened the phone and began to read. He read the text that had come in first, and the message sent a chill up his spine.

"Follow the instructions. Do not waver. I know how you work. Look at your hand for a reminder of why it would not be smart."

Harlan looked over to his hand and at first, he didn't see anything. But once he did, he froze in absolute fear. There, right in the middle of his right hand, the hand he used to do his work, was a flickering red dot. The voice had set not only his sights on Jack, but now on Harlan, too. And all it would take was one false move, one slight deviation, and the voice would pull the trigger, and Harlan's world would explode even more.

Harlan was in shock. He felt paralyzed, helpless. Now he felt like he had no choice but to do what the instructions said. Not because he might get himself shot, but because he already had all the motivation he needed to do what needed to be done. His kids. His patients. Their health and safety mattered more to him than his own. But because the voice was close by and watching his every move, he was trapped.

He looked at his remaining texts. There were only two. He thought that there would be a few more. He was terrified he was about to read some extremely specific instructions so hard to follow that med school would look easy. He slowly opened the first text and read it.

"You only need to do two things. First, do everything they ask of you. Everything."

Easy enough, Harlan thought. There was a legion of cops sitting in front of his house. He wasn't about not to what they wanted. He wasn't that stupid. If the second instruction was this easy he would pass this test with flying colors. With that thought it mind, Harlan read the next text. It was only five words long, but those five words changed everything.

"Blame it all on Cole."

Chapter 35

No. Harlan wouldn't do it. He would not blame Cole for anything. Not a single thing that had happened. Not a chance.

He read the text again. *Blame it all on Cole.* What was it? What things would he even need to blame on Cole? Blame the murder of John Samson on Cole? How would that even work?

"Well, officer. My friend, who hates sports and doesn't care about what was said on some Twitter account, murdered John Samson for fun. Now that I've figured out your case for you, Detective Foxy, let's make out." The voice, it turns out, was not only insane, but an idiot, too.

Harlan knew it was a long shot, but he decided to respond to the text. Maybe he would get some clarification. Or maybe he would just end up getting himself killed.

"Blame him for what? And how? Explain your crazy plan."

He pressed send but expected no reply. He was just going to have to go into this blind and hope he didn't screw up the instructions.

As he was about to drive to his house, the phone rang.

"That was a quick response," Harlan said as he answered.

"Don't call me crazy. Don't you dare do that again." Anger. There was anger in this voice that Harlan could not remember hearing at any point. Like Emily on that fateful night, he wasn't yelling. The calmness made the anger more obvious and more jarring.

"I didn't . . ." But the voice cut him off with even more edge.

"Don't try it. I'm not an idiot." The voice was getting louder now. It was the first time Harlan could think of him not being in complete control. He had obviously hit a nerve. Should he keep pushing on it or back off?

Before he could decide what to do or even respond, the voice broke the silence. "I have this awful feeling that I've underestimated you. I thought you were smart. I thought you could follow instructions."

"I can. I have this whole time, haven't I?"

"You've done just fine, however, suddenly you've grown a spine. I didn't choose you because you are tough. I chose you because you've always been weak and easy to manipulate."

"What do you mean, chose me?" But as Harlan said it, he knew the answer. He didn't want to think about it, to believe it, but he had to. It meant that everything that was going on, with his patients, with John Samson, wasn't random. It was meant for him. He was the target.

"No more questions. None. You do as I say. With exactness."

"Why? It seems no matter what I do, you'll always be watching. Always using me for something. Like I'm your puppet."

"Don't be so full of yourself. Once I've got what I want, I'll move on. But only once I've gotten it, and you have done what I've told you."

Harlan had had enough of this voice. He'd had enough of listening and doing what he was told. He also didn't believe that once this was over, whatever it was, he would be left alone. The voice knew Harlan. He knew his strengths. He knew his weaknesses. He knew what he did. He knew who mattered to Harlan. He truly was, in every sense of the word, the voice's puppet.

"I'll do what I need to do, not what you tell me. You're just a coward who won't even show his face. You hide in the shadows and make others do all the work for you."

Harlan was yelling, louder than he had ever yelled. He felt like a lunatic, and it felt good. The good feelings didn't last long, because before he could say another word the rear passenger's side window exploded.

"That is your final warning. The next shot will go through Jack. Then Leslie. And then, once your life has hit its ultimate low, through you. Now go to your house. Do as I say. Blame it, and you will soon understand what it is, all on Cole. Don't you worry, I've made this simple. Even for you."

The voice was gone and, once again, so was Harlan's spine.

Chapter 36

Jack couldn't sleep. He looked at the clock in his room for the thousandth time that night. It hadn't changed since he stared at it a few seconds ago. Still 2:45. He glanced at his phone, willing it to ring. Or at least have a text show up. He knew it was unlikely, especially since it was the middle of the night, but he still hoped. It was unlike his dad not to call or text after everything that was going on with their beloved Mariners.

Normally, at least in the last six months, his dad would have called during Jack's lunch break at school to talk to him about even the simplest of things. Especially when it came to Luke Masterson. But now there was nothing. Silence. Only one simple text a few hours ago.

His mom was furious. Jack didn't understand why she got that way, but it had been happening a lot more lately. Anything his dad did made her agitated and angry. This, the lack of phone calls today, put her over the edge. She had been ranting all night about how irresponsible and idiotic their father was.

Their father. Come to think of it, it was the first time Jack could ever remember his mom talking like that about him in front of Leslie. She had always either kept it to herself and complained to her friends or had private conversations with Jack about what was going on. He didn't like this new attitude of knocking their dad so loudly in front of Leslie.

Jack could take it, but he never agreed with it. He never understood why a parent would rip the other one in front of their kids. What good would it do? First, kids are smart enough to figure out if someone sucks. Second, that's their parent, someone who matters to them. Why would anyone think that making themselves look better by tearing someone else down was ever a good idea?

Not only that, but Jack's dad didn't suck and neither did his mom. They weren't perfect, no, but they didn't suck. And Jack had never, not once, heard his dad say a single bad thing about his mom. He wasn't sure he'd even thought a negative thing about her.

His mom, on the other hand, didn't seem to have a positive bone in her body when it came to his dad. And Jack kind of understood why. The drinking. The late nights. The not being around when he said he would be. It had taken its toll, and he got it. It still didn't make it any easier to take.

Jack remembered when he decided it was time that he break free from his mom and finally spend time with his dad again. She flipped out when, after a few weeks of Jack sneaking out to have lunch or hang out with his dad, she found out. She had never wanted it. In fact, she was the reason Jack had avoided his dad for so long, but he would never let his dad know that. It was better for him to think it was just some dumb teenage phase that kept them apart. It was really the only option.

Tonight, Jack was thinking about sneaking out and going to his dad's place. It was a stupid idea. He had no way of getting there. But he wanted to find a way. He was worried.

He wasn't just worried about his dad, which was why he hadn't tried to go out tonight. He was just as worried about his sister. How was she taking all the things she had heard from her mom about her hero tonight? Was she still awake after hearing things like "worthless drunk" and "pathetic idiot"? He wasn't sure she could take it, so he decided it was time to go check on her.

As Jack got close to Leslie's room he could hear crying—sobbing, actually—but it wasn't coming from Leslie's room like he thought at first. It was coming from the top of the stairs.

"Mom?"

"Oh, hey honey," Emily said without looking away from the phone in her hand.

"Are you ok?"

"No, no I'm not. I'm not. I can't do it anymore."

Jack sat down next to her and put his arm around her. He hoped it would help but didn't think that it really would. Especially in her current state.

"Can't do what anymore?" Jack sat and stared at his mom while tears continued to stream down. It didn't seem like an end was in sight. As if a faucet had been turned on, broke, and would never be fixed.

"Lies. It's all been lies. I can't lie anymore."

Chapter 37

Harlan slowly pulled into his driveway, concerned with multiple things. First, the least important but still a little terrifying, was how to explain to Clara about the damage to her car, her baby. He figured she would understand. It's not like he asked someone to shoot at him tonight. Or ever, really. But it was still not a conversation he was looking forward to. Second, what was waiting for him, and how in the world was he going to handle it?

He felt like an animal in one of those traps where it didn't matter which way he turned, it would hurt. But this was worse. He wished that, like one of those traps, either way he went it would only hurt him, but it wouldn't. It would hurt, or possibly kill, someone he loved.

He had thought about calling Cole and warning him. Letting him know he had no choice. Maybe then Cole could get out of Dodge quickly and not get caught in this mess. Harlan knew he couldn't do that. The voice would know and then who knew what would happen. This trap was getting tighter and harder to manage every second.

Ultimately Harlan knew what he had to do and was ready for whatever happened. At least, he convinced himself he was.

Harlan was finally ready to face the music when his phone rang. It startled him and he may have let out a tiny squeal that would make a toddler proud. After he composed himself, he saw it was the hospital calling. Dang. It would have to wait. He needed to take care of this issue first.

As Harlan got out of his car, the two detectives approached. Neither looked pleased to see him, or maybe it was the exhaustion of being up at this hour. He just wanted it to be over. Please make this easy for him, he thought. Cut right to the chase.

"Dr. Allred. So good to see you again," Stumpy, Harlan still loved that name, said with too much of a grin on his face. Like he knew something. It made Harlan feel incredibly uncomfortable.

"I'm pretty sure that I told you earlier today to call me Harlan, Detective."

"That's right. I'm sorry for my mistake."

If there was one thing that Harlan had learned from cop shows it was that a sarcastic cop was never good. This could spell trouble, with a capital T.

"Well, what can I do for you all this time of night?" It continued to rain, and Harlan started walking inside, hoping they would follow. He had no desire to be outside. It wasn't the rain that bothered him, but the fact that his neighbors didn't need to be a part of his interrogation.

"How about you make this easier for everyone involved and don't play dumb. You know why we are here." Stumpy had an air of arrogance about him that made Harlan want to give him a high five. In the face. With a chair. Probably not the best idea, but it would be exactly what he needed. Both Harlan and Stumpy.

"I'm not playing dumb," Harlan said as they walked into the house followed by two of the uniformed cops. Both stood there silently staring at him. One of them, who had a beautiful Tom Selleck mustache, looked like he was hoping Harlan would make a mad dash for the door so he could flex his Magnum, P.I. muscles and take him down. Harlan was tempted to test it.

Harlan exhaustingly sat down, but Stumpy remained standing. Foxy, oddly, didn't sit across the table from Harlan, but right next to him. Like she was being interrogated as well. At first, he thought they were playing the good cop, bad cop routine. But everything about Foxy's body language told him differently. She looked dejected and lost. Like she didn't know why they were there. Harlan tried to make eye contact with her, but she wouldn't look up. She just stared at her shoes. Strange.

"Come on, Harlan. Do you think we are fools? How can you not know?" Stumpy laughed and so did the mustache. Kindred spirits those two.

"Because I don't know. Is it about Samson? Did you crack the case and want to celebrate with me?" That got Foxy's—he should probably learn her name as it wasn't quite as fun as Stumpy—attention. She looked right at Harlan and wordlessly pleaded with him to stop, to play the game. He got it.

Stumpy slammed the table with his fists. This guy was trying too hard to be the bad cop. He was not going to make it easy for Harlan to avoid making sarcastic remarks.

"You wanna play it that way? Fine. Where were you tonight? Can you tell me that?"

"Starting out with the tough questions, I see. I was at the hospital, checking on my patients. And then with a few friends. Now I'm spending the night with you. How lucky can one guy be?" He obviously wasn't going to stop being an idiot. Stupid coping mechanism.

"Hilarious. Keep this up and you might have a few blind dates by the end of the night. Now, when were you at work?"

Harlan did not like where this was going. He looked to Detective Rodriguez, finally remembering her actual name, for help. Guidance. Anything. But there was nothing there.

"Why don't you just tell me why you're here. This is ridiculous. It's almost three in the freaking morning, and you show up at my house. Not just with your partner. Nope, you've got four more cops with you. And two are outside waiting for me to run. At least you could have left Magnum, P.I. out there so I didn't have to look at his ugly mug. Now what in the world do you want?"

Stumpy turned bright red, stomped over, and pointed his finger right in Harlan's face. "You want to know why we are here? Do you? Then answer me one more question. What is your relationship with Dr. Josie Silver?"

Harlan was not expecting this at all. Josie? What did she have to do with anything? What had happened? He needed to be honest here. They probably already knew the answer.

"Not good. She and I don't see eye to eye on anything at all. Why?"

"Did you argue with her today?" This time Rodriguez asked the question. Like she was trying to calm him down and help him out.

"Does the day end in y? Then most likely. Like I said, we don't really agree on anything."

"Interesting." Stumpy liked this answer too much. "And what was today's altercation about?"

"Altercation? That's an interesting word for two adults disagreeing. But if you must know, it was as I was coming to see you today. She was waiting for me and made a remark about the cops wanting to see me and how pathetic I am. When I told her to back off, she grabbed my arm and threatened to make sure my life would be miserable. That was it. Not exactly your normal work-place conversation, but not out of the ordinary for her either."

"That's not how we heard it," Stumpy said with too much excitement.

"That's too bad, because it's what happened. Besides, I don't see what this has to do with anything at all. We argued today. We probably argued yesterday. She most likely argued with other docs today, too. And I'm pretty sure we will argue tomorrow."

"I doubt that," Stumpy said with a smile that was mirrored almost exactly by Magnum, P.I. "Dr. Silver is dead. She was found murdered in her office."

Chapter 38

This was taking much longer than Cole thought it would. He thought it would be pretty simple to test Stacy's blood and find something there. He had done it before—don't ask him why, but he had—and it was never this difficult.

When they got into his apartment, Clara was taken aback by the hospital-quality lab that took up half of his spare bedroom.

"Why do you have all this stuff? I get having the microscope and beakers, but who would need their own blood spinner? And, are you kidding me? That's a blood chemistry analyzer. What is this place? Why do you have all this stuff?" Clara asked with ever-widening eyes.

"Breaking bad," Cole said, and Clara nodded. "That show came out and I was convinced it was a great idea. It wasn't. I lasted a few days trying to put together something and, well, it just felt wrong. So, I stopped. Don't tell Harlan. He thinks I did it for longer. It's fun to push the limits with him."

"You can say that again. But if you don't use it, then why do you still have this stuff lying around?"

"Underneath this devastatingly attractive man is a huge nerd. No way I'm getting rid of it. In fact, I've just kept adding to it. Good thing, too. You all would be lost without me tonight." Cole smiled his toothy, cheesy smile. Clara just stared at him, trying to figure out if he was for real. Most people spent their time trying to figure Cole out when they were around him.

Now here they were, after three a.m., and he still could not come up with anything. He ran a few different tests looking for something obvious that was being missed. White blood cells. Red blood cells. Clotting. You name it, he looked. For something. Anything.

Exhausted and frustrated, Cole lay down on the floor and let out an exasperating sigh. He was failing. And he hated to fail. He never failed. As soon as he thought that, he disagreed with himself, because, well, he failed a lot. Mostly because he overthought a situation and stressed himself out to the point of implosion. In fact, he was doing that again right now. It was just like the SAT, but with much larger stakes on the line: the lives of twelve children. They were counting on a washed-up genius who never met his potential and they didn't even know it. Poor kids.

"What are you doing? Get your butt up." Clara was standing over Cole staring right down at him. He had never felt more intimidated in his life.

"I've got nothing. I don't know what I should even be looking for."

"You're not going to figure it out lying on the ground. This blood is not going to test itself. You hear me?"

Cole took that not as a suggestion but a straight-up command, reminiscent of when his mom said it was time to come inside. He knew if he didn't sit up soon, she would be counting down from three and then getting the belt ready. Ah, the joys of childhood.

"Yes sir, I mean ma'am," Cole said as he shot up and headed back over to the blood samples to start again.

"This is the last tube of her blood. Let's make this count."

"Thanks. No pressure or anything. Love the support."

"Come off it, dude. You're some kind of genius, right? Use that big brain of yours. I'm sure you've got tons of weird facts up in there. What are you missing?"

"I am a receptacle of useless information. Maybe some of that will come in handy now." Cole started pacing the floors. He did his best thinking when he was moving.

"We don't know what we are looking for, right? Some unidentifiable substance, right?"

"Right," Clara said. She didn't want to say too much. She could tell he was starting to get on a roll.

"I think I see our mistake. We need to start with what we do know and work from there. Tell me again what the kids are going through. Every symptom."

"It's been all over the place. Almost like everything you could possibly experience. It's been slightly different for each of them, but not too much. They've had some intense headaches, so bad they scream like they've been shot. For a while they will be stiff as a board, as if they're paralyzed. Sometimes it's the whole body, and other times it will be a specific body part. Then it just vanishes."

"Good. Good. What else?" Clara could see the wheels in Cole's head were turning. They might finally be getting somewhere.

"Lots of vomiting. Painful, horrible vomiting. It's awful." Clara felt like she was living it all over again. It was difficult to talk about, but she knew she didn't have a choice.

"There has been one thing that's been constant for all of them though. They shake a lot. I don't mean light shaking either. It's seizure-like. They are out of control, and it's more intense than anything I've ever seen before in a patient. Like a convulsion earthquake."

Cole stopped pacing and stared at Clara. "What did you just say?"

"I said, it's like they are having seizures . . ."

"No, the last part. What did you say?"

"Like a convulsion earthquake? Is that what you mean?"

"Yes! That's it. That's it! I could kiss you!"

"Take a number, buddy. Now, what are you talking about?" Clara wanted Cole to let her in on what he had discovered, but before he said anything more, he ran out of the room and was rummaging through a closet in the hall.

After a few minutes of trying to get through the mess, Cole pulled out a large red storage bin and quickly ripped off the top. It was filled with items Cole had collected from all over the world. He knew it was in here somewhere. It had to be.

After what seemed like an eternity, he discovered what he was looking for. A metal box and a plain white binder.

"Got it. I've got what we need."

"Great. Are you going to clue me in?" All Clara could see was a box and a binder. They didn't seem like the keys to anything, let alone something that would save the patients' lives.

Cole opened the box and carefully pulled out a few clear glass containers filled with some sort of colorless liquid. He set them down and opened the binder and began to read.

"What is that liquid? Come on, Cole. What is going on?" But Cole just stuck his finger up and kept reading. Normally someone doing such a thing to Clara would have ended with their finger being detached from their body, but she needed that hand to stay intact. At least for tonight.

"This is it, this is it! Right here in my notes. Victims may experience headache, nausea, vomiting, collapse, convulsions (especially in children), paralysis, blood clotting, and kidney damage. This is it!"

"What is it? What did you find? And what is that liquid?"

"That? That's snake venom." He said it in such a matter-of-fact way, like it was no big deal to have bottles of snake venom lying around.

"Snake venom? You have snake venom?"

"Oh, not just any snake venom. These come from the deadliest snakes all over the world. This one here is from the coastal taipan, my personal favorite. It's the most dangerous snake in Australia."

"Why? What? Why?" Clara was at a loss for words. A rare experience for her.

"We don't have time for me to explain. Let's just say I went through a phase that led me to travel and study the world's deadliest animals."

"Who hasn't gone through that phase at least once in their life?"

"But it has led us here, hasn't it? That thing I just read you? Those are symptoms of someone who has been bitten by a coastal taipan. You named most of those."

Clara *had* named most of those. "There is no way. This makes no sense at all."

"I know. But this has got to be it. The part that set me off was the convulsions. It happens especially with children. And it's the one constant among all of them, right?"

"You're right. Holy cow. You're right." Clara couldn't believe it. "What do we do next?"

"There is a test I can run. It's super nerdy and technical so I won't bore you with it. But, luckily, I've got the tools for it and I've done it before. Give me a few minutes."

Cole took the bottle of snake venom he had earlier pointed out and went to work. Pulling out trays and plates and anything else he could find. He was like a man possessed. He was in his element, and he loved it.

Once he had it all ready to go, Clara's phone rang. She didn't want to take it. She wanted to watch Cole figure this out. But when she saw it was the hospital, she decided it was probably important.

"Clara speaking."

"Clara? It's Lucy."

"Why are you whispering? I can barely hear you."

"I can't talk any louder. Something is going on here. Are you with Dr. Allred? I've been trying to call him all night." Clara had never heard Lucy sound scared before. All Clara could think was that children had taken a turn for the worse.

"I'm not actually. What's going on? Has something happened to the patients?"

"No, it's not that. It's Rex."

"The lab tech? What is going on with Rex?"

Lucy quietly and quickly explained the whole thing. About the lab tests. About how she asked him about it. What he said. And then what he did. How he ended his life, right in front of her. It was all Lucy could do to hold back the tears.

"Something is going on. I don't know what, but the way it's all being handled . . . Something's not right."

Clara could hear yelling in the background. It sounded like Dr. James. She was trying to make out what he was saying, but before it got clear enough for her to hear him, there was silence and Lucy was gone.

She didn't know what to make of this whole situation. Nothing made sense. Why would Rex change the results? What was all for his wife? What was going on that was so horrible he chose to kill himself?

"Confirmed," Cole said from behind Clara. "They've been injected with coastal taipan snake venom. It's genius, in a twisted way. These snakes don't live here, so no one would even think to look for this. Plus, they were injected with just a little bit. It's been diluted or something. That's why it hasn't killed them yet."

"Killed them *yet*? When will it kill them?" Clara said as tears began to well up in her eyes. She just couldn't hold them back anymore.

"Are you all right? Who was that on the phone?"

"It was the hospital looking for Harlan. Something has happened there. I'll explain later. First, let's focus. When will it kill them?"

"It all depends on when they were injected. Any ideas?"

Clara thought for a second and then remembered what Harlan had discovered. “They all had lab work prior to their appointments. Either the day before or that morning. It must have been then.”

“All right. Then, and this is a pretty rough guess, but I think it’s close. The average time it normally takes to kill someone who has been bitten is about three hours. From what I can tell, the venom was diluted to about five percent of its strength. Whoever did this wanted to maximize the suffering. Sick.”

“Cole. When will it kill them?”

“Right. Sorry. Well, based on all those factors, they . . .” Cole hesitated for a moment, not wanting to believe what he was about to say. “They have less than ten hours.”

Chapter 39

Harlan's head began to spin faster than ever. If he weren't already sitting down, he would have passed out. Josie was dead? Murdered? Right in her office? But how could that happen? It didn't add up.

But then he got it. They thought he killed her. No, Stumpy was convinced that Harlan had done it. And this, this horrible crime, is what the voice wanted Harlan to blame on Cole. Cole could have easily done it, actually. Cole was his best friend, and he had always been overly protective of him. There had been more than one time when Cole had beaten up someone who had crossed Harlan the wrong way.

In fact, and the voice would know this, Cole had been in jail a few years back from beating someone to the edge of death after a simple disagreement in a bar. Some guy wanted to cut in front to get a round. When Harlan told him to wait in line, the guy shoved Harlan hard in the back. This set Cole off, and it took three men to pull him off his bloody, almost lifeless victim. That would be in Cole's record. His killing someone who wronged Harlan was believable. The voice knew what he was doing.

Once again, just as it had earlier, two roads diverged. Last time he took the wrong road. It seemed right at the time—he needed to save his kids. This time it should be clear which way was right, but it wasn't. Both roads were right there, but he couldn't move toward either of them. The trap was closing on him, and it kept getting tighter. He was stuck with nowhere to go.

"Well, that got your smug face's attention, didn't it? Your boss was found murdered not long after you two fought publicly. You're a smart man. Tell me how that looks?"

"It looks thin and ridiculous. If you are going to base this investigation solely off who argued with Josie yesterday, then you're probably going to have to question half the medical staff. No one liked her, and you'd know that if you were doing your job."

"Like I said before, your story doesn't exactly match up with what we heard happened. You say she initiated it, but those who saw it go down say you approached her and started yelling, calling her all sorts of names. Then, like the big man you are, you grabbed her arm and wouldn't let go."

This made no sense at all. Who was telling the cops these lies? He didn't know if he should defend himself or just let the detective keep going. The look on Rodriguez's face told him to not say a word.

"Well, that caught you by surprise, too. You didn't think we would do our research and find out what truly happened, did you? Lies will always catch up to you, Harlan. And this one got you busted."

Harlan couldn't help himself. "Busted? What are we in middle school? You busted me? Because someone, who may be some imaginary friend of yours for all I know, says I got mad first? Excellent work, Detective. You've busted me. Take me away." Harlan mimed putting his hands in front of him.

Stumpy looked livid now, like this fat, lump of a head would explode. Harlan could almost see steam coming out of his ears.

"Listen, you arrogant prick. In the last twenty-four hours, two people who had conversations with you ended up murdered not too long after. How about you put two and two together for me?"

"It's four. I'm surprised you didn't know that."

Stumpy lunged toward Harlan, but just before he could get a hand on him, Rodriguez grabbed hold of her partner and restrained him. Harlan wasn't expecting that at all. Not that she didn't look tough, but Harlan wasn't sure anyone could stop a rhino going full speed with their bare hands. Miraculously, he just witnessed it.

While she was holding onto Stumpy, she looked right at Harlan and mouthed something so that only Harlan could see. He couldn't make it out at first, and Rodriguez looked frustrated. They didn't have much time before her partner broke free. But she mouthed it one more time and this time he got it.

"She's not dead."

Chapter 40

"That's enough, Mancuso." Rodriguez was still restraining her partner. He didn't appear to be close to calming down. "You're not helping this situation at all. Why don't you take yourself and the other two outside? Cool down. I'll take care of this moron myself."

Mancuso—the perfect *Law and Order* cop name—looked a little taken aback by Rodriguez's request. Maybe because it wasn't really a request. It was more of a command. He didn't seem like the type that took orders from women all that well. Harlan wondered if he was going to have to jump in and restrain his new best friend next.

Then Stumpy stopped scowling, smiled, and winked at his partner. Harlan had never felt so confused, uncomfortable, and scared before. Those were emotions he had felt a lot the last few days, but not all together. He didn't like it.

"All right. I got ya. I'll go 'calm down' while you do your thing," Stumpy said, even using finger quotation marks. This guy was a pro. He winked again, and then gestured to the other cops to follow him out. Magnum, P.I. was smiling, too, as he walked out. What were they playing at?

Harlan wasn't sure what to expect next now that he was alone with this gorgeous detective. Under normal circumstances, whatever normal meant anymore, he wouldn't mind being alone with her. But tonight, when he was being accused of the murder of someone who apparently wasn't even dead? He'd pass. Not that he had a choice, but he would like to.

As soon as she was sure the other cops were outside, Rodriguez turned to Harlan. "Tell me what you know. And hurry. We don't have a lot of time."

"Me? Tell you what I know? About what exactly? About how in the last twelve hours you and your partner have accused me of two murders. And then in a five minute period I was told that Josie Silver was murdered in her office, by me of course, then found out she is actually not dead! How about *you* tell *me* what is going on?"

"Keep your voice down. Let's not give my partner any reason to come back in here. I can't help you if he does."

Harlan just stared at her, trying to figure out what she was about. Could he trust her? Or was this just a part of their routine? Is this how they got him to confess?

For Harlan, reading people was never easy, especially with so much on the line, but there was something about the look on her face that made him believe she could be trusted. She looked scared, worried, and confused. She looked how he felt. She was on his side.

"Look, Harlan, today has been confusing for me too. I get it. One second Mancuso is telling me and all these other cops that this Dr. Silver is dead and then the next second he is pulling me into another room to let me know she is alive and well. He won't tell me why he's lied about it, but I've got to trust him and follow his lead. It makes no sense. Now you've got to calm down and work with me, Harlan. I am on your side."

"I'm sorry. It's just, these last couple of days, and then this. I don't know what to make of anything anymore."

"What else has been going on the last day, Harlan? I need you to clear up a few things for me, and then maybe this will make some sense."

"My patients, everyone's patients actually, are dying. I don't know why. And then John Samson dies, and Twitter makes me a suspect. And . . ." He had already made the decision to trust her, but he still hesitated. He sure hoped he was right about her. "Now I get phone calls from some random voice. Threatening me, my family, everything . . ."

Before Harlan could say anymore, Rodriguez cut him off. "Random phone calls from some voice?" Harlan couldn't tell if she believed him. She was giving no sign at all whether she thought he was crazy or just insane. "How long have they been coming in?"

"The first call was a message to my cell phone right before I met you guys today."

"Then why didn't you say something about it at that time?" She was glaring at him in a way that made him want to run for the hills.

"He threatened to make my son suffer the same way my patients were if I told you. What choice did I have?"

"You could have said something. You should have. I get it, but you still should have trusted us. But that's done. Let's move on." Harlan felt grateful for that. He was preparing himself for the kind of lecture of responsibility that, as a child, he often endured from his parents. "This voice called your phone. Has he been calling you on that phone the whole time?"

"Just the first time he did, but then I found this in my car." He pulled out the phone and showed it to Rodriguez. "They've all come to this one since."

She immediately stood up and began to pace the floor. It looked like she was talking to herself, trying to piece some things together.

"Will you sit down? You're making me nervous."

"Yeah. Sorry about that. Force of habit." She stopped pacing, but she didn't sit down. "That phone. I've seen that phone before."

"It is a pretty common phone, so I can imagine you've seen it a lot," Harlan said, trying to figure out what she was trying to say.

"It *was* a pretty common phone. You rarely see flip phones anymore. But I've seen that same type of phone today." She started pacing again. Harlan didn't think it made much sense to stop her now, but he couldn't just sit there and wait for her, so he kept talking.

"The last phone call. He told me that you all would be here and that whatever you guys said, I needed to blame it on a friend of mine. And I could. It would make sense. But I don't want to." He was just rambling now, trying to keep from going crazy.

"Interesting." Harlan couldn't tell if she was talking about what he had just said, or if it was something she had thought about. "You're saying this voice knew we would be here?"

"That's exactly what I'm saying. He knows everything."

That seemed to trigger something because Rodriguez stopped pacing and sat down next to Harlan. The look in her eyes changed. It was now a mix of excitement and terror. Like she had figured something out but wished she hadn't.

"The phone. My partner. He has one, too."

Chapter 41

After what Luke had done to Josie last night, it made sense that she was lying in an uncomfortable hospital bed. What didn't make sense was the location. She was not in one of the hospitals in Seattle that served adults. No, she was in the basement, stuffed in some surgery room in a children's hospital. Her children's hospital. All by herself.

That male detective who came to investigate what happened told her this was where she was going to stay. When she tried to ask why, he just made some stupid "it's for your protection" remark and the two cops, who seemed to be alive to do the detective's bidding, took her downstairs.

They set it up just fine, and she even had some outside nurse and doctor checking in on her. They had made sure her arm was fixed, and she was resting comfortably. But she still didn't understand why they had her down here. She didn't need their protection. It was more likely that they were going to need protection once the Matsuis found out where she was.

Come to think of it, Josie had not heard from anyone within the Matsui family for a while. Nothing at all. This would happen very occasionally, but not during an important time like this. They had completely abandoned her.

The only people she ever heard from, it seemed, were Luke and that voice. That stupid voice. Always calling her and giving her demands about what to do next. Showing up at her office, while she was walking to her car, or even when she was out to dinner, but never showing his face. Threatening to expose her secrets. Threatening to hurt those she loved. Threatening to take away everything she had worked so hard to achieve.

Now she lay in a hospital bed, stuck with no help. All because of Luke. What had snapped inside his head to make him do what he did? Why was everything falling apart and she unable to get out and fix it? And where was the nurse with more pain meds?

Just as she was about to scream out for the nurse, the door opened.

"Thank goodness. Where have you been?"

"You really need to work on the security at this hospital of yours, Joserin."

Josie froze. It wasn't a nurse or a doctor or anyone she wanted to see. *Please no*, she thought. Only one person called her by that name.

Luke.

Chapter 42

Harlan looked at his phone then back at Rodriguez, then back at his phone again. He didn't think this day could get more strange or confusing, but it just did. Why did Mancuso have the same phone?

"Over the last day or so this phone showed up. He tries to hide it, but I've seen it more than once." Rodriguez was still sitting, staring off into the distance.

"Are you saying that he's the voice? That he's the one who's been calling me?" Harlan felt his blood boil just thinking about it.

Rodriguez just looked at Harlan and laughed. "No. No way. Are you kidding me? He's not smart enough to pull off something like this."

"Then what? What are you getting at?"

"Normally he doesn't care about taking any calls in front of me. Work or personal. But then last night, when we were at the hospital, this phone rings, and he says he needs to take it somewhere else. When he comes back he looks like he's seen a ghost and tells me he's got it from here. So, he kicks me out. And when he calls me back in he says Josie's dead and you, Harlan, are the one who did it." Rodriguez paused, got up, and started to pace again.

"The voice is calling Mancuso, too? He's controlling him, too?"

Harlan wanted to get up and walk with her, but his legs felt like Jell-O. If he stood up he would collapse, and he wasn't sure he would be able to get back up. The voice wasn't just terrorizing Harlan, but others. And in the process, terrorizing Harlan more. What was this guy's game?

"What am I going to do? I can't blame a murder on my friend. But, if I don't . . ." Harlan didn't want to say or even think about what would happen. "If I don't, Mancuso will tell the voice. I'm trapped."

Rodriguez stopped walking, sat down, and put her arm around Harlan. He could get used to all these beautiful women giving him attention. Not for the reason he was getting it now, but still. He would not protest.

"I need to get back to the hospital. My patients. We are so close. They are working on it right now. I have to get out of here." Harlan stood up and began to walk toward the door, but Rodriguez grabbed his arm and pushed him back down to his seat.

"Not your best idea, Doc." It wasn't, that was true, but Harlan was not exactly in a rational place. He didn't believe anyone would be rational after what he had been through the last few days.

"Then what? What do I do?" Harlan did not want to break down. Not now. Not ever. He could usually hold his emotions in check. But his control was slowly leaking. Drip by drip. Soon it would break open and everything would flood out. If that happened, how could he save his patients and keep his family safe? He couldn't. He needed to stay strong. Sticking with the water analogy, he needed to dam them up. So, he did.

"First, breathe. There are options. I know my partner. I can get to him and keep him at bay."

"But do you know the voice? Do you know what he could have said to get Mancuso to do all of this? This guy knows everything."

"No one knows everything, and everyone has a weakness. This is beatable if you trust me. Do you trust me?"

Harlan was glad he had decided the answer to that question earlier, because if he'd had to decide at that very moment, it would be tough. But not with all he had found out since.

"I do. I don't know why, but I do." He needed to trust her. It felt like his only option and everything told him it was the best option, too.

"Good. We have two ways we can do this. First, we call him out. You tell him that you're having the same stuff happen to you. We get him back to our side of things."

"Please tell me your second option is better. Please. I just can't see that happening."

"Harlan, Mancuso is a good man and a good cop. I know that sounds cliché, but it's the truth. He's no saint, but this isn't him."

"You're right. It isn't him. It's something else. Someone else. Someone much worse. I just don't see how that will work

"All right, fine. Then we will have to go with this. I tell him you know who did it. That you've got this friend..." "No. No way. I'm not doing it. I can't." Harlan was surprised she was even mentioning it. Hadn't he made himself clear?

"Shut up and let me finish. I tell him you've got a friend that you are sure did it, but you need proof. And we are going to let you get it."

"Do you think he'll buy that? I don't think I would."

"He will because he trusts me. Besides, I'm guessing this voice told him you would blame it on your friend. He's waiting for it."

She had a good point. *I guess that's why she's the detective,* Harlan thought. The whole keen, sharp mind thing.

"Ok. That will work. Do you think it will take long to convince him?"

"Convince me of what?" Harlan and Rodriguez slowly turned around. Mancuso was standing behind them with his gun pulled.

"Convince me of what, Harlan? Come on. Convince me of what?"

Harlan wasn't sure how to respond. If this was a surgical room and a patient were coding, he would have all the answers. But now, he was a blank.

He needed to say something though. Mancuso didn't look like he had much more patience left. As he opened his mouth, hoping that something intelligent would come out, Mancuso seemed to notice something that diverted his attention.

"Where did you get that? Where did you get that phone?" Mancuso looked like his worst nightmare had come to life. He slowly pulled an identical phone from his pocket. "Why do you have that same phone?"

Harlan looked at Rodriguez. She smiled and nodded. He turned his gaze back to Mancuso.

"The voice. I got it from the voice. The same voice that's been calling you."

Mancuso collapsed in a heap on the ground. He sat there and stared at his phone like he was expecting it to explode at any moment.

"This can't be. If he finds out, if he knows, it's all over."

Harlan leaned down to get level with the terrified detective. "What's all over? What is he doing to you?"

"Me. I'm done. Everything is done. Everything. Everyone I care about. It will all be gone."

Harlan looked at Mancuso, trying to let him know it would be ok. He didn't actually believe it himself, but

Harlan needed him to be strong. He needed the detectives' help.

"What do you mean? Why will it all be gone?"

"My secrets. He will expose all of my secrets."

Chapter 43

He used to love it when people called him the voice. There was so much power and mystery to it. It still worked, but ever since that singing show with the same name debuted on TV, it just didn't feel the same. And he couldn't go with the shadow—that was taken. So, he stuck with the voice, and it still worked. It still struck fear.

Now, even though it was the middle of the night, practically morning actually, the voice sat in the office of his day job. He hated this part. The waiting, the patiently waiting, to find out if people would do what they were told. He was always so careful when he selected the people who would help him get what he wanted, and it rarely failed. But when you're dealing with human beings you never know what they will do. They have brains of their own, which leads them to do stupid things and force his hand.

And he hated that, too. He hated when he had to keep the promises and threats he made. Why couldn't people just walk the line and do what he said?

Take Harlan, for example. The voice had never vetted anyone as thoroughly and intensely as he had Harlan. He thought he knew this man and what made him tick. What buttons to push. What weaknesses would get Harlan to do what he wanted him to do. But he was wrong, which meant he needed to get Harlan back on track.

And since verbal threats weren't working, the voice had to escalate the process. Harlan needed to know that he meant business. Which was why the voice got someone—just another person whose weaknesses led him to do whatever he was told—to put a gun on Harlan and blow out his back window. He hated doing things like that, he hated violence in general, but this was a case of the ends justifying the means. And he hoped that these actions had awakened Harlan from his slumber of stupidity.

But he didn't know that, which meant he had to wait to see what Harlan would do.

It was times like these that the voice wished he didn't have morals or boundaries. To him a person's home was a sanctuary, a place that should be left alone. He never crossed that line. He never entered their home, put bugs or cameras all over, or placed a tap on a home phone. Everything else—cell phones, offices, cars—was fair game. The home was sacred, and the one place where people deserved their privacy. So he gave it to them, but right now he wished he hadn't. Not being able to see what was going on in Harlan's home was making the waiting even more unbearable.

The other wild card was Luke. He never expected Luke to be easy to control, but the voice thought they were on the same page. That they had the same goals. Unfortunately, everything Luke had done over the past few days showed otherwise. Luke could ruin this whole thing, everything they had been working for.

Josie had assured him that she could keep Luke in line and look where that got her. In a hospital bed, stashed away where she couldn't be found and completely screw this up. When the first part of this plan was over, so was she. Her usefulness had run its course.

Or maybe it hadn't. She could do one more thing. She could draw Luke out. She could still deliver Luke to him. She would finally do something right without even having to try. A perfect task for her.

The voice smiled. This was going to work out. It always did. He shouldn't doubt that. When had he ever actually failed?

He stood up, grabbed his phones so he could still check in with his new buddies, and left to go pay the good Dr. Silver a visit.

Chapter 44

Harlan took a step back, unsure of what to do next. He knew now that the only option was to try to get Mancuso on their side. He wasn't sure how he would do it, but he knew that was the only way out now.

It was obvious that Rodriguez could sense Harlan's concerns, so she stepped forward and grabbed Harlan by the arm. Almost like she was trying to steady him.

"You can do this," she whispered in Harlan's ear as Mancuso continued to stare into his hands. Harlan looked at her, confused. Hadn't she said earlier that she could get Mancuso to flip? That he trusted her? Why did she now expect Harlan to be able to handle this delicate and time-sensitive situation?

"Me? Why?" Harlan whispered back.

"You two are connected by this voice. I don't get it. You can help him. I'm right here to back you up."

"What are you two whispering about?" Mancuso was still not looking up, but he was there. He wasn't going to wait much longer. Harlan needed to push forward now.

"Just about this whole situation. How horrible it is. How difficult this must be for you."

"No, you weren't. You don't care about me. Don't you try to lie to me." Mancuso had finally looked up. There were no tears, only a mixed look of pain and anger. Harlan decided that honesty was the only way this would work. One hundred percent honesty.

"You're right. I'm sorry for lying. But I wasn't lying about being concerned about what you're going through, it's just not what we were talking about."

"Then what? Spill it, Doc."

"How to get your help. How we can get you to help me get out of this and take care of my patients."

"You're on his side?" Mancuso quickly shot up and Harlan jumped back as the detective stormed past him to confront Rodriguez. "How can you do that? You're my partner."

"Because this isn't you. This isn't the person I know. You're better than this." Rodriguez stood her ground and even tried to reach out to Mancuso, but he just swatted her away.

"You don't know anything about me. You don't know what I'm capable of. What I've seen."

"But the voice does." Harlan walked over and inserted himself between the two detectives. "Right? The man who calls you. Who knows all about it. He's threatening you if you don't do what he says."

Mancuso stared back at Harlan with a look that Harlan couldn't quite read. "Yeah. And I don't have a choice. No one can know about me. No one."

"Do you actually think he is going to let you go free when this is done? That once this is over he will never use you again? Come on now. This voice knows your weaknesses. He knows my weaknesses. He needs both of us, and that won't end. People like him prey off the weaknesses of those who have the power he needs. He will always need us. It never will end."

Harlan hoped his little speech had worked. The look on Mancuso's face told him it might just have. When he looked at Rodriguez it seemed that she thought so, too. She motioned to Harlan to keep going, to take advantage of any progress he had made.

"He's hurting my patients. Killing them. He's threatening my family. If I don't do what he says, if I don't follow his instructions perfectly, he said he will kill my son. My sixteen-year-old son. Does this sound like someone who will care about you after this hell is over?"

"No, it doesn't. It doesn't sound like that at all."

It was working. Mancuso was going to help them. He would be on their side. This crazy plan might just work.

"But it also doesn't sound like someone who will be forgiving if I don't do exactly what he says."

Quicker than Harlan had ever seen, Mancuso pulled his gun and pointed it right at Rodriguez.

"You should have kept your nose out of this. You should have let me do my job. This would already be over." Mancuso was ranting, but his gun never moved off Rodriguez. As insane as he sounded, everything else about him looked eerily calm.

"What are you doing? You don't have to do this, Rick. You can get out of this if you'll just listen." She was trying not to look scared, like it was normal for her partner to pull his gun on her. But it wasn't working. She couldn't hide her fear.

"Are you kidding me? You can't honestly be so naive as to believe that."

"It's true," Harlan said. "There is a way out. We just need you to tell the voice what he needs to hear. That will give me the time I need."

Mancuso paused for a moment like he was thinking this through. He even started to lower his gun a little bit. Again, Harlan had hope that they had Mancuso where they needed him.

But just as quickly as the light of hope entered the room, it was gone as Mancuso pointed his gun at Rodriguez and pulled the trigger.

Chapter 45

All Harlan could hear were bells blaring in his ears from the explosion of Mancuso's gun. He had never had so many close encounters with guns as he had that very night. He didn't like it, and he was hoping this was it. This time the shot was fired right next to him. This time he could see who pulled the trigger. This time he could feel the bullet in the air and hear the gun's explosion. The explosion that was so loud he couldn't see straight. He couldn't see what had happened.

Once he gained his bearings he saw Rodriguez lying on the floor. Tears began to fill his already blurry eyes. Harlan was the reason she was lying in a pool of her own blood. He had killed her without pulling the trigger.

"Rodriguez!" he yelled as he ran in her direction. "I'm sorry. I'm so sorry. You didn't deserve this."

"What in the world are you crying about?"

Harlan stopped running and looked at Rodriguez. Was that really her who just spoke to him? Maybe he was dead, too, and they were in heaven. That had to explain it.

"I'm fine, Harlan. It's just a flesh wound. The bullet barely grazed my shoulder. It's Mancuso who needs some help." She pointed toward the detective, who was on the floor covered in red.

"But . . . he shot you. I saw it. He had his gun pointed at your chest. He shot you."

"He did. And he would have killed me had Officer Bennett not shot him first." A young officer, who looked like he should still be in high school, was sitting next to Rodriguez putting pressure on her shoulder. Harlan recognized him as one of the cops who had been waiting outside earlier.

"You? What? How did you? What?" Harlan was stammering like a broken record. He couldn't stop himself. "Is he dead?"

Rodriguez gave Harlan a knowing look that he couldn't read. Before he could ask again, his phone rang. He had never gotten this many phone calls in his life.

Again, it wasn't the voice's phone, and it wasn't his phone. It was the loaner. This was getting hard to keep track of. It was Clara. Or Cole. He couldn't be too sure.

Harlan stepped away into another room and answered. "This is Harlan."

"You sound horrible. What is going on? Are you still at your house?" It was Clara this time. He was hoping she had something good to tell him.

"I'm still here. And I don't know how to explain what has happened. I'm not even going to try right now."

"Is that Harlan? Did you finally get him?" It was Cole in the background. He sounded excited, and Harlan could hear him trying to grab the phone away from Clara.

"Yes. Calm down and give me a second . . . Sorry about that. Your buddy needs to talk to you. How do you put up with him all the time?"

"I don't. It's impossible. But we make it work."

"I hear that. Before I give him the phone, have you talked to anyone at the hospital?"

"No. Why?" This question made Harlan nervous. What had he missed? What should he have been there for?

"You know Rex, right?"

"The lab tech? Yeah. Why?"

Clara paused. It felt like an eternity before she opened her mouth again. "He killed himself. Right in front of Lucy. He was involved in this whole mess. Something happened to him that got him involved."

Harlan grabbed hold of the nearest chair so that he wouldn't tumble to the ground. Rex was involved in what was happening to the kids? Good, fun, hardworking, trustworthy Rex? Just another thing that didn't make sense to Harlan. Until it did.

"The voice. The voice got to him, too," Harlan said as he sat down, hoping he wouldn't pass out. "His wife has been sick. On her deathbed for a few months. Up until recently, he had been so worried about how she was going to get the treatment she needed with the little money they had. But he seemed better lately. The voice. He knew."

"We have to stop this person, Harlan. Whoever or whatever it is."

"I know. He's tied to all of this. But the kids first."

"Which is why Cole is freaking out, waiting to talk to you. Here."

"Venom. It's snake venom." Cole didn't say hello, he just went straight for it. And it made no sense to Harlan at all.

"Snake venom? Slow down and explain."

So Cole did. He explained everything he had discovered. Harlan didn't know how to respond. It was crazy. Too crazy? Maybe. But it sounded right, too. Sometimes it paid to have a crazy genius for a friend.

"Now aren't you glad that I went on that insane trip a few years back? It finally paid off."

"It finally has. One of your eccentric fetishes has some good to it. So, what now? There's an antivenom, right?"

"Yup. But . . ."

"But what? There's an antivenom, so this should be easy." At least that's what Harlan was hoping would be the case. But why would it be?

"I've got enough for one person. I got it while I was traveling. But, it's a snake found only in Australia. That's the only place that has it."

"Of course. But you can make some? You can take what you have and make more? It's easy, right? Please tell me you can make some."

"I can, but not from what I have. You can't just do that. It takes months to make. And we only have . . ." Cole paused. He hadn't told Harlan this part yet. "The kids have less than ten hours."

Harlan was glad he was sitting. He was at a complete loss. Once again, that light of hope was ripped from his grasp.

"Then why were you so excited? Because you figured it out? Congrats on that, Cole. But they're still going to die. Stacy is going to die."

"There is a way, but you might not like it. You remember Fang, right?"

Fang. Cole's friend with whom he traveled the world. His friend that first introduced Cole to drugs, had almost gotten Cole killed on numerous occasions and in many different ways. Normally Harlan wouldn't even allow the thought of Fang to come into play, but if he could help the kids, Harlan didn't care. He needed whatever help was out there.

"I take that silence as a yes. He's got a farm of sorts a few hours north. It's a snake farm. He's got snakes from all over and he replicates their habitats. It's fascinating. You should see it."

"Cole. Get to the point."

"Oh yeah. Sorry. Well, you can't surround yourself with that kind of danger and not be prepared. So, he's got some of the antivenom we need. I don't know how much, but I know he's got some."

"And we can use it?" The ray of hope was back.

"I haven't asked yet, but I'm sure we can. Are you game for getting Fang's help?"

"I'm game for getting anyone's help right now. I don't care whose."

"Good. I'll call him. Meet me back here as soon as you can."

"On my way." Harlan was about to hang up and run out the door, when a thought came to him. "Wait. This snake. Where did you say it's found in Australia?"

"The coastal taipan? Mostly on the Gold Coast. Why?"

That was what Harlan was hoping Cole wouldn't say. He was hoping that this snake was found anywhere else. But it made sense.

"That's where Luke Masterson is from."

Chapter 46

Very few things made Luke happier than terrifying someone simply by walking into a room. Watching the fear on Josie's face was perfect. That kind of control and power was the greatest rush he could experience. That and taking someone's life. And he may just be able to do both right now. It really was up to Josie.

Luke reached out and began to stroke Josie's hair. She flinched as he did it. Just another thing Luke loved.

"Don't be scared, Joserin. I just came to pay you a visit and make sure they are taking care of you."

"Don't be scared? What else would I be? You're the reason I'm here."

"And I am truly sorry, but you must admit that you were asking for it."

Josie was shaking like a pet dog that had been left out in the cold all night. Luke couldn't tell if it was out of pain, fear, or both. No matter what, he had caused it. And he loved that.

"Let's not talk about that anymore. What's done is done. These things happen. What other clichés work in this moment? Live and let live? That's a good one, too. Besides, I need your help."

"What makes you think I would ever help you again?"

"Because you're not a fool. Because you know you actually want to. And, most importantly, you don't have a choice." Luke pushed down on her broken arm to emphasize his point. Josie screamed out in pain, but Luke quickly covered her mouth.

"No, no, no. No yelling or screaming. Not that it will do you any good. It's just you and me."

Luke moved his hand from Josie's arm back to her hair. From her reaction, he couldn't tell which place she hated him touching more.

"Now, like I said, I need your help. You're going to help me find a few people. First, let's start with Kenji."

Josie gave Luke a vacant look of confusion. "Kenji is dead. Did you already forget that you killed him?"

"When I left him, he was still alive. I didn't see him die. And now I hear he's walking around the city, trying to ruin my life."

Josie continued to stare at Luke, dumbstruck. Like he had completely lost his mind. Like he was some sort of crazy lunatic.

"That's not possible, Luke. When they got there, he was barely holding on. He mumbled something about you. About something you said. Then he died. He's dead, Luke."

"No! He's alive and you know where he is. Tell me where he is!"

Luke slammed his fists repeatedly against the wall. All the control he ever had was gone. He couldn't think clearly. Nothing made sense. He had never let Josie see this side of him before. He wished he weren't now, but he couldn't stop himself.

"He found my parents. He brought them here. I saw them and it's because of him. Where is he?"

"I saw Kenji's body. You gave him no chance of survival. And your parents are dead, too. You killed them, just like you killed Kenji."

"Then how did I see them? How? Explain that."

Josie did not answer right away. Her pause made it seem possible she was coming up with a response. She just didn't know the answer that she should've known right away. Luke hated when people did that. It made him want to break everything in his path. Including Josie.

"Did you see your parents die? Did you actually see their dead bodies?" Now he was the one who hesitated before he answered.

"No, I didn't. I left them to suffer and die the slow death they deserved. There is no way they could still be alive. None. How could they have survived?" Luke was spinning out of control. Had his whole life been a lie?

Josie flashed a smile. It was quick, but not quick enough, because Luke caught it.

"What was that smile for? Do you think this is funny?" He moved back toward Josie's bed with a manic look in his eyes. But Josie didn't look scared now. Why didn't she look scared for her life?

"I don't. It's not funny at all. I was just thinking about why I've liked working with you so much in the past. The punishment always perfectly fit the crime."

Luke stopped moving toward Josie and smiled, too. He did have style. It was good to hear someone else say it.

"Then maybe your parents didn't actually die. Maybe you really did see them today."

Before Luke could grasp what Josie was saying, the room went completely dark. He couldn't see anything at all. Not even his hands right in front of his face.

"No," Josie whispered.

Luke was trying to look around, trying to adjust his eyes quickly. Coming from one of the corners of the room, someone started to clap. Slowly and loudly, someone was clapping.

"Excellent performance, Josie. Academy Award winning."

"Who's there? Show yourself," Luke yelled in the direction he thought the clapping was coming from.

"It's him," Josie said between sobs of fear. "The man I was telling you about. The voice."

"You're always so dramatic. You can stop the performance now. You've done everything I needed you to do." The voice said calmly.

"What do you mean everything? I can still do so much more for you!"

"I'm sure you can do so much more, but not for me."

Luke had no idea what was going on. He had no idea where this voice was. Every time he spoke it came from a different part of the room. He was somehow bouncing from place to place. Now, however, Luke could hear footsteps inching closer to Josie's bed.

"How about this? How about I do one last nice thing for you. Right before you die, right before your last worthless breath leaves your body, I'll show you my face. You've earned that treat."

As soon as the voice finished his sentence, Luke could hear Josie kicking and struggling for air. And just as her struggle was slowing down, just as her life was about to end, the lights burst on. Luke looked at Josie as she saw the face of the man who had tormented her for so long. The voice, as she called him. In that brief second, Luke saw fear flash in her eyes. And something else. Recognition.

She knew him. The look on her face said she knew him well. Intimately. Before Luke could ask who he was, Josie was gone.

The voice turned and faced Luke. "I hate doing things like that. So pointless." He smiled at Luke, like they were sharing some inside joke. "Now, you come with me."

Just as Luke was going to laugh at this idiot for thinking he could boss him around, a lightning-quick fist slammed into Luke's chest. And for the second time in a matter of minutes, the room went completely dark.

Chapter 47

"What about Luke Masterson?" Rodriguez was standing right behind him, which made Harlan jump. He had forgotten he wasn't alone and wasn't sure what to tell her, especially with so many others in the room.

"I think . . ." He looked around the room and saw the cop's eyes glued on him and Rodriguez. Harlan even thought he saw Mancuso stir. No one had answered him earlier when he asked if Mancuso were dead, and now he wished they had.

"Wait. Did Mancuso just move? Is he alive?"

"Yes. I only shot him in the arm. Not on purpose, mind you. No one is that accurate with a gun." It was the first time Bennett had said anything. He even sounded like a teenager, squeaky voice and all.

"Oh. That's good. Nobody needs to die over this. Look at all that blood though. Let me help. At least get him to a hospital."

"Soon. We've got him stable." Rodriguez stood tall in front of Harlan, like she wanted to make sure he knew she was in charge. That she had it under control. "Quit changing the subject. What about Luke Masterson?"

Harlan looked around the room once more. As relieved as he was that Mancuso wasn't dead, Harlan still didn't like the idea that he could hear this conversation.

"Can we talk about it in another room?"

"Yeah. Sure. But make it quick. I don't want to leave Bennett alone with him for too long." As they walked into the living room, Rodriguez looked back at Bennett. "I'll be in the next room for a second. He may be handcuffed, but don't underestimate him. Watch him carefully."

As soon as they were out of earshot, Rodriguez didn't hesitate. "Now spill it."

Harlan told her about his conversation with Cole about the snake venom, all the while looking over his shoulder to make sure no one could hear his crazy theory.

"I think Luke's involved in what's happening to my patients. He's spent a lot of time at the hospital, especially with one of the phlebotomists. And now Luke's missing. And the snakes originate from where he's from. You must think I'm crazy."

"I do, but not because of this. I think you're right. I really do." She paused and looked past Harlan with a look of deep thought. "Are you saying Luke Masterson is this voice that's been calling you and Mancuso?"

In the few seconds since he made the connection, Harlan had thought about that possibility. "Maybe this will confirm my being crazy to you, but I don't. I saw him earlier, walking out of the hospital. He pretended to be someone else with not the strongest American accent I've ever heard. It's not him."

"You saw him? Why are you just now telling me this?"

"I don't know, but there's something about being accused of murder that makes one forget things."

"Touché. I am sure that would mess with anyone's mind."

"Are we done? I need to go. There isn't much time for my patients." Harlan started to walk toward the front door.

"Where do you think you're going?" It was Mancuso. His voice was weak, but it still had authority. It almost made Harlan stop and stay. Almost.

"To do my job. Something that you should try doing, too."

"But what about the voice? If you leave, he will know I screwed up. My secrets. Everyone will know."

This did make Harlan stop. He turned around and got right in Mancuso's face.

"I have to stop hiding and do what is right. For my patients and for my family. They all need to be safe again. I don't care about your stupid secrets. Right now, I kind of hope they do get told. You've earned it." Harlan stood up and walked out the door, spine firmly back in place.

Chapter 48

It wasn't very often that Harlan found himself standing up to anyone, much less a cop. Most of the time he would just back off and take the blame. He would allow the person to get angry and yell at him. He would be everyone's punching bag.

Maybe that was why the voice chose him as a target. Not just as a target, but the main focus. The person who was key at every turn. Without Harlan's 100 percent cooperation, nothing the voice wanted to do could be done. At least that's how it felt, and it just seemed to be heading that way more and more every second.

But something had changed in Harlan over the last few days. He couldn't put his finger on it or identify when it happened, but something had changed. Maybe he changed when Cole finally put him in his place. But after a lifetime of being everyone's favorite puppet, he was finally cutting those strings and being his own master. It felt good. And unnerving. And he hoped it would continue to help him as he faced what was coming next. Whatever that would be.

As Harlan got closer to Cole's house, he realized meeting Cole there might not be a great idea. Would the voice be watching his place and know that Harlan hadn't blamed everything on Cole once he saw him there? Maybe he already knew. Maybe it didn't matter what Harlan did next. Maybe it was already over.

Harlan brushed those thoughts away. He had to stay focused and positive. And he needed to take care of his patients, which meant he needed to still play the game. He picked up the loaner and called Cole.

"You getting close?"

"Yes, but I'm not coming. It's not safe."

"Is this just you being paranoid again? Come on. It will be fine."

"It won't be. If I come there, he'll know, and I don't know what will happen then." So many scenarios were running through his brain. Would his family be killed? Tortured? Would the voice do something to Cole, too? Harlan couldn't risk it. Any of it. "If I come there he will know, if he doesn't already, that I didn't do what I was told."

"What are you talking about? You've done everything he's asked, haven't you?"

"No. Not anymore. He wanted me to blame murders on you. I couldn't do it."

There was complete silence on the other end. Harlan wished he could see Cole's reaction. It would make it easier to know what he was thinking.

"Wow. Here I thought my life was strange, but in comparison to yours, mine seems pretty normal."

"True. Who would have thought that would happen? But here we are." Wherever here was, they were there for sure.

"Have you called Fang yet? Please tell me something good."

"I did. And he's got it. He says he's got plenty, and we can have it all. Dude's a big softy when it comes to kids."

"With a name like Fang, what else would he be? How are you going to get it? Is he coming down?"

"I was waiting for you before heading up there to get it. I'll leave now and take Clara. What are you doing?"

"I want to go and get a hug from my mom and have her tell me it's going to be ok. But I'm going to go to the hospital to see what I can do."

"Ok. I'll keep you updated, and you do the same. See you in a few hours, and then this will all be over. And everything will be ok."

Harlan wasn't so sure if this would ever be over, or if everything would ever be ok again.

Chapter 49

He didn't expect Luke to go down so easily. A big, tough athlete like that? Sometimes the voice didn't know his own strength.

As a result, he ended up stuck with the body of a person that people were looking for, and he still had more work to do. So, he did what any logical person would do. He stuffed Luke in a janitorial closet in the basement of the hospital. Perhaps it wasn't actually logical, but it would have to do for now. He couldn't waste any more time. Luke had wasted enough of his already.

The voice stepped back into the room where Josie lay dead. It was her best look by far. As much as he hated violence, he liked the outcome. One less person to deal with.

He picked up his phone and decided he would call Mancuso first to see if he had done his simple task. Mancuso had secrets that gave the voice power, plus having a detective in your back pocket was a valuable thing. He figured he could use this guy to get what he wanted for years to come.

"Hello?"

"You sound weak, Rick. Is everything ok?"

"I'm fine. Everything's fine. I'm just tired. It's almost 6:00 in the morning, and I haven't slept. Been running myself ragged for you all day." He sounded more than tired, but the voice decided not to push it. He only needed a bit of information from Mancuso now, no reason to drag this conversation out longer than it needed to be.

"I can imagine. But don't you worry. Soon this will be over for you. Your secrets will be safe, and you can sleep well again." Of course, none of that was true. Not a single word. People will believe anything when a threat is attached.

"I'm looking forward to that."

"I'm sure you are. So, how did it go tonight with Dr. Allred?"

"Exactly as you said. He turned on his friend. It took a little bit, but I worked my magic, and we got him."

"Perfect." The voice was smiling. Another one of his plans was working to perfection. "Have you arrested his friend?"

"Not yet . . ."

"Why not? This better be good, Rick. Give me a good reason." The smile was gone as quickly as it had come.

"No judge would give me a warrant without evidence. I tried. You've got to believe me."

"I believe you. I'm just not sure you tried hard enough." The voice decided the next person he needed in his grasp was a judge. That should be easy enough. Lots of corruption and weaknesses there. "What's the plan? You better not just be sitting there on your thumb, Rick."

"Harlan is getting the evidence for us. He said it would be simple. I bet by noon Cole will be behind bars."

"Good. Now get some rest. You've earned a few hours."

He had been right about Harlan. The pushover would do whatever he wanted. And while he planned to use the detective for a long time, he could not say the same for Harlan. Once he was done with him, once Harlan was stripped of all his abilities and accolades, once people saw him for who he really was, Harlan would be begging for death. And his wish would be granted.

Chapter 50

Harlan pulled into his parking spot at work and glanced at the clock. It was just after 7:00 a.m. He honestly wasn't sure what he was doing at the hospital right now. He had not slept for a full day; his brain was fried and he couldn't do anything to help his patients until Cole got back with the antivenom. When would that be? Had Cole told Harlan where Fang and his snake farm were? But he just couldn't think of anywhere else to go while he waited. Or anything else to do. Maybe he would just take a quick nap in his car. That sounded like a good idea. The best idea he'd had in a while.

Before his eyes were closed all the way, he saw Lucy walking toward the parking lot. It was obvious that she had been crying, and why wouldn't she? After what she had witnessed with Rex, he would be concerned if she weren't He was amazed though. Even with her eyes all puffy, her hair flying all over the place and her makeup smeared, she was still gorgeous. Now may not be the time for thoughts like this, but he couldn't help it.

Harlan rolled down his window and called to Lucy. She stopped and stared, trying to see where his call was coming from. So, he got out of his car so she could see him. What a gentleman he was.

"Lucy. Over here." She spotted him and started to walk his way. He was pretty sure he even saw a tiny smile come to her face, which caused a smile to come to his face, too. What had gotten into him?

"Hey, Dr. Allred. What are you doing here so early?"

"Couldn't sleep. Too much going on. How are you doing? Clara told me what happened."

"It was horrible." Lucy started to cry again and dug her head into Harlan's chest. "We see difficult things all the time, but nothing like that. And then . . ." She trailed off as tears kept streaming down her face and onto Harlan's shirt. He didn't care. It was worth it. He wanted to ask her to keep going, but he had learned years ago that sometimes people just need to cry. We think it's only kids who can't stop crying once they've started, but it's adults, too. Once they're done and ready to talk, they will.

A few minutes later, Lucy looked up at Harlan with a look of gratitude in her eyes and smiled again. "Sorry about your shirt. That's nasty."

"It's ok. I've got plenty." I've got plenty? Very smooth. "Um, yeah. So, what else has happened?"

"Dr. James happened. Once I finished speaking to the police, he cornered me and flipped out. Yelling at me for questioning Rex's test and probably screwing up everything for the patients. Telling me to do my job as a nurse and just make sure the patients are comfortable. That I should leave the medicine, the real work, to the doctors."

This attitude that some doctors had toward nurses always made Harlan want to scream. He never understood it. They would be lost without nurses, and, if doctors didn't know that, then they should probably find a new profession.

"Why would he do that? It wasn't my fault that Rex, that Rex . . ." The tears exploded again and back went her face into his chest. He could feel every sob, every movement, every part of her pain.

"Why can't more doctors be like you?" she said as her tear-filled eyes gazed up at him. He got lost in her beauty as he glanced back. He didn't know what to say. Or do.

"Why can't more people be like you?" He wiped the tears away from her face and leaned in close. She still smelled like heaven. Like everything he was missing.

Before he could think better of it, he kissed her. This time because he wanted to and for that moment the world stopped, and he couldn't remember anything else. Everything that happened over the last few days left him. The kiss was all that mattered.

"Wow," Lucy said as they pulled apart.

"I couldn't have said it better myself."

The moment was abruptly ended by a loud ringing coming from Harlan's pocket. The phone. Of all the things to end his bliss, it was the voice. His timing was equal parts impeccable and maddening.

"I'm sorry. I have to take this. Trust me, I'd rather stay right here." Cheesy. Incredibly cheesy. Harlan hardly recognized himself right now.

Harlan took a few steps away from Lucy before he answered the phone, hoping she wouldn't overhear anything. This was not something he felt like explaining again.

"Hello?"

"Much better, Harlan. It seems you've found your manners. Now let's find out if you are still obedient."

Did he really not know what had happened that night? Was this another test for Harlan? He hated not knowing the answers when he entered a test. Especially when the wrong answer could result in devastation for all around him.

"What else would I be? That's why you chose me, right? Because you knew I would do whatever you asked."

"Such a smart man. Another reason I picked you. Intelligence never hurts. How about you tell me what happened with the detectives?"

"No."

"No? What do you mean, no?" The anger in his voice should have stopped Harlan from going any further, but he didn't care anymore.

"I mean no. The opposite of yes. Do you need me to spell it out for you? 'Cause I will. N-O."

"I don't think you have a choice. You tell me everything. Now. Don't be stupid."

"Not on the phone. Only face to face. Come out of hiding, and I will tell you everything you want to hear." Harlan didn't think this would work. There was no way. But he knew the reaction would make it worth it.

"You idiot. Do you really think you have any leverage here? That you can tell me what to do? You have no power. None."

"I have something you want. Information. I think that's pretty good leverage."

"Do you really believe that I don't know what already happened? Have I not known every step of the way? The only thing that's stopping me from killing you right now is that you did what I asked." Bingo. Stumpy came through. The voice walked right into that.

"That's great to hear. Look, as much as I enjoy talking to you, and I really do, I need to go. I still have so much to do. Evidence to make magically appear. Patients to save. Can we catch up later?" Harlan was probably just being foolish now, but he wasn't about to stop.

"We will talk soon. There is no doubt about that."

"Great. I'll be waiting by the phone in anticipation."

Harlan began to hang up when the voice chimed in. "Good luck with your patients, Harlan. You will need it. Because while this may just be the end for them, it's only the beginning for everyone else."

The phone went silent. Harlan was left confused, wondering what that was supposed to mean, but more sure of what he needed to do.

"What was that all about?" Lucy startled him as she put her arm around his waist.

"It's hard to explain."

"Try me."

"I will, but not now. I need to go to work, and you need some rest." Lucy looked disappointed. Harlan did not like the idea of making her feel that way. "But I am going to need your help in a few hours. Get some rest and call me when you get up."

"I guess if the doctor ordered it, I'll do it." She was cheesy, too. He liked that.

Lucy reached up and kissed Harlan on the cheek before she walked away to find her car. He stood there for a few minutes and enjoyed the view. McHotty Pants indeed.

As soon as she was out of sight, he snapped out of it. Focus. He needed to focus. There was still so much to do.

Harlan was about to enter the hospital when he realized he needed to text Jack. He said he would, and he didn't want Emily to be right about him.

"Jack! Sorry we haven't talked yet. Can we do lunch tomorrow?"

Harlan waited for a moment before he walked into the hospital. He wanted to get a reply from Jack before he went on with whatever was waiting for him. But it seemed like that might not happen. The one minute that passed nearly convinced Harlan he had ruined everything with Jack again. He so often allowed the smallest things to cause him the most grief. Just another thing he wished he could change.

His phone let out a beep and Harlan exhaled again. Phew.

"That would be great."

And another big exhale, followed by another beep.

"You need to talk to Mom. Soon."

That was strange. Jack had always stayed out of things between the two of them. Plus, he was writing every word out. It must be serious for him to get involved.

"Ok. Why? Is everything ok?"

Jack responded quickly this time. "It's not, and I don't know why exactly. Will you please talk to her?"

"Of course. I'm walking into work. I'll call her in a few hours." He wasn't sure what he could help her with. She had just yelled at him yesterday. But he would do it for Jack.

"Thanks, Dad. I really appreciate it."

Burdened now with this new issue that he did not understand, Harlan walked through the front doors of the hospital, waved to the volunteer at the front desk, and made his way to the elevator. As he rounded the corner, a loud voice boomed in his direction.

"Seriously? What the hell are you doing here?"

"Is that the only question you can ask me? If you must know, the answer has not changed from last night. I'm doing my job, Alex. What else would I be doing here? It's certainly not for the food."

"Hilarious. Such a funny guy. You know what I mean, Harlan. I'm on call. This is my shift. You keep coming in during my shift. You're here to steal my glory when I figure this out."

"What is wrong with you? I don't care about that and neither should you. These are my patients. It's about the patients. Not about the credit." Harlan started to walk away. He couldn't stand another minute with this clown.

"Spare me the speech. I know what you're about. I know how you work."

That made him stop. *I know how you work.* That wasn't the first time Alex had said that to him tonight, and those weren't the only two times Harlan had heard it that night either.

The voice. The voice had said those words to him, too.

Chapter 51

Clara and Cole finally got out of the car and approached the strangest looking home she had ever seen. It wasn't a long drive to Fang's farm in Lake Stevens, but it was nerve-wracking. Clara wasn't exactly excited about going to a farm filled with dangerous snakes, especially when the owner had a name like Fang. It didn't really promote safety or sanity.

"Can I just stay back at the car?"

"I wouldn't do that. You never know what could be lurking around the corner."

"Are you serious?" Clara stopped walking and started looking around for something to jump out from among the trees.

"No. You should see your face right now though. Classic," Cole said through his laughter.

"And you should see your face after I'm done with you. This is not my world." The laughter quickly stopped as Cole could see she was not joking about rearranging his face to look like a Picasso painting.

"There's nothing to worry about. I'm serious. This is the safest place you'll go with wild animals running around."

"This is the only place I'll go with wild animals. Unless you count the one club downtown, The Zoo. You ever been there?"

"Yup. It's always nice to be in the presence of a fellow zoobie. We should go there together sometime."

And for the first time, Clara didn't think Cole was insane. Now she knew he was, but it was her kind of insane.

"Sounds good to me. But please don't call me that. Zoobies are the worst. We should get Harlan to come. Can you imagine?"

"Actually, I can't. And I'm not sure I want to."

Just as Cole was about to knock on the door, it flung open and Fang came bounding out. He was actually skipping with delight as he gave Cole a big bear hug. He was not exactly what Clara pictured when she thought of someone named Fang. There was no spiky hair or face tattoos. There wasn't jewelry coming from every part of his body. He looked like someone who worked in banking, not snake farming. He was proof you couldn't judge a book by its cover, or its name, in his case.

"Cole. It has been way too long, my friend." Once their very manly hug had ended, Fang saw that Cole was not alone. “Who is this exquisite creature, and why have you been keeping her all to yourself?” Clara wasn’t sure if she should roll her eyes or blush. Blush won out, however, and there was nothing wrong with a compliment. Especially one so true.

“Clara. And you aren’t too bad yourself.” Now Fang blushed a little.

“I’m going to throw up. Everywhere. Especially on your white couch over there. Can we please come in and move past this?”

“How do you expect me to move past this sweet being?” Fang grabbed Clara by the hand. Cole gagged.

“By shutting up and remembering why we are here.”

“Fine. Always the rule-keeper, Cole. Let’s go get the antivenom.” Yes, the antivenom. For the kids. That was much more important than some guy she’d just met. She would just have to come back for a visit.

They walked through Fang’s massive home and into the backyard. As soon as they set foot outside, Clara’s skin began to crawl. There were snakes everywhere—on trees, in the grass, on top of the house. And she was sure they were crawling all over her skin, too.

“Don’t worry. You are perfectly safe. Stay on this path and you won’t disturb them. Snakes don’t get enough credit for how smart they are. They are very well-trained. They know their boundaries.”

Clara planted herself right in the middle of this lifesaving path and walked straight as an arrow while

Cole and Fang laughed and joked like they weren't in the middle of a death trap. She would not even allow her head to swivel to the side. She just wanted to get the antivenom and get out of there. No matter how cute Fang was.

They walked into a little cabin in the middle of the huge yard. The place was covered in two things: pictures of Fang with wild animals from all over the world, and vials upon vials of liquid.

"Here we are. All the antivenom I've got."

"This is it? You could run out any day if you're not careful," Clara said eyes wide open.

"You can never be too safe. Plus, it takes forever to make some. You've got to milk the snake of its venom."

"Milk the who of what?" Clara needed to get back to the city where there was no milking of anything. Ever. "Snakes have milk? Snakes have *nipples*?"

"Yeah, they've got milk, but it comes from their teeth. Then you inject it into a horse, diluted of course, and about two to three months later the horse has produced antibodies that fight the venom. After some purification of the horse's blood, voila! You've got your antivenom."

Clara was both fascinated and terrified. The wonders of science would never cease to amaze her. Miracles every day.

"Awesome. So, where's the stuff from the coastal taipan?" Cole was straight business right now. Clara was impressed.

"Coastal taipan? I thought you said inland taipan. Shoot."

"Shoot? Please tell me you have antivenom for the coastal, too."

"I do. Just not as much. Give me a second. I just need to find it."

Fang pulled out a ladder and started to climb. When he got about halfway up, he stopped and started moving some tubes around. Clara was beginning to get nervous. Maybe he didn't have any. Maybe there wasn't any hope for these kids.

"Found it!" Fang yelled. "I knew I had some." He climbed down the ladder, filled a box with some vials, and handed it to Cole.

"How much is in here?" Cole asked as he looked through the box.

"Enough for ten kids. You remember how to use it, right?"

"I do. But, how much did you say again? It looks like a lot more in here."

"There are about fifty vials in there. Based on what you told me about the amount of venom and the time it's been in the kids, they will need five each. Minimum."

Clara looked at Cole as they both realized what this meant. This couldn't be happening. There were twelve kids that had been injected with the venom, and with Cole's own stash, they only had enough to save eleven.

Chapter 52

Harlan was afraid to look back at Alex. Afraid that if he did, Alex would know Harlan had figured out who he was. That Dr. Alex James, a man Harlan had worked closely with for almost ten years, a man who had sworn an oath to take care of his patients, was the voice. He was the one terrorizing Harlan and so many others. And, most importantly, he was the one who was killing these patients. All these innocent kids. It didn't make sense.

Harlan began to walk again and this time, he didn't stop until he made it to his office. He needed a few minutes of peace and quiet. He needed to figure out what was going on and what his next steps would be. Nothing in his life had prepared him for something like this. Nothing at all.

What would possess Alex to do something like this? He was never happy and most days he did not seem to enjoy his line of work. He treated the staff poorly and often fought with other doctors. But the second he walked into a patient's room, he was a different person. Kind and compassionate. Decisive and confident. Everything a doctor should be, until he walked out of the room again.

The one constant complaint that Alex had was lack of credit. He never felt like anyone paid attention to the work he did. How many medical staff meetings had he rolled his eyes in or made an offhand comment when someone was praised? Too many to count. But how many times had Alex been called out in front of the staff for excellent work? Harlan couldn't think of one. Not a single time.

Harlan began to feel guilt all over his body. Had he helped create this monster Alex had become? Had his lack of support and acknowledgment caused Alex to do what he did? What if he had just been kinder or pointed out when Alex had done something fantastic? Would it have been so hard to give credit where credit was due?

Harlan was doing it again. Just like Cole had said, he was taking the blame for someone else's actions. He knew it didn't make sense, but no matter how hard he tried, he still felt he had pushed Alex to become so desperate for attention that he would do all of this.

That was enough wallowing in self-pity. There was no time for this. Harlan had an important piece of the puzzle figured out. He knew who the voice was. He was now a step ahead of the game, and this would help him to save his patients.

But, Harlan thought, how would he even get to them? Alex would be there every step of the way, wouldn't he?

He would never allow Harlan to be alone, let alone inject them with antivenom.

Maybe if he knew why Alex was doing this, what his motivation was. That fact alone would help a great deal. Then he could use it against him when it was time to get to distribute the cure. Now he just needed to figure that out. That might be the hardest thing he had to figure out yet—the motivation of a madman.

Harlan's phone rang, a number he didn't recognize. Who could this call be from now?

"Hello?" Harlan answered hoping it wasn't another part of Alex's game or another call from the cops.

"Hi, Harlan." It was Lucy. This was a phone call he was glad to be getting.

"Lucy? What's going on? Why aren't you sleeping?"

"I can't sleep. Not with everything going on. Every time I close my eyes, I see Rex. I see the kids. It's horrible."

"I know. I'm sorry. But you need to sleep." Harlan realized the irony in this, seeing that he hadn't slept a moment the past twenty-four hours.

"I know I need to, but how am I supposed to do that? You're the doctor. Tell me. What do I do?"

"Take some drugs?" He waited for her laugh. She didn't. No amount of joking would be able to break this level of stress.

"I can't just sit at home and wait. You said you would need my help. Can I help you now?" While there was still shakiness in her voice, as she asked to come in, she sounded stronger. But he couldn't ask her to come in now. Not in her current state. Not with Alex walking around.

"I will. But not until you rest. Without that you won't be able to give these kids the attention they need." He was lying. He knew she could come in and work on little sleep. She had before, and she could do it now. But he felt a need to protect her, to keep her safe, which was something he hadn't felt since Emily. And that terrified him.

He could hear her start to cry. "Lucy, I need you to be ok. I can't explain it, but I do. I will call once I need you here. I promise."

"Ok. Thank you." There was some strength back in her voice now—his words of needing her to be ok had filled her soul with what it had lost that day. "Thank you for caring about me."

Confused by what had just happened, by what he was feeling right now, Harlan pushed the button to end the call. The number he hadn't seen before, Lucy's number, flashed across the screen. This made him stop and think about all the calls he had received from Alex over the last day. What was the number on the caller ID?

He opened the phone and looked at his received calls. "Unknown caller." Dang. Dead end. He was hoping to use that to get hard evidence that Alex was the voice and use that to his advantage. He would have to come up with another way.

Wait, Harlan thought. The text messages. He was positive he couldn't receive texts from a blocked number. There had to be something there.

He found the texts from just a few hours ago. Each had the same number attached to it. This was it. Except, yet another except for the day, it wasn't a string of ten numbers like a normal phone number. Why would it be? It was seventeen numbers. And letters. It wasn't something he could use at all.

Needing to clear his brain and start over, Harlan decided to check his email. Maybe that would distract him enough to have a clear thought again.

There wasn't much in there, thank goodness. He hated reading his work email. It was usually just a bunch of meeting reminders, fundraiser announcements, and notices from IT about their medical records being down or upgraded—which was another way of saying, "Sorry for all the shortcuts you've made to make your job easier. They're all gone."

That's what it mostly was today, too. One was from Joe Graffis, the best IT guy Harlan had ever worked with. Dude knew his way around technology. He had fixed Harlan's home computer and cell phone on numerous occasions. He was a lifesaver.

That was it. Joe. He could take the phone to Joe, and he could do whatever it was that he did and learn Alex's number.

Harlan hurriedly walked to the basement offices and knocked on the door outside of IT. It was a little after 8:00, so he hoped that meant Joe was already in. He was probably being optimistic; these guys were never here at 8:00, but he thought he would try.

"Dr. Allred. I'm guessing you're here about the email I sent you?" Joe was here. And the email Harlan saw wasn't some notice, it was an email with something for him. Now he wished he had read it.

"Um, no. Was it something important?"

"Not really. We are getting new laptops and wanted you to get first dibs."

"Thanks for thinking of me. That would be perfect. I could use something new."

"I wasn't just thinking of you. These computers will be better protected and harder to break. This is more for me not having to help you so much when you screw things up."

"I would call you a jerk, but you're right. I do take a lot of your time." That was an understatement. Harlan was the king of viruses, pushing the wrong key, and making something explode.

"I'll get you first on the list then. What else do you need?"

"It's a strange question," Harlan said as he closed and locked the door behind him. "Can you hack into a phone and figure out a number?"

"Depends on the phone and how much info you've got. The older the phone the better. They are not quite as secure."

Harlan pulled out the phone and handed it to Joe. "This I can do. I believe this is a Motorola from about ten years ago. What do you need me to look for?"

"Before we go any further, this doesn't leave the room, got it? Don't say a word." Harlan realized how cliché that sounded, but he needed to say it. He trusted Joe, but he wanted to make sure.

"You got it. It's just you and me, Doc."

"It's in the text messages. There are two from a strange number that uses both numbers and letters. I've never seen anything like it before."

Joe's eyes widened as he looked at the number. Harlan couldn't tell if it was a good look or not. Maybe this really would be a dead end.

"It has been forever since I've seen something like this. Back in my past life, before I went legit, these used to come up all the time. I even used these to get away with, um, stuff." Joe often alluded to this past life. At some point, Harlan was going to get him to go into more details.

"Is that a good or bad thing? Can you break it?"

"It's a good thing. It won't be easy, only because it's been a few years, but I can break it."

"Great. How fast can you have it done?"

"I will make it my top priority. Give me an hour. Tops. I'll text you on your cell when I'm done."

Harlan felt a rush of hope as he walked out of Joe's office. Something he hadn't felt for a long time.

That hope lasted until he reached the fourth floor of the hospital and heard the unmistakable screams of Stacy coming down the hall.

Chapter 53

Harlan sprinted down the hall faster than he had run in his life. Had anyone gotten in his way, he would have plowed them over without a second thought. He only had two thoughts during that short trip. First, to get there as fast as he could. Second, where in the world were Cole and Clara? The kids couldn't wait much longer.

As he entered Stacy's room, he could tell something was wrong beyond her screaming and thrashing around like she was running away from some sort of monster. Something was out of place.

"Where's her dad? Where is Stacy's dad?" The two nurses in the room turned and looked at him. Neither seemed to have any idea what he was talking about. Harlan could feel his blood boiling with frustration, and while he promised himself he would never yell at a nurse, he was getting pretty dang close. Luckily, they were saved by Clarence, another RN, entering the room.

"He went to get something to eat and take a walk. I thought it was a good idea."

"It was a great idea. You all did great. Now, what is going on? Why is Stacy screaming?"

"We don't know." This time Lydia spoke up. "She's been sleeping, and now she's screaming. It doesn't seem to be pain, but something else. She hasn't even woken up through all of it."

The nightmares. She was in the middle of one of her nightmares. She was running away from a monster. The horrible monster of reliving her mother's death over and over again.

"I'll take it from here." All three nurses looked at him, convinced he had lost his mind. "I'm serious. I'll call if I need you. And please close the door on your way out."

Harlan sat down next to Stacy and grabbed her hand. This did not calm her down, but it was a start. He had to do something more.

He knew her favorite song, at least a few years ago, was "Twinkle, Twinkle, Little Star." Maybe she had grown up and moved past this song, but it was all he could think of. So he cleared his throat, hoped no one was standing within earshot, and sang.

Twinkle, twinkle, little star,

A tear rolled down Harlan's cheek. This little girl was that star.

How I wonder what you are.

What are you? Strong. Stronger than anyone Harlan had ever met.

Up above the world so high,

That was Stacy. Always watching over others, even in her struggles.

Like a diamond in the sky.

The tears were flowing now. The world needed more diamonds like her.

Twinkle, twinkle, little star, how I wonder what you are.

Through his tears, Harlan hadn't noticed Stacy had stopped screaming and was perfectly still.

"You remembered that's my favorite song. Thank you, Dr. Allred." She looked up at him, wiped away a tear, and smiled.

"What are doctors for?" Harlan smiled back. "Are you ok now, Stacy?"

"I guess. The nightmare is so horrible. And so clear now. I can see everything. Every detail."

"Your dad told me that. I'm sorry." He wanted to ask her if that meant she could see the person who had caused the accident, but he knew it wasn't his place. His place was to heal her. That was all.

"How have you been feeling? Any more pain?"

"Lots. And it doesn't go away like it used to. Do you know what's wrong? That other doctor doesn't seem to know anything. Or care."

And the other doctor didn't care. He was the one causing this. He was the reason she was here.

"We are getting close. I really believe we are." And he did, but he was afraid they were running out of time. It was close to 9:00 now. He was sure that meant they had less than four hours left.

"I knew it. I've been telling everyone you would figure it out."

"Thanks for the faith in me, kiddo," Harlan said as he ruffled her hair. Kids and their unwavering belief in others. At what age do we get that beaten out of us?

Harlan's phone buzzed in his pocket. It was a text from Joe.

"Got it. I'll bring the phone up." Perfect.

"I need to go for a minute. Tell the nurses the second you need me. Ok?"

"Ok. Dr. Allred? Thank you for the song. It really helped." She flashed her award-winning smile at him. It was exactly what he needed to give him hope that all would work out.

"Anything for you, Stacy."

Harlan walked out and back to his office only to see the nurses, every last one on the floor, standing there, smiling at him as he walked by.

***

Harlan sat at his desk trying not to lose his mind waiting for Joe to show up with the number that he would use to prove Alex was the voice. And then what? What would he do with this information once he knew? He hadn't thought that far.

This wasn't some movie where he could just walk up to him, tap him on the shoulder and say, "I figured it out. You're the voice, and I've caught you. Now turn yourself in and save the kids." Then the credits would roll and they would all live happily ever after.

He needed a plan. He wasn't good at things like this. Cole was. Cole could come up with something on the spot. Where was Cole? Shouldn't he and Clara be here by now? Harlan's paranoia kicked in and every worst-case scenario started to run through his head. If only there was some sort of technology he could use to make sure everything was ok.

As if Cole was thinking the same thing at the same time, the loaner rang.

"Where have you been?"

"Geez. Sorry, Mom. I didn't know I had missed my curfew."

"You know what I mean. I just got worried that something had gone wrong."

"We were in the middle of nowhere and didn't have reception. I would have called. I know how you worry about me."

"Yeah, that's it. I'm worried about you. It has nothing to do with the cure that you may or may not have with you right now."

"I always knew you loved me for my brain. I feel so used."

"Will you two quit flirting," Clara yelled from the passenger's seat.

"You're not getting jealous, are you?" Harlan was not sure he liked this playful banter between the two of them. He didn't need them ganging up on him.

"What's the story? Did you get it? Did Fang really have what we need?"

"Slow down, tiger. We got it. Except . . ."

But Harlan was too excited hear the last part. "Are you serious? He came through. Things are finally looking up."

"Yes and no."

"And I know who the voice is. I just have to prove it." Harlan wasn't listening to a word Cole was saying. The fact that he now believed they were finally in the home stretch and an end was in sight made it difficult for him to think of anything else.

"Harlan. Calm down. There is something else I need to tell you. Something you might not want to hear." Cole sounded serious. Something that made Harlan feel more worried than anything else.

"We only have enough antivenom for eleven kids." Silence. Both ends of the phone went silent. No one knew what to say. Harlan put his head on his desk, not wanting to ever move again.

"Harlan? Harlan! You still there?"

"Physically? Sure. But everything else is gone. We can't play God and decide who lives and dies. If we can't save them all, what's the point?"

"I know. I know how this must tear you up. But you can't let them all die just because one won't live. You have to know that."

"I do. Of course, I do. But it doesn't make it any easier. It doesn't make it right or fair. How do I decide?" *How could anyone decide something like this?* Harlan thought. This wasn't why he had become a doctor, and after all of this, after all the disappointment, he wasn't sure why anymore.

"You'll know. You always do, my brother. I don't know how you do it, but you always find a way."

"Thanks for the vote of confidence. Now hurry up. I could use your support."

"We are fifteen minutes away. Hold tight and don't do anything stupid until we get there."

Harlan hung up and put his head back down on the desk. It would be impossible for him to do anything stupid when he didn't plan on moving anytime soon.

His dreams of lying there until this was over, until this nightmare was finally in the past, were swept away by a knock on his door.

"Didn't mean to startle you, Doc," Joe said as he walked in and Harlan jumped up. That's right. The phone.

"Sorry. My mind is still with the patients."

"I'm sure. Sorry about what's going on. Everyone feels it here when so many kids are suffering. Hardest part about working in a children's hospital, ya know?"

"I do." There were plenty of days that Harlan wished he hadn't chosen pediatrics as his field. The pain of kids was devastating. "You got something for me?"

"You bet. It was a tough one, too. Whoever did this is didn't want his number to be found."

"But you got it, right? You're one hundred percent sure?"

"Yup." Joe handed Harlan a piece of paper with just ten digits and the phone, too.

"Did the phone ring at all while you had it?" Harlan hadn't thought of that before. What if Alex had tried to call him while Joe had the phone?

"No. Not once." Harlan exhaled. "Hey, Doc? I saw the texts. They didn't say much, but at the same time, they said a lot. What's going on? Why did you want me to do this?"

"It's hard to explain. And I don't think I could if I tried. But this will help. More than you can possibly know."

"Glad I could be of service. And if you need anything else, let me know."

If he did, Harlan would. It was good to have another person he knew he could trust. He would repay this guy as soon as he could.

Harlan stood up. He had no idea what he was going to do once he knew for certain that Alex was the voice, but he would figure it out as he went along. Just like he did in times of crisis for his patients, he would find a way.

Chapter 54

If someone had told Rodriguez yesterday morning that over the course of twenty-four hours, she would take part in faking someone's murder (unknowingly, but still a part of it); blame that murder and another one (a two-for-one special of the worst kind) on an innocent doctor; discover that Luke Masterson may have been involved in those murders and even the deathly sickness going around the children's hospital; find out there was some voice manipulating not only that same doctor, but her partner; and then, to put a bow on it, she would get shot by her partner for trying to stop him, she would have told them that they'd been watching too many Lifetime original movies. But now she sat next to her partner's hospital bed trying to figure out what had happened that day and how it had gotten away from them.

Her shoulder hurt, but it would heal, and it would heal fast. Mancuso, on the other hand, was in it for the long haul. That rookie, Bennett, had saved her life with his quick shot. And his poor aim had saved Mancuso's life, too, but the wound would take a long time to heal. Though not as long as the mental and emotional wounds Mancuso had from his actions. Those might never heal.

Had Mancuso not smartened up and told this voice character the lie that she and Harlan had come up with, she might not be sitting next to him now. Forgiveness had never come easily for Rodriguez. Not now or ever. She was learning. Not easily, but she was getting there.

It also became easier to forgive Mancuso when he told her the secrets he was trying to keep hidden. Had they been hers, she would have shot her own mother to make sure they didn't get out. Especially ones he had hidden so well, not just from his family, but from himself.

Earlier, right after Harlan had stormed out of his house, Rodriguez stepped hard on Mancuso's wound. He screamed out in pain and looked at her like a child who didn't know why he was being scolded.

"What is wrong with you?" She removed her foot, but left it hovering over his arm as a warning.

"You don't understand. You can't."

"You're right. I can't understand. I can't understand how anyone would do what you did tonight. We all cut corners, but this was more than that."

"My secrets. He will tell everyone. My life. Ruined."

"So you would ruin another person's life to save your own? What secret can be so bad that you would do all of this?"

Mancuso looked up at her. "Do you really want to know? Ok. Bennett? Outside. Now."

As soon as Bennett left the room, Mancuso began what may have been the most horrible and heart-wrenching story Rodriguez had ever heard and it didn't take long for her to know why he would do anything to keep this hidden.

"When I was twelve, my mom died. She got mugged and didn't have enough money, so the guy killed her. He was so high, I'm not sure he even knew where he was. My dad took it hard. He was a cop who couldn't keep his own wife safe."

She had never heard Mancuso talk about his family before. It explained why he cracked down harder on drugs than any cop she had ever worked with.

"And I get it, ya know? It was horrible. But he still had me. He just forgot about me. Wouldn't even look at me. He went back to work the day after the funeral. Didn't even take a leave of absence. He left me to fend for myself, no second thought at all. Right away he gets put on this intense case, like his captain thought it would help him move past it or something. Stupid, if you ask me. Anyway, it was the huge child porn ring that had exploded in Seattle. This was about the mid-nineties, and the Internet was starting to get big. It made it easier for perverts to hook up."

Rodriguez was maybe seven or eight when this case happened, but she still remembered it well. Kids were getting kidnapped and then vile, graphic pictures of them were sold on Internet chat rooms. It was all over the papers, and her parents were constantly warning her about not going anywhere alone and the dangers of any and all strangers. They didn't have a computer in their home, and she wasn't allowed near one without adult supervision.

"Dad became obsessed with the case. He even bought a computer and started using the Internet to find out more about it. If he wasn't at work, he was in his room. Working. Looking at child porn."

Mancuso grimaced. Rodriguez couldn't tell if it was from the physical pain or the mental anguish of the memory.

"He started chatting these guys up. A lot. I'm sure at first it was for the job, but then he couldn't get enough of it. He was no longer a cop trying to crack a case. He was a pervert, too. But the other guys started getting angry when he never sent them any pics. He was getting death threats all the time. He could have just left that world behind and moved on. He had the chance. Why didn't he take it? Why didn't he choose me?"

Rodriguez had a feeling where this was going. She hoped she was wrong. She prayed she was wrong. Yet, she knew she wasn't.

"He had me. Me. His son. His own flesh and blood. With no one to protect me. He would take me to the basement. Make me undress, take off everything. He would yell and scream and hit me until I did it. He wouldn't let me eat or go outside until he got the pictures he wanted. And those guys, those perverts, never got enough. They were always asking for more. My dad started charging more and more. He was making big bucks off me. And then, that was no longer enough. Not for any of them."

Mancuso paused and looked past Rodriguez like he was trying to see beyond the memory. Hoping it would fade and never come back.

"One guy offered a lot of money for me to sleep over at his house. My dad didn't even question it. He just drove me over and dropped me off. He let some guy have his way with me. All night. Then he picked me up, like nothing had happened. He sold me for sex, and he didn't even care."

Rodriguez had a hard time imagining something like this could really happen. How could anyone do this to a child? To his own son?

"Once word got out, I was with someone different almost every night. Passed around like a sack of potatoes. Like something to be bought and sold. Because that's all I was. They even started taking me on vacations all over. Paying tons for the chance to take me away and rape me for hours. My dad got loaded. This went on until I was fourteen. Two whole years. Then it just stopped. I guess I got too old for their liking. I was no longer useful to them. Or my dad."

Rodriguez just stood there. Stunned. Mortified. She couldn't comprehend what Mancuso had been through. What he still went through. He could have shot her a thousand times to keep the truth from coming out, and she still would have forgiven him.

"Can you imagine what would happen if anyone found out about this? My wife and kids would be devastated. They could never look at me the same way again. My career would be over. A detective who was sold for sex by his father? No one would take me seriously."

More than anything she wanted to tell him that wasn't true. His family would still love him. None of the other cops, especially those that mattered, would care. He would be fine. But it wouldn't do any good. Devastation, traumatic, horrifying devastation like Mancuso had been through warps the brain. Makes you believe you are worthless. Makes you think no one could love you if they knew.

"And those guys that did this to me, I don't want them to find me. I don't want to see them ever again."

Rodriguez finally did put her arms around him, and they sat like that until the ambulance arrived to take them away.

"You're not crying over me, are you?" Mancuso had woken up from the drugs they gave him for pain and startled her back to the present.

"No. No way. Me? Cry over you? Never. Good to see you're awake though. How are you feeling?"

"Horrible. But, it's ok. I deserve it. I've been thinking about what Harlan said about Luke Masterson."

"I didn't know you heard that."

"That house was so empty. Everything echoed. We could hear everything. Anyway, what do you think? Think Masterson has something to do with this?"

"I do. I think he has a lot to do with it." She expected Mancuso to laugh at her and call her out for her stupid theory. But he didn't.

"Me, too. I think we find him, we will find the voice, too. Then all of this will stop."

"I know. But how? What do we do? How do we find him?"

"Not we. I can't go anywhere. You. Go, find Masterson and the voice. And put an end to this now."

"Yes sir!" she said with a sarcastic salute. That got a little smile out of Mancuso. "Where do you think I should even start?"

"Harlan saw Masterson at the children's hospital, right? Go there. Everything that has happened the last few days leads there."

Chapter 55

Harlan paused and sat down on a bench as he made his way to the fourth floor. As much as he was ready to do this, he was unsure of how it would go and if it would even matter. He told himself that knowing for certain that Alex was the voice was essential for him to save his patients. He needed to remove Alex from the situation. Once Alex figured out that Harlan had the cure, the chance of actually getting the antivenom into their bodies was slim to none. He would block them at every turn.

The question was how would he get Alex out of the way? Harlan didn't have a clue. He didn't have a relationship with Alex, not even much of a working one. He didn't know enough about him that he could use to get him out of the picture and do what he wanted.

Harlan's mind was clouded by Cole's revelation. One of the patients would not get the antivenom. One of them would die. There was no way around it, and that crushed Harlan down to his soul. Even if he found a way to get past

Alex, it wouldn't matter. One of those families would go home without a child.

"Harlan, are you all right? You look like death." Harlan looked up and saw Dr. Diana Baxter, another one of his fellow pediatric surgeons. She was the opposite of Alex. Friendly, calm and helpful to all. She even had a good relationship with Alex. Harlan had no idea how she did that.

"Thanks for the compliment. That's the exact look I was going for when I got out of bed this morning." Diana laughed. She always laughed at his jokes, mostly because she was too nice not to. "Other than looking horrible, I'm all right. This stuff with our patients is difficult to handle right now. Harder than it has ever been."

"I know. It has been for all of us." Diana sat down next to him and locked her arm with his. "Why did we go into pediatrics again?"

"I ask myself the same question all the time."

"Me, too." That was the first time Harlan had ever heard Diana not be completely positive. "This has been the most difficult few days for me. I feel lost. Do you have any ideas about what's going on?"

"I might. I need to look at one more thing, and then I'll know for certain."

"That's good news, Harlan. What do you think it is? How can I help?" Harlan didn't want to tell her. He was afraid she would tell Alex, which would make sense for her to do, but he couldn't risk it.

"I'm afraid if I say it out loud it will jinx it, and I'll be wrong." That was lame. He used that same logic all the time when watching sports, like having to get food and be in his seat before the game or sitting a certain way on the couch or his team would lose. It was lame then, too.

"I get that. Everyone has their ways of doing things. Most of them are insane, but whatever works, right?"

"True. We are all a little insane."

"I need to go, but good luck. Let me know what you find out and how I can help." Diana got up and began to walk away.

"I will." Harlan now had an idea of how he could do what he needed to do.

Harlan stood up, filled with confidence. He finally had a plan to get Alex.

As Harlan got closer to his destination, he pulled out the loaner. He knew that if he used his phone or the phone Alex so graciously gave him, Alex would know it was him calling. He also figured that Alex wouldn't answer his phone from a number he didn't recognize.

Harlan didn't want to talk to him anyway. What would he say? "Alex! It's me, Harlan! Caught you sucker!" There were no scenarios where Harlan saw that going well. All he needed to do was hear Alex's phone ring and see him look down at it. This would confirm what Harlan already knew.

The only thing he worried about now was that Alex wouldn't even be there. With the way the last few days had gone, that would make sense. Why would it be this simple?

He rounded the corner and was glad to see Alex standing near the nurse's station. As he thought about it, he realized there was no way Alex wouldn't be there. How would he ensure that the patients continued to suffer and die if he took off? He needed to be close by. He needed to have that control.

Harlan saw Alex was talking to Barry. Perfect. After he proved Alex was the voice he could enlist Barry's help. Barry would do anything to make sure Alex was out of the way, and the kids could get their care.

Harlan stood around the corner, just out of Alex's eyesight but still where he could see his every move. He wondered how strange it had to look for a passerby to see a doctor hunched, peering around a corner. It wasn't going to stop him, but he could imagine they would think he was losing his mind.

He opened the loaner and dialed the number Joe had given him. Of all the tense moments Harlan had been through the last few days, waiting for the call to start ringing and connect with Alex's phone was toward the top. Not to sound overly dramatic, but everything that had happened came down to this moment. All the pain and suffering would almost be over. Soon he would move forward, get rid of this heartless idiot masquerading as a doctor and take care of his patients. This was going to be over soon.

Finally, Harlan's phone started to ring. His stomach flipped a little with the anticipation of it all. He peeked a little harder in Alex's direction, not wanting to miss a movement.

But, nothing happened. No phone rang. Alex didn't move at all. He just kept talking to those around him. What if Alex hadn't even brought the phone with him to the floor? What if Harlan was just completely wrong? Everything pointed toward Alex. Every single thing.

Harlan began to hang up his phone, but then a phone started ringing near the nurse's station. He looked at Alex, waiting for him to reach into his pocket and pull out a phone. But he didn't.

Barry did.

Chapter 56

Luke woke up surrounded by darkness. He tried to look around for signs of where he could be, but he couldn't see a thing. Where was he, and how had he gotten there?

He felt something brush up against his arm. And then his legs. Wherever he was, he wasn't alone. He thrashed his arms around, trying to make contact and maybe kill it, but he hit nothing. Just air.

A loud hiss came from between his legs as it brushed up against him again. Was that a snake? Was he in a room filled with snakes?

"Don't be such a pansy, Luke," his dad's voice boomed out next to him. "It's just a snake. One of those coastal taipans you're obsessed with."

"I hate those things. Why are you always chasing after them, honey? They could kill you." Now his mom chimed in, too. How were they here again?

"Come on, Luke. Pick it up. Show me how much of a man you are."

"Fine. Then will you stop treating me like an idiot? Will you play catch with me again?"

"Of course I will. Pick up the snake, and you'll have your dad back." Luke could tell by this tone that his dad was smiling. Maybe this would finally be the turning point in their relationship.

Luke felt the snake brush up against his legs again. He reached down as quickly as he could to grab it before it got away, but he missed.

"You always had horrible reflexes. Slow as anything I've ever seen." His dad was laughing now. And not the laugh of a dad playing with his son, but the laugh of one who enjoyed watching him fail.

"Shut up, Dad. Shut up. I'll get it. I'll get it!" Luke swung his arms around like a crazy man just trying to make contact with something. Anything. The more he tried, the harder his dad laughed. The harder he laughed, the angrier and wilder everything Luke did became.

"Stop it, honey. You don't have to prove anything. You're a man in my eyes." This only made Luke want to catch this stupid snake more. It only made him want to prove his parents wrong again.

"He can't catch it. He can't catch anything. He couldn't catch a cold if you sneezed right in his face. Worthless. He's worthless."

"I'm not worthless. You are. You're nothing but a washed-up nothing. I'm everything you couldn't be. I made it when you failed. I'm the man and you're just a stupid child who's never done anything."

Luke punched his father as hard as he could. If he hadn't killed him before, he would kill him now. Only he didn't hit his dad. He connected with a concrete wall with all his power—like one of those crash test cars that would explode the second it made contact.

Luke felt blinding pain surge through his whole body as he collapsed to the ground. He couldn't show this hurt. He couldn't let his dad see he couldn't take it.

Only there was no laughter coming from the room like he expected. Or cries coming from his mom either. Just as quickly as they had come, they were gone, and he was alone. Like always.

Luke looked down at his hand, and it was now more like the claw of an eagle than anything a human would have. He reached down and screamed as he popped each finger back into place. It was still disfigured, but it would be of some use to him. At least to get him out of there.

His eyes had finally adjusted a bit to the dark and now he realized he was in a small empty closet. He was all alone. There wasn't room for a snake or two more people at all. Luke was losing it.

As the room was becoming clearer, so was Luke's memory. That voice person put him in here after he killed Josie. He thought he could somehow trap Luke Masterson. What a fool.

As he turned around, Luke found the door. He turned the handle. Nothing. He tried again, harder and with more violence, but nothing happened. He was locked in. Whoever that man was, he wasn't going to make it easy for Luke to get out, but he had to be stupid to think Luke couldn't figure out how.

He looked around the closet for something he could use. The room seemed spotless, but people always made mistakes. They always forgot some detail.

In the corner of the closet something shiny caught his eye. This could be it. He reached down to pick it up and noticed it was attached to a piece of paper. A note. His nemesis had left Luke a note.

"Now that you've had time to think, isn't it time to stop playing this game and come back to our team, Luke?" He turned the paper over and there was a key. The key to the door. The key to Luke's freedom. The key to the voice's demise.

Chapter 57

As a kid, the fictional character that gave Harlan the most nightmares was Harvey Dent, or as he was better known, Two-Face, someone who could change who he was and what he would do at the drop of a hat. In the case of this particular villain, it was the flip of a coin. Whenever Two-Face showed up in one of the Batman comics Harlan used to read, he would dread the coin flip. Dread the fact that if it landed on the wrong side, people would suffer and die.

He would even dread knowing that if it landed on the right side, Two-Face would do something great and right some wrongs. That anyone could do this - change who he was so quickly -was harder for Harlan to swallow than someone like the Joker. To him, Two-Face was evil in its most real form.

And now he stood staring at a real-life Two-Face, and he couldn't believe who it was. The one person Harlan had truly believed was on his side couldn't have been further from it.

Harlan blinked, hoping he was wrong. But he wasn't. It was Barry staring at his phone. It was Barry who, after a moment of confusion, pretended like nothing happened and nonchalantly put the phone back in his pocket. Barry was the voice.

Realizing he was still staring, Harlan tried to walk away. But he couldn't. He was, once again, frozen to the ground in fear. Everything just got more complicated. Every idea he had to overcome the obstacles vanished, and he was lost. And now, so were his patients.

After his body decided moving was something it had permission to do, Harlan began to walk toward his office. He wanted to get away from there as fast as possible. But do what exactly? Hide? Bang his head against the wall? What good would he be to his patients if he ran? They needed him close by. Especially with Barry so close. How could it be Barry?

Harlan took out the loaner and sent Cole a quick text. "Don't come inside until I tell you to." He wasn't sure why, but Harlan felt the need to keep them away from this until he understood more. Maybe it was to keep Cole and Clara safe. What if Barry saw Cole at the hospital? Why hadn't Harlan thought of this before?

Knowing that walking past Barry and Alex would cause suspicion—his paranoia was way out of control at this point—Harlan walked right up to them, trying hard to steady his voice.

"Alex. Barry. How are we doing today?" Very smooth. Casual. Calm. No sign of the fact that he was doing everything in his power not to pee his pants.

"All right, Harlan. Alex has just been updating me on what's been going on here. Sad stuff."

"We would be lost without Dr. James though. He has done amazing work." This statement had the exact effect Harlan hoped it would. Alex looked happy, like a kid who had received a gold star from his teacher in front of the whole school.

"Is that right? It's good to hear you two working together. It's what the patients need."

"It's more like I'm following Dr. James' lead on this one. He's the reason I believe these kids will live." Harlan saw Alex's chest puff out, and his smile grow. Harlan knew how Barry was getting Alex to do his bidding. It wasn't through threats. It was pride. Alex's need to get credit and be the man of the hour. Now Harlan needed to get Alex alone. They needed to talk and straighten this out.

"I'm about to make some rounds. Dr. James, will you join me? I'll need your expertise."

"Of course. However I can be of assistance to you and the patients." Harlan wanted to throw up, but at least this was working. The ego is such a frail thing.

"Seeing that you two have this handled, I'm headed back to my office. Need to keep this out of the press. Twelve kids dying at our hospital from the same thing would not look good. Keep me up-to-date."

Harlan knew he was seeing Barry differently now, but something about what he just said rubbed him the wrong way. He didn't know what or why, but it did. Barry was planning something.

"Where would you like to start, Harlan? Where can I help you the most?"

"The break room." Alex gave him a disgusted look. "Not like that. What is wrong with you?"

"I knew your flattering was too good to be true." Alex dug his heels in and wouldn't budge.

Harlan got close, and as he flashed the cell phone from Barry, whispered, "I know what you're doing. I know you're involved. I will expose you and not lose a second of sleep." He didn't know for certain if this was true, he had been wrong a lot lately, but he didn't have time to dance around the subject either.

Before Harlan knew it, they were both in the break room. Door locked. Blinds down. Alex didn't want there to be any chance someone could walk in. Harlan had obviously slammed a very sensitive nerve.

"You don't understand." Harlan had heard that a lot lately from people. As if that excuse would get anyone off the hook. They seemed to believe they didn't have the ability to choose for themselves.

"I don't understand what exactly? Why don't you try me?"

"You don't know what it's like to work as hard as I do and never get any credit. Not once. I live in your shadow. For once, I'd like the spotlight on me."

"You would kill innocent children for the spotlight? Are you kidding me? Because some voice promised you fame if you did? That makes zero sense, Alex."

"Kill them?" Alex looked at Harlan with eyes wide open. Like a deer caught in headlights, unable to understand why they were coming at him. "I'm not going to kill them. I'm going to save them. The voice is going to let me save them."

Chapter 58

Harlan sat down. It was either that or collapse. Alex was insane. Harlan had been right. The only reason he was involved in this whole mess was for fame and fortune. Pride. It always comes before man falls thousands of feet to his own self-inflicted death.

He wanted to reach across the table and strangle Alex. Show him just how stupid he was being. How stupid he had been.

"You're angry, Harlan."

"You're damn right I am."

"Watch your language, Doctor. There are children around." Harlan shot out of his chair and began to move toward Alex, fists up, ready to strike and knock that smug look off Alex's face once and for all.

Just as he was ready to, as his dad would put it, punch Alex's lights out, he stopped and took a step back. What good would it do? Sure, it would probably feel fantastic, but the patients would suffer more. And, as much as Harlan hated to admit it, he still needed Alex.

"You're right, Dr. James. I don't understand what it's like to deal with what you have. You deserve better. I should have treated you better."

"Are you lying to me again? Trying to get on my good side?"

"No and yes. You do great work, and no one points it out. I never have. That's the truth." Alex seemed to relax a bit at this admission. "But I am trying to get on your good side. I still need your help."

"How? And, why would I? You're just trying to get in on saving the kids, so you can steal my credit."

"Believe what you want. But I know what's wrong. I already have the cure."

"You know what's wrong? How? I don't even know that. The voice just told me to stay close by and when the time is right, when everything was in place, I would get the cure with instructions on what to do. Did he tell you what was wrong? Has he been lying to me this whole time, too?" Shock and confusion were exploding from Alex's face.

"No, he didn't. I figured it out."

"Then what do you need me for? You can save the day all by yourself. Like you always do."

"Because I can't do it without you. The voice is here. In the building. Alone, I can't get to the patients with him here."

"He's here? How do you know? Who is he?"

"It doesn't make a difference. It doesn't change what we need to do. Are you in?" Harlan looked at Alex with that horrible feeling of hope that had messed with him so much.

"In for what? You won't tell me anything. And you'll still get all the credit."

"Will you come off of that? I don't give a crap about the credit. You can have it all. I will make sure everyone knows it was you who saved the kids."

This made Alex stop and think for a second. Harlan hated how much this mattered to Alex. He hated that Alex's life was so miserable that he needed credit for something like this to be happy. It didn't matter though. Harlan would do whatever it took to get what was needed. And he didn't care that that made him just like the voice.

"I don't believe you, Harlan. You'll screw me like you always do. I'll do it my way." Alex stormed out of the room leaving Harlan wishing he had just knocked him out when he'd had the chance.

***

Harlan quickly checked on the patients before heading back to his office. Nothing had changed. They were still in pain. They were still going to die soon. Even though he had the cure, how would he get it to them? So many roadblocks and not enough time.

And he may have just created the biggest one yet. He believed that he could get Alex to see the error of his ways. Now Alex knew Harlan could cure the patients and take away his glory. Harlan got the feeling Alex would do anything to make sure that didn't happen, even tell Barry what Harlan planned to do.

He was about to enter his office when the loaner buzzed.

"Are you ever going to let us up?"

Harlan had forgotten what he had told Cole and Clara earlier. How many things had he forgotten over the past few days? How many things had he missed?

"Sorry. Got distracted. Come up now. Be careful. It's not safe for Cole here. I'll explain."

As he entered his office, Harlan pressed send and looked up at his desk. And he was glad he did. If he hadn't, he wouldn't have seen someone sitting in his chair.

"Dr. Allred. We have got to stop meeting like this, mate"

Harlan flipped on the light to get a better look, but he already knew who it was. Luke Masterson.

Chapter 59

"Why don't you close the door and take a seat." This was not a suggestion, but a command. A command that if not followed would have consequences Harlan couldn't even fathom.

"Good," Luke said as Harlan sat down. "I think you know why I'm here."

"I don't. Should I?"

"Harlan. May I call you Harlan? Don't play stupid with me. I know what you're capable of. I know what you already know."

"Are you here to make sure I don't cure these patients you've poisoned?" Harlan couldn't even look at the man that just two days ago had been his idol.

"I poisoned? I did no such thing. You will not find my fingerprints anywhere near any of this."

"Maybe not physically, but they are all over this no matter what."

"Shut up!" Harlan jumped. He braced for Luke to yell at him more, until he noticed Luke wasn't looking at him at all. He was staring at the wall behind him.

"I didn't poison anyone, Mom. But if you're not careful, I will not hesitate to poison you. How many times and how many ways do I have to kill you two?"

Harlan had been in a constant state of confusion the past few days, but this put him over the top.

"Quit laughing at me, you fool. You washout. You failure. You were never half the man I am." Luke swung his fist hard and connected with a picture of Harlan's family. This seemed to wake him up.

"Now for why I'm here and how you will help me." It was as if nothing had happened. As if Luke had not just been yelling at his parents when they were nowhere to be seen.

"I still don't know why you are here." Harlan was afraid he would send Luke into another fit of rage. He needed to choose his words carefully. "But, you're right, I am here to help you."

"You are a smart man. I knew I could come to you. I need you to help me find a man. This man." Luke held up a picture he had drawn to exactness. It was a perfect likeness of Barry. Every detail perfect. "You know this man, don't you?"

Lying would not do any good. Luke obviously knew Harlan knew who he was. If he wanted this madman out of his office, he would have to give him what he wanted.

"I do. Why do you need him?"

"You know why, Harlan. This man, who wants everyone to call him "the voice", needs to be stopped. You want that, don't you?"

"I do." But Harlan wasn't sure that Luke was the right person for the job. He also wasn't sure that he wanted to cross Luke's path either.

"Then where is he? Where can I find him?"

"Last I saw him he was going to his car. Probably for a meeting." Harlan chose to tell a little lie to buy him more time. Time for what, he didn't exactly know.

"Then I'll wait for him right here. You'll keep me company, won't you?" Not the best of ideas for Harlan. He needed to get Luke out of there now. He didn't have time.

"As much as I would love to have you here, how will you know that the voice is back? His office is on the eighth floor. Go and wait in the room with the glass doors right outside administration. You will be able to see as soon as he returns."

"A perfect idea," Luke said as he stood up to leave. "Don't go too far. I'm sure I'll need your help again soon."

***

"Was that Luke Masterson walking out of your office?" Cole said as he and Clara walked in.

"Yup." The shock had finally caught up to Harlan. He had very few words left.

"What was he doing here?"

"Looking for Barry."

"Why would he be looking for Barry? Clue us in, Harlan." Clara was standing right in front of Harlan, demanding an answer.

"Barry's the voice."

Clara was speechless, an event that deserved its own national holiday. Cole looked how Harlan felt: dumbfounded.

"And Alex is in on it, too. There is no scenario where I see this working."

"There has to be, Harlan." Clara found her voice. But there was very little conviction in it. "We've got all this antivenom. This isn't over."

"It is. Even if we get past Barry, Alex, and whoever else in this place is a part of this, someone will die. I can't live with that."

"But eleven kids will live." Cole crossed over to Harlan and grabbed him by the shoulders. "You can't forget that."

Harlan knew Cole was right, just like when he tried to convince him earlier. It didn't make it easier to swallow. It didn't mean he liked it. However, it did mean that he needed to end his pity party and grow a pair.

"Ok. Now we just have to figure out how to get past Barry and get the kids the cure."

"Why don't you call the cops? Tell the press? You could end this thing now and get to the kids without anyone in your way," Clara said.

"Don't you think I've thought of that? Who would believe me, an alcoholic idiot, over a well-respected CEO of one of the top children's hospitals in the country? And what about the evidence I have and how I got it? I stole blood from a patient and had it tested on a home chemistry kit. All my credibility is gone."

They sat in silence. No one had a clue about what they should do now. It was like they thought getting the antivenom would be the end. Once they got it, the path would be clear. Instead it had become harder to navigate.

"It's more complicated than I've let on. But . . ." Harlan had an idea. It was not ideal, but it could work.

"But what, Harlan? Spit it out."

"It involves you, Cole," Harlan said as he pulled all three phones out of his pockets. "I just need to make a few phone calls."

Chapter 60

Harlan began the long journey to the eighth floor. Not long because of the distance, but because the weight of what was next pulled him down. Everything was in place for his plan except for two things, and that was where he was headed now. If these two important parts failed, all the rest of the work they had done wouldn't matter. The road would still be blocked. No pressure at all.

He looked through the glass doors of the room next to administration and saw that Luke was still in there. Pacing. Talking to himself. Looking like he was about to lose whatever was left of his mind. Harlan couldn't decide if Luke would be the easy or hard part. Or if he could even distinguish between the two.

"Luke?" Harlan whispered as he walked into the room. He was terrified a loud, sudden noise would set Luke off again. "Good. You're still here."

"I've been waiting forever for this voice to show up. Where is he?" There was both power and fear in Luke's voice. This scared Harlan more than anything.

"He's on his way back, but he won't be coming here."

"What do you mean? You told me to wait here, and he would show up. Why did you lie to me?" With his one good hand, Luke picked Harlan up by his shirt and slammed him up against the wall. Harlan felt every last drop of air rush out of his body.

He tried to talk, but nothing came out. This only made Luke more furious. Effortlessly, as if Harlan were just a feather, Luke flung Harlan across the room. Harlan slammed onto the floor and felt his body explode in pain. Harlan knew that this was it. This was how it all ended.

Luke approached with a terrifying grin and stood over Harlan. He was about to crash his foot into Harlan's throat when Harlan miraculously found his voice.

"Wait. Please listen," Harlan said weakly, but loud enough that Luke paused. "The voice is not coming to this office, but it will be better. I can deliver him to you."

Luke's eyes widened. Harlan hoped that was a good sign, that he believed what Harlan said and would spare his life.

He reached down and Harlan flinched figuring the final blow was coming. Instead Luke grabbed him by the hand and lifted him up.

"Sorry about that, mate." In the blink of an eye, Luke changed to the polite, articulate person he always had appeared to be, that he had always so flawlessly presented to the world. "Sometimes I allow my anger to win out before I listen. I'll let you finish."

Harlan took a deep breath, which hurt in every part of his body. "Go to the fourth floor. There is a hallway there that because of construction is rarely used, except for as a shortcut by hospital staff. Wait there, and soon he and I will walk through. He'll be all yours."

"You really are a smart man, Harlan. Have I told you that lately? This could be the start of a beautiful, long-lasting friendship," Luke said as he walked out the door.

Don't count on it, Harlan thought. He had, however, begun to feel sad for Luke. Over the past few days he had started to believe that Luke was a monster driven by deep-seated hate for everything. But that wasn't it. It was deeper and much worse than that.

To Harlan it seemed Luke suffered from a serious and most likely undiagnosed mental illness. Left unchecked, it could not be managed and was dangerous for everyone who crossed his path. There was no doubt that people had used this to their advantage for years. Barry had exploited it. This made Harlan sick. Just another example of how poorly those with mental health issues were treated. Tossed out or manipulated. Sure, Luke was still responsible for his actions. There weren't really any excuses for what he had done, but he needed help. And Harlan hoped, when all of this was done, he would be able to get it.

But he couldn't worry about that now. He had to focus on part two. This part should be easier, but he had to be believable. He could not be flustered.

As Harlan started to open the door to administration, he was hit hard by what had just happened. He had almost been killed. Murdered. Gone forever. Was he walking into another death trap? Would his actions eventually lead to his death? He had never thought about those things before. He had worked around sickness and death for a long time, but never took a second to question his own mortality. And now he was forced to.

He closed the door, took a step back, then pulled out his phone and called his parents. He didn't want the last they heard from him to be his canceling breakfast plans. And Harlan knew he was being a bit over-the-top, actually, way over-the-top, but facing death does that to a person. At least, that was his excuse.

After several rings, his parents' voicemail picked up. Shoot. He wanted to talk to them, but a message would have to do.

"Hey Mom and Dad. It's Harlan. Just calling to say hi, and I love you. I'm so sorry about breakfast yesterday and for screwing up so much, so often. You deserve a better son. I'll work harder to be that from now on. I'll call again this afternoon. I love you guys."

He hung up, but kept his phone on. Harlan remembered his promise to his son. He said he would talk to Emily. There wasn't time now, but he should do something. It meant so much to Jack. Even a text would be good enough.

"Just wanted to say hey. And if you ever need anything at all, call. I'm here."

Not sure if that was the right thing to say, he pressed send and made his way toward Barry's office once again.

He smiled and waved at Grace, Barry's assistant, while she talked on the phone about who knows what. She motioned for him to go ahead in. He wasn't sure he was ready, but it didn't matter. He was here.

"Barry! I need to talk to you. Something you should know." Harlan burst in out of breath, needing Barry to think he had run frantically to his office. It appeared to work.

"What? Sit down. Take a breath. What is going on?"

"No time. The police are on their way back. I'm afraid it will be a scene, and I don't want that with everything that's happened here. It's my fault."

"Harlan. Seriously. You've got to calm down. I can hardly understand you. What police? And why are they coming?"

"The detective from yesterday, remember? She is coming to arrest my friend Cole." Harlan thought he saw the hint of a smile flash across Barry's face. Just enough for Harlan to know he had him. Then Barry was back to business.

"What for? And why here? Why not somewhere else? We don't need this now."

"It was the only way. He killed Josie. He did it because of me, because we hated each other. The cops thought I did it, but I knew it was him. I just had to prove it. And I got him to come here so he would have nowhere to run. I didn't want you to be surprised."

"This must be so hard for you, Harlan." Barry put his arm around him. Harlan wanted to snap it in two pieces and hear Barry scream in pain. "Do you want me to be there when they come? For support?"

"Yes. That would really help."

It had worked. To perfection. And in a few short moments, the road ahead would be shorter and hopefully smooth.

Chapter 61

Rodriguez was surprised when Harlan called her. She thought that going to the hospital was the right idea, but this seemed too good to be true, which always made her nervous. But Harlan sounded confident as he explained the plan and gave her every detail she needed to succeed. She wasn't sure if it were because he really was confident, or if he were putting on a face, doing what doctors do so well—putting the patient at ease even when they don't completely know the answer.

She had watched her doctor father do that for so long until he snapped from the pressure of pretending he was something he was not. Pretending he had the answers when he didn't. And then having to deliver the bad news when everything they tried didn't work.

He was why Rodriguez became a cop. To get justice for those falsely imprisoned for crimes they could not, in their right mind, have committed. The man she knew would have never wandered into the corner drug store in just his underwear in the middle of the day. He would have never tried to walk out without paying for his fifty-cent candy bar. And when he was confronted by the store owner never would have stabbed him repeatedly until someone pulled him off the poor severely injured man. He shouldn't be in some prison surrounded by all those criminals. He wasn't one of them. He needed help. Serious mental help. And he wouldn't get it locked up for fifteen to life.

Maybe that's why she was so invested in this case that made absolutely no sense. Harlan reminded her of her father. Caring and compassionate. Someone who worked hard to make a difference and covered up his feelings of inadequacy with sarcasm, especially in the most inappropriate moments. Maybe if she could solve this case and allow Harlan to save the patients, she could save Harlan from wandering off like her father had.

Would what she was about to do work? She didn't know. Would she lose her badge for it? She didn't know that either, but she didn't care. Sometimes you have to bend the rules a little bit to get the right outcome. Her mom always said, "Rules are meant to be followed, unless a broken one mends more than it breaks."

As she pulled into the hospital parking lot, she knew now was one of those times. If all went according to plan, and she had no idea if it would, she would be able to do a lot of mending. Not only for others, but maybe finally for herself.

Chapter 62

Harlan and Barry silently walked back to Harlan's office. Normally they would be talking about baseball or work or anything really, but now Harlan didn't know what to say to this man he had once looked up to and had considered a friend and mentor. A personal savior, even. He was convinced that anything that came out of his mouth would come out wrong, give him away, and end this whole thing.

As they turned the final corner Barry turned to Harlan.

"It takes a strong man to do what you did today. Turning your friend in. You have come a long way these past six months. I'm really proud of you."

Two days ago that would have been the perfect compliment. Now Harlan felt his blood boil to explosive levels. The ease at which Barry lied was effortless. It just rolled off his tongue.

"Thanks, Barry." You lying, murdering scumbag. "That really means a lot." What I wouldn't give to inject you with all the snake venom in the world.

"Anytime. Now let's go catch us a bad guy."

You'll get your turn, Harlan thought as he gave Barry a surprisingly convincing smile of gratitude.

"Harlan!" Rodriguez was waiting outside Harlan's office door. "Is this where the suspect is?"

"Yes. Right in my office."

"And he has no idea I'm here? This isn't some cruel joke, is it? Trying to get me back for accusing you of all this earlier?"

"He's there. He thinks we're meeting for lunch. I promise."

"He better be. Now back up."

Rodriguez pushed Harlan out of the way, pulled out her gun, and slowly opened the door.

"Harlan? That you? I thought you wouldn't be back for another half an hour."

Rodriguez barged in and pointed her gun at Cole, who looked sincerely terrified. Harlan couldn't tell if he were that good of an actor, or if he had forgotten for a split second this wasn't real.

"Don't move. Don't even think about running. It won't do you any good anyway. If you cooperate right now, this will all be easier for you." How many horrible cop clichés could Rodriguez fit into one statement? She only forgot, "we've got the place surrounded." Maybe she would get that in next.

"Cooperate about what? I have no clue what you're talking about."

"Don't play dumb with me." Another excellent use of cliché. "You murdered Josie Silver. We have evidence and motive. And we have your best friend to ensure you go away for a long time."

"No, I don't believe you. Harlan would never do that to me."

"You left me with no choice, Cole. You did it. I can't lie for you anymore. You're on your own now."

"See, Cole? Not even your friend believes in you. Sad life you live. And now it's over. It's all over."

Cole put his head down and looked defeated. He slowly walked toward Rodriguez ready to surrender, his hands out ready to be cuffed.

As Rodriguez reached down to pull her handcuffs out, Cole saw that moment and took full advantage of it. He threw Rodriguez hard against the wall and ripped the gun from her hands.

"You're next," Cole said, pointing at Harlan. "When you least expect it. You're next."

Before Harlan or Barry could react, Cole bolted out the door and took off sprinting down the hall right into the middle of the hospital.

Without hesitation Harlan took off after Cole. He could hear Rodriguez yelling at Barry to get off his butt and go for help. She was playing her part to perfection. Within moments Barry was right next to Harlan as they sprinted down the hallway.

They stopped as they came to a section where a few halls crossed. Cole could have gone in any direction.

"Where would he have gone?" Barry looked concerned. Harlan could see Barry's mind moving with all the possibilities. Losing Cole would be devastating to Barry. For some reason, Cole was a huge part of this game they were playing.

"I think I know. He knows a lot more about this place than he should. Follow me."

Harlan took off again with Barry right behind. They finally got to a little-used back staircase where Harlan once again stopped.

"I'm sure he's up this way. It's loud back here though. Everything echoes. He's got a gun, so walk quietly and slowly. Got it?"

Barry nodded. The concern seemed to vanish from his face now. The confidence was back, but now with an edge of cocky. With an edge of the voice.

As they were halfway up a flight of stairs, Barry slipped and one of his phones fell out of his pocket. The sound of it hitting the floor echoed throughout the stairwell. They froze, waiting for Cole to pop out at any second. But, just like Harlan knew, Cole would not be appearing anytime soon. He was nowhere near there at all.

Harlan gave Barry an all clear thumbs up and pointed toward the door leading to the fourth floor. As they approached, Harlan put his hand up to stop Barry.

"He will be somewhere in this hallway. Let me talk to him. Try and convince him to stop. That should distract him enough for you to take him down."

"Are you sure? Seems risky."

"I am. I know him better than anyone. He will listen to me. I know just what to say."

Barry nodded in agreement again. Harlan gave him another thumbs up, and they slowly opened the door.

As they turned the corner, someone was standing looking right at them, and it wasn't Cole. It was someone that Harlan had been running into a lot lately, only this time Harlan wasn't surprised. Barry stared, shocked, as Luke smiled.

Chapter 63

There was silence as the three of them stood together in the hall—the type that meant you could hear a pin drop. Harlan waited to see who would break the silence first, for what lie Barry would tell next. To see where this would go.

Harlan had often heard the phrase "this silence is deafening" used in uncomfortably quiet situations, but this was the first time he really understood what the phrase meant. This silence was loud. It screamed tension and fear. The longer it lingered, the louder it became, and the harder it was for Harlan to keep his mind clear and focused. Someone needed to say something. And these two psychopaths seemed intent on seeing who could keep this going the longest.

Harlan didn't want to be the one to say something first, but the clock was ticking on his patients' lives. He couldn't wait any longer.

He opened his mouth, hoping that the right words would magically form, but he never got the chance to find out.

"Can you believe it, Harlan? Luke Masterson is in our hospital. People have been looking all over for you."

Luke laughed at Barry's attempt at conversation. Harlan just stared in disbelief. Did he honestly believe he could lie his way out of this? Perhaps when you've lied for so long without consequence, you begin to believe you're untouchable, that you can get away with whatever you'd like.

"Is this guy for real?" Luke asked while continuing to laugh.

"What are you talking about?" Barry looked at Harlan but didn't get the response he expected. He still believed that Harlan had no idea.

"Stop, Barry. I know who you really are," Harlan said as he pulled the loaner out of his pocket.

"What is that supposed to mean? Have you lost your mind? Are you drunk, Harlan?"

"Nope. My mind is completely clear." Harlan opened the loaner behind his back and pressed send.

"You don't sound that way. You sound . . ." But he was drowned out by the loud ringing coming from his pocket. Barry didn't move. He was pretending he couldn't hear a thing.

"You should answer that. Didn't your mother ever tell you it was rude to ignore a phone call?" Now it was Harlan who had the smile on his face.

"Fine. I don't know why I should. But if it will get you back to normal, I'll do it."

Barry opened his phone and answered. "Hello?"

"Hi, Barry."

Barry dropped his phone as he heard who was on the other end.

"What's the matter?" Harlan's smile grew as he saw Barry's reaction. "How does it feel to actually have to face someone and not hide behind your voice?"

Barry turned around and looked straight at Harlan. Harlan had expected a look of shock or surprise or maybe confusion. That's not what he got. Instead, Barry looked angry. Angrier than Harlan had ever seen anyone. He looked like the voice sounded.

"Aren't you so clever, Harlan?" Barry began to slowly walk toward him. "Not smart. If you were smart you would have known that figuring this out would only make horrible things happen for you."

"Because the last few days have been fantastic, right? Why would I want to go and ruin that?"

"It can always get worse. You should have just played the game."

Barry quickly bent down and pulled a gun from his sock. It was something Harlan only thought happened in movies.

"I hate doing things like this. I hate the violence. Why do people make me do this?"

Barry pointed the gun at Harlan with a look of complete disgust. Harlan started to run in the opposite direction, knowing it wouldn't do any good, but also not knowing what else to do. He braced for the pain that would soon explode through his body.

Nothing happened. Harlan couldn't figure out why until he heard a loud thud come from behind. He turned his head and saw Barry pinned to the ground by a smiling Luke. Luke had saved Harlan's life.

"The moment has arrived, Barry. Can I call you Barry? Or would you rather Mr. Voice?" Luke said as he glared right into Barry's eyes.

"You can't call me anything. You're the reason we are here right now. If you would just have cooperated. Stuck to what you were told to do."

"I don't ever get told what to do. We are here right now because you thought you could control me. You thought you were in charge."

Harlan could see Luke's grip tighten on Barry's shoulders. Any harder and it looked like they would snap right off, but Barry didn't flinch at all. He looked like he felt no pain.

"No, no, no. Do not kid yourself. Your instructions were simple. Important? Yes. But simple. This has never been your show."

"It's always been my show. Everything is my show." Luke was no longer smiling. His anger now matched the anger Barry had shown before.

"Keep thinking that, Luke. It doesn't matter now. You've lost."

"I have not. I don't lose. You still need me. How do you expect to get into the other children's hospitals without me? I'm your way in."

"And what good will it do if you stop us from curing the disease here? The point wasn't death, Luke. The point was suffering, so much suffering that people would pay any amount of money to get the cure for their kids."

"This was all about money?" Harlan yelled from down the hall. "You injected kids with deadly snake venom for money? You put these kids through all of this, you put me and countless others through this, just to get rich?"

"And fame. Why else? What other reasons are there? But this loser tried to stop the cure from being given to the patients. He wanted them all to die."

Harlan didn't know or understand what was going on. He didn't know which of these two men made him angrier. Both weren't worth a penny.

"I'm not a loser, Dad! You are. You're the one who beats his wife and child. You're the loser." Luke was once again yelling at no one. Harlan remembered again why he had felt bad for this man. And why he hated Barry more.

"Shut up, Mom. It was your fault, too. You let this happen to both of us. I was raised by fools who deserved what they got."

Barry used this as a chance to push Luke off him and get free. He grabbed his gun, but didn't point it toward anyone. He looked calm. Like nothing had happened at all.

"This has been fun, but I can't stay any longer. I need to get ready for all the interviews I'll be doing once this 'new' disease and its miracle cure leaks to the press."

"What would stop us from going to the press and cops first?"

"Come on, Harlan. You know why. It's probably why you haven't gone to them already. Who would believe an alcoholic whose ineptness is the reason his patients are dying and a missing baseball player whose finger prints are all over this tragedy over a well-respected, never-had-any-problems CEO?"

"I'm glad you asked," Harlan said as he held up his cell phone. "Say hello to Detective Rodriguez."

Chapter 64

"The look on your face. Priceless. I wish I had a way to take your picture," Luke said with a laugh. He was back and lucid again. "The once mighty voice is reduced to a whisper."

Barry moved his glare from Harlan to Luke. Without hesitation he grabbed Luke and slammed his head hard into the concrete wall. Harlan watched as blood splattered all over, covering Barry's clothes. Barry slid his finger through the blood on his shirt and stared closely at it, like he was admiring his sick handiwork.

"Such a waste of talent," Barry said as he pulled the trigger, putting a bullet through Luke's brain for good measure.

"Who are you? What kind of person does the things you do? Even after you've been caught. You're done, Barry. Done."

Barry's rage grew as Harlan taunted him. He looked like a man who had never been defied before and did not know how to handle it.

He, once again, pointed his gun at Harlan.

"Why do you insist on making me do this? This was all so simple. But you had to be a hero."

This time there was no way out. There was no Luke to save him. At least Harlan's death would serve a purpose. The patients would be saved, Barry and his voice would be silenced. No one else would have to suffer because of him. That was all that mattered now.

"Look at me. I want to see the life leave your worthless body."

Harlan heard footsteps coming from behind him. This had been one of his fears. That someone would walk in, and another innocent person would die.

The footsteps stopped. He wanted to know who it was and warn them. Tell them to run. Get away from here. But Harlan was too afraid to turn around. He looked at Barry, whose eyes widened with his smile.

Barry fired twice, but both bullets flew past Harlan's head and into the person who had the bad luck of stumbling into their own death.

Harlan took that moment and charged, slamming Barry hard into the ground. Barry tried to push Harlan off, but Harlan wouldn't budge. He was filled with strength he did not know he had and anger he had never felt before.

Harlan picked Barry up and flung him against the ground again. And again. And one more time. Until he knew Barry could not move. He stood up and to emphasize his anger, wound up and kicked Barry right in the kidney. Barry screamed out in terrifying pain, a noise Harlan had never enjoyed until that very second.

"Why are you doing this? How can you know so much about so many people?"

"It's pretty simple," Barry said through his pain. "Everyone has secrets. Most of them are damning. And everyone thinks they can bury them without anyone ever finding them. I learned when I was young that once you found out a person's secret, you had them for life. They would do anything and everything you wanted to keep that secret from getting out. So, I created a whole army of idiots who would do anything for me. Kill for me. Steal for me. But mostly dig up dirt for me. Dirt that I could exploit for more power, money, and fame. And here we are again and even though it may not look like it, I will get what I want again. I always do."

"Why me? Everyone knows my secrets. Why did you choose me?"

Even through all the pain, Barry managed a smile. "Ask your ex-wife."

Harlan kicked Barry hard again. Barry writhed in pain while laughing at his continued control over Harlan.

Harlan saw Barry's gun on the ground and made a decision that he never thought he would be tempted to make in his life. He picked it up and aimed it at Barry. He felt an uncomfortable power coursing through him. Countless times he had held life in his hands, but never like this.

Harlan slid his finger onto the trigger. He did his best to steady his shaking hand and focused hard on his target. A chill went through his spine and into his whole body as he stared at Barry's soon-to-be lifeless body in front of him.

"Harlan! Don't do it. He's not worth it," Rodriguez yelled as she sprinted in his direction. She got to his side and grabbed his hands. "Put the gun down. Walk away. Your patients need you. So many people need you."

"Give me one reason why I shouldn't. He deserves this. He deserves his life to end."

"You're right. He does. But you don't. Pull the trigger and your life is over, too."

Harlan slowly lowered his arms, while Rodriguez slid the gun out of his hands. He looked hard at the gun, unable to believe what he had almost done. What he would have done.

"Thank you. I don't know. I don't understand. I'm sorry."

"I get it. Everyone gets it. Now it's over, and I've got it from here. I'll do my job, and you go do yours."

Harlan looked at his watch. It was almost noon. If Cole were right, and he usually was, those kids only had about an hour left to live. And it could easily be less than that. He nodded at Rodriguez and left to go to the floor where Clara would be waiting with the antivenom.

He knew this meant he would have to pass the body of the unfortunate person that had been killed by Barry. At least by Barry's bullet, but because of Harlan's actions. Because Harlan had brought the gun fight into the middle of the hospital.

Harlan couldn't make out the face at first, but as he got closer it became perfectly clear. And as it became clearer, his vision became blurry. His heart sank. His knees buckled as he collapsed to the ground next to Cole.

Chapter 65

Harlan lay down next to Cole's body and put his arms around him, hoping that somehow that action would give his best friend his life back. He didn't care how it looked to anyone at all. He didn't care how crazy it sounded. He just wanted Cole to roll over and make some horrible joke again. Breathe. Be alive.

"He kept his promise," Harlan whispered to no one at all. Just himself. Just a reminder that Barry had kept the promise that he would ruin Harlan's life. Take everything away from him that mattered. And he probably wasn't done yet.

"Wake up. Wake up. Why won't you wake up?" Harlan was hitting his fists against the ground. Yelling at the top of his lungs. "Why were you even here anyway? You weren't supposed to be here."

"He was worried about you, Harlan. He didn't know why it was taking so long. He thought you had to be dead." Rodriguez sat next to Harlan and laid her head on his shoulder. He could tell by the wetness on his shoulders that she had been crying, too.

“Why didn’t you stop him? Why didn’t someone stop him?”

“Everyone tried. Clara, Lucy, Dr. Baxter, you name it. They tried. He wouldn’t have it.”

“And now he’s dead. Because of me. Because I wouldn’t just listen to Barry and play my part. The only person in the world who never gave up on me is dead. I killed him.” The tears just exploded from Harlan’s eyes. There was no end in sight.

“You’re not the first person to lose a friend like this and feel this way. And you won’t be the last. Barry killed him. Not you. Barry.”

“You should have let me kill him. You shouldn’t have stopped me.” Harlan stood up and began to walk toward Barry’s still, handcuffed body. “I still can. I still can.”

“No, you can’t.” Rodriguez grabbed Harlan and held him back. “What good would it do?”

“He’d be dead. That’s all the good we need.” Harlan struggled, but she wouldn’t let him go. He couldn’t budge at all.

“And Cole would have died for no reason. Do you get that? Make his death mean something.”

“How? How can I do that now? He’s gone. My best friend. My best friend. Gone.”

Rodriguez loosened her grip and turned it into a hug. She just let him cry. He wasn't sure how long, but he didn't really care. He was sure he would never stop.

"Go save those kids. Don't let Barry win. Don't let your hard work, Cole's hard work, everyone's hard work, go down the drain. Make Cole's death matter."

Harlan stared at Barry's body and then back at Cole's. What a contrast. One had everything. The other nothing. But, had you looked at their lives, even examined them closely, you would have gotten that mixed up. Rodriguez was right. Cole's death would mean something.

"Thank you again." He hugged her a little harder, then turned and went to work.

Chapter 66

Harlan was just moments away from putting what just happened behind him and concentrating on his patients. He was usually good at this. It usually came easy. But he had never watched his best friend die before. This was uncharted, rocky, and unfair waters.

He turned the corner and saw the patients' rooms. Soon they would be ok. All of them, except one. One would die. Another person would die, because of him. How much blood could one person have on his hands? Harlan sure felt he was testing the limits.

He noticed there was a buzz about the floor. Nurses, techs, phlebotomists, everyone was running around. All of them looked out of sorts. Lost and confused. Including Clara who was running toward Harlan.

"What took you so long?" Then she stopped and stared. "You're covered in blood. Is that . . . is that yours?"

Harlan hadn't even thought about the blood. He didn't even think for a second that his clothes would be covered from holding Cole just seconds before.

"No. It's Cole's."

"Cole's? Is he . . ." She didn't have to finish her sentence. She could tell by the look in Harlan's eyes. "I'm so sorry, Harlan. How?"

"Barry."

Clara looked shocked. Then angry. Then devastated. She looked how Harlan felt. She mirrored him in every way.

"Will you get me a lab coat? I've got to cover this blood up. Can't let the patients see this."

"Are you sure? Can you do this?"

"There's no other choice. I can't sit back. You know that."

"I do. Wait right here." Clara ran and grabbed Harlan a lab coat, and they were back to work.

"Are we ready? Do we have the antivenom? What is the situation?" Harlan beckoned Clara to walk with him. He was in full go mode. It was either that or collapse.

"We've got it. And we need to do it now. Give the orders and you've got a team ready. But, there is one more thing." She grabbed Harlan's shoulder and stopped him. "You do remember we only have enough for eleven of them, right? One of them can't get it. Who?"

"I don't know. I can't decide who lives and who dies. I just can't."

"Dr. Allred?" It was Stacy. He hadn't realized they had stopped right in front of her room. "Can you come here?"

"Of course." He and Clara walked over to her bed, where she was sitting with her dad.

"I heard what you guys were talking about."

"Don't you worry, Stacy. We've got this all under control. Everyone will be fine. You'll be fine."

"I heard you, though. And I've heard others whispering about it. You don't have enough to cure us all." Harlan opened his mouth to protest, to say something comforting, but nothing came out. He had no words. "I volunteer. I'm ok to go."

"No." Tears, once again, filled Harlan's eyes. He wondered if he would ever run out. "I can't let you do that. You have so much life left to live."

"And so do the other kids here. They all can do so much. I wouldn't be able to live knowing I had taken that from them."

"But, your dad. You can't . . ."

"It's ok, Harlan." Phil put his hand on Harlan's arm. "We talked about it. She's right. It's the best solution. I will be ok."

Harlan looked at Clara. She was crying, too, but she nodded at Harlan. Letting him know this was right. It didn't feel right. He knew it never would, but it was what had to happen. If she wouldn't change her mind, then it was all there was to do.

"Ok. If that's what you want."

"It is. It really is," Stacy said with one of her amazing smiles.

"Then sit tight. Don't go anywhere. I'll take care of these other patients and be back. Got it?"

"Got it, Dr. Allred. I'll be right here."

Harlan walked back out into the chaos. As he closed the door he knew he would never see Stacy again.

Chapter 67

Harlan looked at the mass of health-care workers—no one had any idea what was about to happen. Of course, that's what you sign up for when you choose this path. The unknown. Each day, each hour, each second different from the last. It's what had drawn Harlan to it and, right now, it's what was pushing him away.

The one person he didn't see was Alex. This made him nervous. Was Alex waiting to crash their plans? Was he going to allow Barry's legacy to live on by doing what he was told? Harlan kept waiting for him to jump out and ruin everything.

"Where's Dr. James?" Harlan asked Clarence as he walked by.

"No idea. No one has seen him since you two were talking earlier."

This didn't ease his fears, but it didn't mean he could sit around and wait for something else bad to happen. It was time to move this forward and finally save these kids. Except Stacy. Why couldn't he save Stacy?

The next few minutes were a blur, as it often was when life was on the line. Harlan called out instructions, giving anyone available orders to inject the eleven patients with this medicine through their IVs. He never told them what it was or what it was for. Talking about snakes and antivenom would only cause confusion. He needed them to just go. Trust him. Not ask questions.

And they did. Harlan went from room to room, checking on each patient. On each nurse. He saw Dr. Baxter doing the same thing. This made him think about Alex more. His absence was disturbing. Alex had never missed an opportunity to be in the limelight, and this was his chance. His chance to one-up Harlan. Instead, he was nowhere to be found.

Harlan also noticed, as Rodriguez had alluded to earlier, that Lucy had come back. She was working with one of the patients. She was helping to save a life. Just like she had when she tried to stop Cole. This time, however, she would be successful.

After rounding and seeing that things were going well, that it appeared that this would actually work, he rested his head on the nurse's station. Exhausted. Happy and devastated at the same time. He felt a tap on his shoulder and saw Lucy looking back at him.

"Thanks for coming in, Lucy. We couldn't have done this without all these skilled hands."

"You said you needed help, and I knew you wouldn't call." She smiled at him. He wished he could return it, but all he could think about was Cole and Stacy. "Why aren't you smiling? You've accomplished some amazing things today. Enjoy it."

"I can't. Not with . . ." He paused. He didn't want to talk about Cole. He didn't want to say it out loud again. "Not with so much left still to do. It's not over yet."

"I know. But just smile a little. Look at what you've done."

He looked around. He saw happy parents whose kids would be ok. Happy nurses, who knew they had made a difference and saved the lives of children. But he didn't see Cole. He didn't see Stacy. He only saw more failure.

"It's hard. When you can't save them all, it's hard to smile about anything." He put his head back down and cried some more. He hadn't cried this much since he was a child. And even then, it couldn't have been as much as this.

"Harlan!" It was Clara. "Have you heard about Stacy?"

"No. Is she gone already? I didn't get to say goodbye." Clara grabbed him by the arm and dragged him to room 418. She opened the door and pushed him in.

"Dr. Allred! Look!" He looked, and he couldn't believe it. Her IV was filled with medication. It was filled with the antivenom that was now pumping through her veins.

"What? How?" He looked back and forth from smiling Stacy, to ecstatic Phil, to the IV, hoping this wasn't a dream.

"That doctor. The one I didn't like before? He came in, told me what he was doing got it started. Then he left without saying a word."

Alex? Alex had saved Stacy's life.

Chapter 68

Harland tried wrapping his head around something that made no sense at all. An impossible problem that had no answer. Harlan had been through medical school, residency, fellowship, and thousands of complex cases. He had been through marriage, babies, diapers, debt, and divorce. None of those life situations confused him as much as Alex saving Stacy's life.

Harlan knocked on Alex's office door, hoping he would be in there. Hoping to thank him and find out what had changed.

"Come in."

Harlan walked in and opened his mouth to say something when Alex wordlessly pointed to a small box on his desk with a note on top. Harlan picked them up and opened the note.

"Alex,

There is enough for one patient in the box. You decide who lives. Then, as promised, you will get all the credit.

You will live forever as the man who first cured one and then thousands.

The Voice"

Harlan read the note again. Nothing should surprise him anymore, especially not from Barry, but this did. He planned to have Alex save just one and then turn that one into millions of dollars. He planned to turn eleven dead, innocent kids into piles of money.

"I couldn't do it. Once I saw it, I couldn't do it. Just save one? No way. It wasn't worth all the fame and accolades in the world." Alex paused and stared blankly out the window, like he was still trying to wrap his head around all of this, too.

"He wasn't going to give you the credit anyway. He was going to take it himself. He told me that not long ago. He used you."

"I was just going to take off and never come back." He continued like he hadn't heard what Harlan said at all. "And I was on my way, when I heard a nurse say all were going to be fine, except one. Stacy. That little Stacy was going to die."

"But she's not. Because of you. When it mattered most, you came through."

"She was the one who amped my stupidity to the level it is now, ya know? That night. I let that incident cloud my judgment. I was so angry. Thinking I should have been there, and that life would be better for me if I had. At least that's what I told myself."

Harlan had had no idea. It would always amaze Harlan what flipped the switch in people. It was usually something small, something that didn't even make sense. This case was no different.

"I can't believe I was so stupid, Harlan. I was taking part in the murder of eleven kids. And for what? To get back at you? So people would like me?" Alex stood up and walked toward Harlan. "I'm sorry. I'm sorry for letting this happen. For being an absolute fool."

"Me, too. I take a lot of blame for this, too. But, give yourself some credit. You saved one. You are the reason all of them will live."

"But I let someone I couldn't see control me. Because I wanted power. Because I didn't want people to know about me."

This surprised Harlan a little bit. He knew about the power. He figured that was all Barry would need to get Alex, but did he have a secret he was hiding, too? Should Harlan push it and find out more? Did it even matter? Would it change anything? This might be the only time he and Alex were on the same page, but it could also be the start of a better partnership.

"I've said too much. I should go. I don't deserve to be here right now anyway." With that, Alex answered Harlan's question. This would be a conversation for another day.

"Come on, Alex. Stick around. Stacy will want to see you."

"Maybe later. I need to get out of here and think. Figure out what I'm doing with my life. What I almost did."

"Do what you think is best. I know how hard this was for you. Now I know the real you." Harlan reached out and shook Alex's hand. Alex actually smiled a bit.

Just as Harlan was about to leave, his phone rang. It wasn't the one from Barry or the loaner, but it still made him jump. He was going to trash every phone he ever had as soon as he got home.

"This is Harlan."

"It's Clara. You need to get down here now."

"Why? What's going on? The patients, are they ok?" Harlan's heart stopped. They hadn't saved them, had they? He had been wrong again.

"They're fine. Emily is here looking for you. Please come quickly. She won't leave until she sees you."

"Why? Did she say why?" Emily was there? Even when they were married, he couldn't think of one time when she had visited him at work.

"She just says she needs to see you. Something is going on with her. I can't quite put my finger on it."

As Harlan walked back he thought about Jack worrying about her and wanting Harlan to talk to her. He thought about what Barry had said to him earlier. *Ask your ex-wife.* He thought that whatever was coming, he wasn't prepared for it, and he didn't like that.

He wanted to turn and run, not deal with something else. Mourn the loss of Cole alone, something he had not had the chance to do. Part of him was grateful for that, but the rest of him just wanted to grieve. He needed to grieve.

That would have to wait. He couldn't run and hide. He promised Jack he would talk to her. As he rounded the corner and saw her standing there, he wished he hadn't. He wished he didn't have to face whatever this was.

"Harlan. I'm glad I caught you." Emily smiled at him. When was the last time she had done that? Then she hugged him, which confused him even more.

"Is everything ok?" he said as he pulled away from her. "You've never visited me before."

"Everything is fine. I got your text." He had forgotten he had texted her earlier. It seemed like years ago. "Thank you for that. It meant a lot. Can we talk somewhere private?" There were a lot of eyes glued to them, including Lucy's. Those were not happy eyes either.

He led her around the corner to a hallway where they could have some privacy. He didn't want to go with yet another person to the break room. He had been there enough.

"So, what's up?" Harlan said after an uncomfortable silence.

"I guess . . . it's just . . . this is hard." She took a deep breath and looked Harlan in the eyes. "Your text made me realize how poorly I've treated you. Not just lately, but for a long time. I'm sorry."

"It's ok. You've been just fine. You have so much going on." He was surprised by her apology. The way she carried herself, the tone in her voice—she sounded like Emily again. Like the Emily he fell in love with years ago.

"I haven't, Harlan. There are no excuses. You deserve better. The kids deserve better. They deserve us." She moved closer to him. He took a step back.

"What are you trying to say, Emily?"

"I'm saying we need to give this another try. If you want." Again, Harlan was thrown another curve. How many had that been in the last few days? He'd lost count.

"You're being so quiet. Isn't this what you want, Harlan?"

"If you had asked me a few days ago, I would have been jumping for joy. But, right now, I'm not in a place to make that decision. Can you give me time to think it through?"

"Take all the time you need. I'm not going anywhere," she said with a smile. She reached up and kissed him on the cheek.

Harlan walked with her for a second and pointed her in the direction she needed to go to get out. This was confusing, but a good confusing. A confusion he was glad to have in his life.

"Harlan? Can you come here for a second?" It was Phil calling from Stacy's room and he looked concerned.

"Of course. Is everything ok?"

"Who was that woman you were just talking to?"

"My ex-wife. Why?" Phil looked at Stacy and Harlan followed suit. Stacy's eyes were glued to her door. She looked terrified, as if she were living a nightmare.

Harlan sprinted out of the door until he caught up with Emily. She looked surprised and happy to see him so soon.

"Why did you really come here?" Harlan asked, as Emily frowned a bit.

"What do you mean? I already told you. To apologize and make things better between us."

"Please don't lie to me. Why did you really come here today?"

Emily was no longer looking at Harlan. She was staring past him to the patients' rooms. Tears began to fill her eyes.

"It was you, wasn't it? It was you who caused the accident that night?"

Emily collapsed to the floor. She said nothing. She just cried. Harlan turned and walked back to his patients.

Chapter 69

Six months later

If anyone had ever told Harlan that he would miss a Mariners Opening Day, especially one where they would raise an AL West Championship banner, he would have thought they had lost their mind. But it was true. He was nowhere near the stadium. Instead, he sat where he now spent every Sunday night. At Cole's grave.

Harlan would just sit there and talk. A beer on Cole's grave and soda in Harlan's hand. This weekly ritual was one of the few things that kept him sane. It's amazing what you can figure out when you just talk. Even if no one responds.

"They offered Barry a plea deal and he wouldn't take it. I don't get it. I am not sure anyone has ever been caught more red handed than he was, but he still keeps pushing forward. Have I told what they charged him with? Three counts of murder, a whole slew of attempted murder charges because of the twelve kids he'd tried to kill and so many blackmail charges I've lost count. Just take the plea and move on."

Harlan paused and took another drink, thought for a second about what he had just said and listened for any advice Cole might whisper.

"But I guess that makes sense. The arrogance to do what he did . . . He probably just thinks he can get away with it, or maybe he loves the idea of hearing his crimes replayed over and over again for everyone to hear. He is sick and twisted enough."

Sometimes, when Harlan would come visit his best friend's grave, he would talk the whole time and sometimes he sat there wordlessly. Today was one of those days that he spilt his guts. Everything just came flowing out. He just needed to be somewhere else, with someone who understood him completely.

"What he did to all those people . . . I will never get it. I will never understand Josie either. How could that first-class, incompetent jerk have been a high-ranking member of a Japanese mob? She couldn't even tie her shoelaces without help, so how could she have moved her way up that family?"

Harlan paused, looked over at Cole and smiled until the laugh flew out of him. He could actually hear Cole laughing, too.

"I guess Hi-Ho Silver wasn't just her nickname in the medical world!" Laughing sure felt good. He needed to do this more.

"Lucy has been there for me every step of this process. It's weird, man. You should see the way people look at us when we are together. I am surprised she hasn't picked up on it and run to find someone better."

This relationship with Lucy wasn't perfect, and he wasn't even sure what you would call it—mostly because Harlan would often find himself terrified of where this would lead and hide himself away for a few days. Call it PTSD or just plain stupidity, he was happy that Lucy was patient as he worked through his issues.

"Emily calls occasionally, too. Not just about the kids, but to talk. I don't know how I feel about it."

Harlan talked to Cole about Emily a lot. He felt like he was even starting to understand Emily better now, too. Cole helped with that. When he was alive and now.

He didn't know why he walked away from her that day at the hospital. Even then he knew he wasn't doing the right thing. He should have stayed and consoled her, but he couldn't. He couldn't stop and help someone who had ruined a little girl's life and, to be honest, his life, too. He didn't care if it made him look bad. At that moment, he wanted nothing to do with her.

For four years, Harlan had wondered what would happen, how he would react, when they finally found out who had caused that accident. It never crossed his mind it would be someone he knew. Someone he loved. Someone who let him believe he had been the one who had abandoned their marriage. But she had been the one. That very day, it had been her.

When he thought about it, he still got angry. But Cole would just listen, and Harlan would start to forgive. He was getting there. He hoped.

"You should have seen Rodriguez working on this investigation. She's incredible. Every time they try to push the narrative to make it look like it was all Luke, she pushes it right back at them. Have I ever told you about her dad? It makes so much sense why she is such an advocate for mental health. She's done so much good from such a bad thing, really trying to make things better for so many."

Harlan took another drink and stared daggers at Cole. "Dude, that's gross. She's my friend. You can't say stuff like that about her."

Of course, all of it came back to those twelve kids, especially Stacy. That day, six months ago, when Harlan got back to Stacy's room, he expected to see that same fear in her eyes from when he left her. He even expected to see anger etched all over her dad. They finally knew who caused the accident that day. Finally knew who had changed their lives forever.

"I . . . I . . . didn't . . ."

"It's ok, Dr. Allred. Stacy is ok. We are all ok. She feels closure."

"Yeah. Don't worry, Doctor. I'm good. You should be good, too. You saved me. Again! Let's move on."

Once again, this little girl amazed him. He couldn't believe her reaction then, and he still couldn't believe it now.

All the kids were fine today, thank goodness. No side effects or concerns in any way.

"Of course, I still have all the other court cases to deal with. These lawsuits from some of the parents may never end. I get it. I would be mad, too. I am just glad the kids will never feel the pain they were feeling again, and I've been cleared by the medical board to practice medicine, so I can continue to try and help them still."

"I thought I would find you here." Jack sat down next to Harlan and grabbed himself a root beer, too.

"Why aren't you watching the game? It is Opening Day and all," Harlan said as they clinked their drinks together.

"It's not the same without you, Daddy," Jack said with a smile. "Plus, I thought you could use the company."

Harlan looked at his son with awe and wonder. Grateful that after all he had been through, all that had happened, he still had his kids. Still had their belief in him. He was going to need that to make it through tomorrow and every day after that. He hadn't told them about their mom and what had happened, and he never would. They needed her, too.

"Let's go, Dad. We can just walk. No baseball tonight. Nothing but you and me. Sound good?"

Harlan smiled at his son and for the first time in a long time, or maybe ever, he realized he hadn't failed at everything.

Acknowledgements

Before writing this book, I had no idea the amount of people it takes to write a novel. And I am not just talking about the editors. I could not have done this without the help and support of so many who want to see me succeed. There really are a lot of people to be thankful for.

First, and most importantly, my amazing wife Amy, who never stopped pushing and giving me advice to help me get this book finally finished and the best it could be. She also dealt with my out of control stress as I worried about each word I wrote. I am not sure how she does it.

For my mother, Susan, who read each and every draft I wrote with a fine-tooth comb. She found many things that I could do to improve the story and the grammar, all while encouraging me and letting me know she was proud of me.

For my entire family, who spent countless hours reading over every single draft and letting me know their completely honest and helpful thoughts each time.

For Melea Bird, Kylynn Sherry and Melissa Cantwell who took the difficult task of being the first people, outside of family, to read my book. Up until I finished, I would refer to their thoughts to make sure I was still on the right path.